ALL THE THINGS I'M
MISSING
AT HOME

NIKKI-MICHELLE

**All the Things I'm Missing at Home…
By Nikki-Michelle**

"Nothing is true, everything is permitted."—
The Old Man of the Mountain quoted from 'The
Master of the Assassins' by Betty Bouthoul

Perfect Strangers: Rome

Chapter 1

The bass in the club damn near shattered my ear drums when I walked in. I had no idea why she wanted to meet here. It wasn't my type of hype. Quite frankly, I was too old for this shit. But there I was. I paid the bouncers way too much to get in through the VIP door. Paid even more to have my C-Class Mercedes valet parked. Took way too much time getting dressed. The brand new red bottom shoes I had on hadn't been broken in so they kind of hurt my pinky toes.

I don't know your name, but you heard my name
…

I honestly wished Chris Brown would shut the fuck up. I hated that little nigga with a passion. What he did to Rhianna was unforgiveable. Any man who hit women was a fuck nigga in my book. And that was real talk. But judging by the way the young girls on the dance floor were shaking and gyrating their asses, it seemed they didn't care. I guess the same could be said for my sisters who still listened to that dude R. Kelly but had teenage daughters. I shook my head and kept it moving. I'd always been an overly analytical kind of dude.

I took the elevator up, then made my way to the top of the see-through stairs leading to the VIP section. The gold bracelet on my left wrist had chicks eyeballing me. Not because it was some kind of fancy jewelry or some shit, but because it said that I had money and status in this setting. It told them that the VIP section I was going to was exclusive. Gold diggers were vying for my attention even though I was scanning the club for someone else.

She told me she'd be wearing white. That wouldn't have been a problem except she forgot to mention that tonight all the ladies were required to wear white. The wedding band on my hand sparkled in the lights and caught my attention. I took a long look at the thing that tied me to my wife back home. I thumbed my nose, then ran a hand down my face. I had no love for the woman I'd left back home. None. Actually, I hated her if I was to be honest.

I couldn't pinpoint when things between Sheila and I went downhill. It could have been when she finished her doctorate and decided she needed to stay in Atlanta to further her career even though we'd discussed moving to my home state of Florida. Forget the fact I wanted to be near my sick mother who died a year later. Did I mention my wife decided she was too busy to accompany me to my mother's funeral? Or the fact that she made me miss my flight to Florida so I couldn't make it to my mother's bedside? She'd only had a few hours to live so I never got to see my mother before she died. Nah, those things were nothing compared to the fact my wife wouldn't open her womb for me and give me a child.

I was thirty-nine years old and longing for a little prince or princess to spoil. Sheila was thirty-eight, and it wasn't like we had all that much time before her body made it so she wouldn't be able to give me a child at all. I shook my head and then turned to keep going up the stairs.

The place was packed beyond capacity. *Bad bitches* and *thug niggas* flooded the place. Down in the lesser VIP sections, a popular rapper was throwing money around and popping bottles. Naked ass underneath short shorts and even shorter skirts bounced all around him. Food was being serviced to other VIP areas with bottle service. The bar was flooded. Half-naked women of all ethnicities danced in glass cages. I passed other VIP sections at the top level before getting to my secluded area.

"Bottle service?" the pretty waitress asked me like I had a choice.

It was mandatory that at least two bottles of top shelf liquor were ordered to even get into this section.

I nodded. "Two bottles of Armand de Brignac please," I told her.

Smiling, she batted her lashes. I chuckled because of the way she was eyeballing me.

"You here alone?" she asked.

"With two bottles of Ace, mama? Nah," I answered. "Waiting on someone."

She eyed my wedding band. "Your wife?"

I shook my head and joked, "Mistress."

Quirking a brow, she tilted her head. She gave me the once over and looked as if she wanted to say something. I knew I looked good; I was quite handsome to be exact. There wasn't a woman I'd come into contact with who declared otherwise. Dark, butter pecan tanned skin, a chiseled chin, dimples, and coffee-colored eyes made up my physical appearance. Dressed simply in tailored slacks and a purple button down that showed faint hints of all the time I spent in the gym, I put half the men in the place to shame.

Mama was a fine one. Thick in the thighs, childbearing hips, bountiful breasts, and naturally coiled hair that she had pulled up into one of those cute, natural styles sisters wore these days. Skin as rich as dark chocolate with light eyes that sparkled with mischief.

"If this is how you treat your mistress, I can only imagine how you treat your wife," she commented.

She had no idea how I treated my supposed mistress. She was basing her opinion solely on the fact that I could afford top shelf bottles. She, too, was a gold digger. I could have kept talking to her all night, but I didn't want my date to show up and feel awkward.

"Those bottles, mama. Let me get them," I told her.

She playfully rolled her eyes and moved on to get what I'd asked for. After adjusting my slacks, I took a seat on the white, leather sofa. I checked the Movado watch I had on. *She should have been here by now*, I thought. I was a little nervous and I hated to admit that shit. Grown ass man that I was shouldn't have been nervous about meeting any woman. But Piña was different. I'd met her on a chat line with no expectations of *actually* meeting her.

Khemetic Konnections was a new thing going around in ATL. I'd come out of my office building one day to find the flyer on my car. At first, I'd been annoyed as hell. Couldn't stand for a motherfucker to litter my car with their bullshit paraphernalia. But there was something about the beautiful, dark-skinned sister on the flyer that caught my attention. She looked as if she had just walked out of the heavens of the Mother Land. Toned thighs, small waist, rotund ass, and a smile that lured me in. The flyer boasted of discreet phone calls or email exchanges between strangers. They said they only offered conversations. There were no online profiles. It was strictly phone or email only. You call in, listen to people lie to you about what they look like, what they liked to do, what they were looking for in conversation, and go from there.

It was a strange thing, that at the time, I thought had to be one of the stupidest marketing plans I'd ever come across. And for $9.99 a month to join, I wasn't buying the hype. They said anonymity made the conversations and anticipation more intense. I had to be honest, I didn't necessarily think it would be a good idea.

Shit, I could have been emailing a toothless bitch with ten kids and twelve baby daddies. However, I craved that female connection. I needed a woman to validate me at this point. My wife hadn't even sniffed my dick in the last three or four months. I couldn't remember when I'd caught a glimpse of her naked. Being that I was well known in our community, there was no way I could cheat where I lived.

I just needed someone to talk to. Someone to listen to me vent about the stresses of my job. Needed a woman to stroke my ego and tell me all would be well. I knew I said I hated my wife, but it was complicated. On one hand, I hated what she'd turned us into. On the other hand, I loved the woman she used to be. Sheila used to make me feel like a king. Shit, breakfast in bed was one of the things I missed. I would wake up with my dick in her mouth. We used to joke that she would never get pregnant with the way she kept swallowing the chances.

I chuckled to myself as I rubbed my big hands together and watched the club life below me. I would come home from a long day's work at the office and the shower would be running. My favorite lounging clothes would be laid out for me. She would be walking around in something sexy, tempting a brother. Putting on a show as she bent over to pick up something she'd intentionally dropped. She knew I liked the look of her fat, heart-shaped ass that way. So she made it a point to bend over as much as possible in those little, V-cut, lace boy shorts. Her pussy print from behind would be a glorious sight. Damn, I missed those days.

Missed the days when she would be able to look at me and tell something was wrong. Missed the days when she would be stressing over schoolwork, fall asleep at her desk, and I would finish up a term paper for her. I missed washing her hair while she sat in a chair at the kitchen sink. I switched between massaging her scalp, drying my hands, and then fingering her pussy. I'd straddle her in the chair while standing, kissing her, and working up a lather at the same time. Sheila used to come at the sight of me smiling at her from across the room. She'd be running late from class so she would come rushing in the house mumbling to herself about not having my dinner ready.

I enjoyed seeing her shocked, but pleased, face when she saw dinner already on the stove. I'd take her hand and lead her upstairs to the bedroom where her hot shower awaited her.

I sighed. Those were the days. We were in love and madly in lust. Now, I barely saw her. She was director at a psychiatric hospital and ran her own private practice as she was a psychologist. The last time she'd been home before eleven was about five years ago. Sex seemed to be more of a chore when we did have it. Neither one of us wanted to give in to the other, but just to keep the peace, I fucked her, she fucked me, and then we went our separate ways.

I got tired of the constant arguing and begging for my wife's time and affection. That was where Piña came in. I went through countless voicemail profiles until I found one who intrigued me. Her voice was like silk. She had that Girl 6 thing going on that made my dick jump to life. Said she'd been a member of Khemetic Konnections for a few months and had yet to find anyone who intrigued her enough to make her respond. She said she was switching to email exchanges since she was tired of dudes telling her they jacked off to her voice.

"Have you ever craved something so badly that if you didn't get it, it threatened to drive you insane?" she crooned. "I have. In fact, I'm craving it right now. All I need is a little bit of attention. I need male stimulation to bring out that feminine energy I haven't felt in months. I need you to talk to me. Tell me all the things you'd like to do to me even if you know there is a possibility that it will never be. I need you to make my pussy wet without asking me for anything in return. I need you to make my nipples harden and breasts swell in anticipation of your velvety tongue paying homage to them. I just need excitement. I need to … feel … something. I haven't felt in so long. I need to know I'm alive. I need to know I exist. Make me feel alive. Light those pressure points and erogenous zones without ever having to touch me. So, if you're interested, send me an email. I will no longer respond to voicemails. I need written word. If you move me, I'll respond. If you don't, no hard feelings …"

I listened to her message over and over, her slight accent pulling at my curiosity the more she spoke. She sounded like me in a sense. All I was looking for was the attention I wasn't getting at home. *I will probably never meet this woman in person*, I thought, *but if she can get me off with just our imaginations, give me that feeling I crave, the one I used to get with Sheila, that'll be enough.*

At least, that was what I'd thought. Piña and I started exchanging emails. Days turned into weeks. Weeks into two months. Harmless flirtation turned into thoughts of what if …

I want to see you*,* she sent me in an email one day.

You know we can't do that*,* I responded.
She doesn't have to know.
And what about him?
Fuck him. He pays me no attention anyway. I tried to touch him last night and he pushed me away. I got a new hairstyle, and he didn't even notice. But I bet if he was needed at his job, he would have been lucid enough to do that.

I'd been sitting in a meeting at work, emailing a woman who wasn't my wife. She had a husband. Brother man didn't pay any attention to her. She said she was sure he was cheating on her. Told me about how a few weeks ago she walked in on him jacking his dick, but when she tried to have sex with him earlier that morning he acted as if he was too tired. I found myself becoming jealous. I'd never seen her, but the connection she and I built was strong.

I found I wanted to be the one she offered sex to. I wanted to be the one to make her pussy wet. I wanted to be the one to slip between her folds and sink deep into the tightness that I was sure would pull me in. I told her as much.

I sat around my office waiting for her to email me back. I knew I was crossing the line but fuck it. My dick swelled at the thought of seeing her. I prayed she was as fine as her voice portrayed. I'd be pissed if she wasn't but satisfied if she was at least a five in the light. That meant I could make her a seven in the dark.

It took her over two hours to email me back.

You sure about this? she wanted to know.

Weren't you the one who just offered the same to me?

Yes. Lol, but still, are you sure?

I am. I need to see you. Need to put a face with the person behind the emails.

Where would we meet? What if you don't like what you see?

I pondered that last part hard before responding. I had no doubt that I would like what I saw, but just to put her mind at ease, I responded with something she could agree to.

We can figure out a way to spot one another from a distance. If neither one of us like what we see, we can leave and the other one never has to know.

Another twenty minutes passed by before she responded.

Okay, but I pick the place.

I grinned like a fox in a hen house. **Deal.**

Club Egypt. Saturday night. I'll wear all white.

I didn't like clubs but had been to Club Egypt a time or two with my homies.

I'll be wearing a purple shirt. And I'll get a VIP section so we can have some privacy. I don't really like clubs, but for you, I'll make an exception.

I'm nervous, she sent.

Don't be.

Scared. I've never cheated on my husband.

Who said anything about cheating?

Come on, Rome. All this sexual tension we've built up, the poems and stories about fucking one another and you don't think we're going to fuck?

LOL, I may be an ugly-ass dude.

And I may be a busted-ass woman.

So what you're saying is, we're going to be two uglyass fucking motherfuckers?

She LOL'ed, then sent me a meme of a woman with her head thrown back laughing hard. I found one similar and sent it back to her.

LOL. If we turn all the lights out, we could still make it work, I sent to her.

True. LOL.

We could have easily exchanged pictures with one another, but the inconspicuousness of it all turned us on more. We had to be honest, we were two married people who'd been neglected by those who took vows to us. All we wanted was instant gratification. Everything else was a prerequisite. Truth be told, I wasn't too keen on cheating on my wife in the beginning. I'd just wanted to play around, tease the idea of fucking another woman. I knew crossing that line meant there would be no coming back.

Piña had given me something that Sheila hadn't in years, though; her undivided attention.

I wanted to know, *So, are we still on?*

Yes, but can I ask a favor?

Yeah, sure.

If you fuck her tonight, will you think about me? Think about me tasting you while massaging your balls. Think about how wet I get when we exchange emails. Think about pulling my hair. Think about me spitting on your dick, then sopping it back up. You like anal. So think about this tight ass taking in all that dick you say you possess. Will you do that for me?

I licked my lips. Looked around the room to make sure no one could see me adjusting my manhood as I sat in a meeting with my partner and potential clients.

Only if you give me the same. No ifs. I want you to fuck him tonight. I want you to think about all nine inches of me sliding into you…slowly. I won't be in a rush. Think about the way I'm going to cup the back of your knees in the creases of my arms and hit that spot you say he hasn't touched in months. Think about the way I'll suck on that pussy and make her squirt for me. I want you to fuck him so good that you think it was me.

Damn, that just made me so wet, she sent back, but this time there was an attachment to the email.

I excused myself and quickly stood, then grabbed my phone. I logged out of my email account, shut the lid on my laptop, and headed to the bathroom. After grabbing a handful of brown paper towels as I passed by the dispenser on the wall, I found the stall on the very end, closed myself inside, and opened my Gmail account on the phone. The attachment was what I wanted to get to. Piña had sent me a picture of her sopping wet pussy. Most beautiful thing a man could see. It was a pretty, dark brown piece of perfection. Her lips were plump. Clit swollen and sat out for me to see.

He manicured fingers spread her lips open so I could see the pink perfection inside of her labia.

I unbuckled my pants and quickly slid them down enough to pull my hardening manhood from my boxer briefs. I placed the paper towel on my lap. My dick was heavy and swelling by the minute. I laid the phone on my thigh, spit on my dick, then started to stroke. The precum had already saturated my fingers. The ache in my balls almost blinded me. My eyes watered I needed that nut so badly.

I imagined myself easing inside of Piña. Imagined my dick fighting the resistance of her tightness until I made her take all of me. Fantasized about her come coating my dick, glazing it, then using her kegels to pull me in deeper. I squeezed and stroked until I could feel my sacks tighten. The muscles in my lower abs clenched, and just as I felt the nut about ready to erupt, I squeezed my dick to stop it.

Quickly picking up the phone, I tapped the icon on the flat screen for the camera. I made sure the setting was on record before I started stroking slowly. I tried to hide my moan as someone else had walked into the bathroom. I bit down on my bottom lip, faced scrunched into a hard scowl as my come oozed out. I kept milking my dick until I had nothing left. I ended the recording. Made sure my face couldn't be seen, then sent it back in an email to Piña.

Chapter 2

That was five days ago. Since then, we'd shared explicit photos and short videos, no more than six seconds of us touching ourselves. She loved the way the vein on the top of my manhood snaked around the shaft. I was fascinated with how pretty her pussy was when it was wet. We never showed our faces. We let that anxiousness build up inside of us until we were about ready to explode with pent-up sexual aggression.

Sheila hadn't been home anyway. The one day she had off she decided to hang out with her girlfriends instead of giving me some quality time. For once, I didn't care. Piña had my mind occupied. She and I had talked to one another about our significant others so much I'd started to tell her fuck her nothing-ass husband and she, in return, told me she could be everything I was missing at home.

I stood, then scanned the dance floor over the railing again. I tried to figure out who Piña could be. Could she have been the light-skinned sista standing in the middle of the floor looking around like she was lost? Or the brown-skinned beauty sitting at the bar staring up at me? Nah, she was neither of those women. I was sure of it. I saw the waitress coming back over with the two bottles of Ace of Spade I asked for. Sparklers were flashing in the top of the bottles. I guess the club wanted everyone to see where the money was.

My phone buzzed, and I looked down to see I had an email. I opened it anxiously.

Are you upstairs? Piña had sent me.

Yes, where are you?

I'm here. Purple shirt, right?

Yes. I needed to know, how will I know you?

I have a purple rose pinned to my white dress.

I smiled because she'd remembered purple was my favorite color. That was all I needed to know. Ignoring the waitress after I gave her my credit card to keep the tab open, I walked back over to the railing and looked down. I was trying hard, scanning the crowd so diligently to spot the woman with a purple rose pinned to her white dress, that I didn't even see the woman walking up as the waitress walked off.

"Rome," shecalled out to me.

Any and everything that had been going on around me became nonexistent at that point. Her voice sounded so different than what I'd heard on that voice recording. Yeah, it was still smooth like silk and had the potential to make God himself question his sanity. Her voice could make a man lose his mind. Something about her being in the same place, the same small space as me, settled into my spine and made me think about what I'd set out to do.

Nervousness settled over me like an obsessed lover. I turned slowly. Started from six-inch, white stilettos, then let my eyes roam over her toned calves and plentiful thighs. The hip-hugging, white dress she had on did its job in making her stand out amongst the other women in the place. She'd snuck up on me so smoothly that I had to wonder if she'd been watching from afar before approaching me. Her hips sat out, rounded like beacons that drew me in to her femininity. Waist not as small as the waitress's, but there was enough definition there to give her a Coke bottle figure. Her breasts sat up high and gave the perfect finish to an already flawless picture.

I swallowed hard as I took in her soft, oval face. Almond-shaped, coffee brown eyes sat out against deep brown skin. Her hair was pulled back into a sleek ponytail, and although she was smiling, there was pain behind those beautiful eyes. She swallowed as she took in the sight of me as well. Whatever music was playing was lost on the both of us. I could tell that she wasn't naturally as tall as I was, but the heels put her eye-to-eye with my six-one frame.

Running a hand through my locs, I studied the woman I'd only spoken to through emails over the last two months. She was nervous, I could tell. There was a slight tremor in her hands as she held her golden clutch so elegantly in front of her. The muscles in my arms coiled and tightened. Pressure points heated up to the point I felt the temperature in the room change.

"I'm glad you made it," I finally said, breaking the awkward tension.

She licked her plum-colored lips and gave a light smile. There was a slight gap in her teeth, but it only added to her beauty.

"Me too," was all she said.

For a few moments, I stood there remembering all the emails she and I had exchanged back and forth. There had been times when I was sending those messages that I often wondered how Sheila would feel if she knew I was so anxious to eat another woman's pussy, a woman I barely even knew. I wondered how she would feel knowing I wanted to lay with this woman and bask in the afterglow of our adulterous affair.

"Want to sit down?" I asked Piña.

She nodded. I placed my hand on the small of her back and then ushered her to the soft leather sofa I'd been sitting on before. I could tell she was a woman of elegance and grace. She sat down like she had been trained on how to be a lady most of her life. Her mother had probably paid good money for those lessons. I wondered what her mother would say if she knew Piña had told me she wanted to suck my dick and give herself a facial with my kids.

I poured Piña a drink, then passed it to her.

She accepted gracefully. Slender fingers wrapped around the wineglass and made my loins tighten wondering what they would feel like wrapped around my manhood.

"Was it hard to get out the house?" I asked.

She shook her head. "No, he didn't even question me when I told him I was going out tonight. He doesn't care."

I visually drank her in again. Watched the way the dress hugged her hips and thighs as she sat there staring at me with innocent eyes.

"He should care."

"Well, he doesn't. Barely looked at me this morning and I walked around stark naked."

"Still think he's cheating on you?"

She sniffed a bit, then sat up straighter as if she remembered a lady wasn't supposed to slouch.

I caught a glimpse of the Eye of Horus tattoo on her right thigh.

She looked me in my eyes. "I think he is. In fact, I feel it strongly, more so now than ever."

"Why is that?"

"Because I need an excuse, any reason to cheat on him tonight."

I took a sip of my drink before responding. I needed time to think about that desperation mixed with hurt I heard in her voice. Was it possible that a man could push a woman to this point? What had her husband done to her that would make her look to another man, that she would need another man so vehemently? Had I done that to Sheila? Was it possible that my wife could have been cheating on me? To be honest, the thought had never crossed my mind, until this very moment.

"Was it hard for you to get away from … her?" Piña queried.

"Nah. Actually, she didn't come home. Tonight was her first night off in a long time, but she opted to go hang out with her friends."

"Why would she do that?"

I shrugged. "I don't know. I asked myself the same thing."

"Do you still love your wife, Rome?"

After setting my drink on the table, I sat back. I couldn't front, shame resided in me. How could I admit to loving my wife but felt the need to bed a stranger? A need that was so strong that I'd stopped at the store to buy condoms because I had made up my mind I was indeed going to cheat on my wife tonight.

"I do."

"I don't love him anymore. I don't. I stopped loving him about a year ago. He's not the same man I married. The man I married wouldn't treat me like he does. It's good you still love her though …"

Awkward silence settled between us before she spoke up again. I stood and turned to look behind me. The club we were in sat atop a hotel in the middle of Atlanta. Most people didn't know or didn't care that it slowly rotated. The view of the Atlanta skyline was beautiful. Piña stood then walked over to stand with me.

"Am I what you expected?" she asked.

I shook my head and chuckled. "No, not at all."

"Do you think I'm beautiful, Rome?"

I looked over at her. "You're beautiful, Piña. Very beautiful. More so than I could have imagined."

"My husband hasn't told me I was beautiful in years. I don't think he even recognizes me anymore."

"Why is that?"

"I gained a little weight when I got pregnant."

I studied her well. She didn't look like she'd pushed out a kid or carried one. But that wasn't unusual as many women kept their bodies tight after pregnancy these days.

"You have a son?"

Tilting her head, she gave me a strange look and shook her head no. At first it confused me, but then I figured she'd lost a child. Sheila had miscarried once, about six years ago. She'd been calling and texting me, but after a long day at the office, I'd fallen asleep and had left my phone in my car. By the time I got to the hospital, she'd already miscarried and the look of betrayal in her eyes told me she would never forgive me for making her endure that alone. The last thing I wanted to talk about was kids, so I said nothing else about the matter.

Piña took my hand and turned me to face her. "I don't need you to love me, I just need you to fuck me. I want to know that I can still turn a man on. Need to know I still possess my womanly wiles."

"Is it that bad at home?" I wanted to know.

"Worse."

"Why?"

"Who cares at this point? We may never see each other again, and I won't kid myself about it. So we have this section to ourselves. Please … touch me. Let me know I'm alive, Rome. Make me feel like a woman."

Chapter 3

"Make me feel like a woman …"

Piña's words collided with the male prowess in me. It wasn't necessarily the words; it was the way she said them. It was as if she was pleading with me, tugging at the animalistic sexual desire that she'd stirred up from the moment she responded to my email.

"Your poem yesterday," she said as I pulled her in close to me.

"What about it?" I asked.

"Did you mean it?"

"Which part?"

"You said you wanted to touch me and stir something within my soul."

I wrapped my arms around her, placed my hands intimately atop her backside, then slid them down to palm and grip her with enough aggressiveness to let her know I wanted her. She moaned a bit, more like purred. I felt the shiver that settled within her. She smelled damn good. Like brown sugar with a hint of something else I couldn't place.

My eyes never left hers. The more she talked, the more I wanted her. I knew she could feel my arousal pressed against her.

"I meant it, but in a sense that once I got the chance to be inside of you, I wouldn't let up until I knew you were satisfied. I wouldn't leave you unfulfilled like you told me he does."

"Do you feel anything for me, Rome?"

"Yes, and you can feel it, too," I answered honestly, referring to my hardening manhood that I was sure she could feel.

She giggled softly. She was here with me, but I could clearly tell when he would creep into her thoughts. No matter what she said, she loved him.

"Donovan."

"What?"

"My husband's name … his name is Donovan."

"Oh," was my response.

We'd said we would never mention their names. It would be easier that way. If we kept them nameless, it would be easier. Since she'd disclosed that information, I knew that after tonight, both of us would have to move on. However, there was no way I could or would mention my wife's name.

"Why couldn't it have been us who'd met one another instead of them?"

I didn't think she was asking me that question more than she was just speaking aloud. I kept my hands on her ass. Leaned down to let my nose trail from her neck to her shoulder. Her skin was so smooth and soft. If one had ever felt cashmere against their skin, then they would know what Piña's skin felt like.

I moved my hands from her shapely rump. Led them up to her waist. She inhaled deeply. I'd found another one of her spots. As she gazed at me, I brought my lips to hers. That first kiss was like a hit to the veins. I squeezed her waist as a guttural groan escaped me. Piña had bragged about her ability to bring a man to his knees with her kiss. Her velvety tongue traced the outline of my lips before she urged me to open my mouth.

She took her time seeking out my tongue. When she found it, she played with it, toyed with the nerve endings there. The sensation traveled down and settled in the pit of my stomach. She was trying to bring out something in me that should have only been reserved for the woman I'd taken vows to. That scared me a bit, so I turned the tables on her. Brought my hand up to cup the nape of her neck, then the back of her head. I took control of the kiss.

Aggressively tongued her down as I pushed her against the wall. I caged her between my arms. Let my hand slip underneath her dress. I needed to feel what she'd teased me with days before. I took my time searching it out until I realized she had nothing on under the dress. I pulled away from the kiss. Looked at her. Her lips were kiss swollen. Eyes watering.

"What's wrong?" I asked.

"Nothing. Please touch me," she asked softly.

I gave her what she wanted. After all, we were two adulterous sinners doing that old song and dance. What we were doing had been going on since the dawn of time. Cheating wasn't some new phenomenon sweeping the country. Did we know it was wrong? Yes. But what were two people to do when the people they had at home wouldn't give them what they longed for? After all the fights, fussing, cussing, and talks of counseling, what was left to do when one didn't want to leave their spouse, but needed to feel something, anything? Even if it didn't come from them.

I slipped my fingers between her folds. Toyed with her that way until my thumb found her pearl. Her head fell back when I slipped a finger inside of her at the same time. She was so wet … so goddamn wet. I couldn't remember a time when my wife had been this wet for me. It almost angered me to know that I could turn Piña on this way but couldn't get my wife to even wet my dick with her saliva.

I kissed Piña's neck while I finger-loved her. I bit down hard enough to make her arch and ask me to bite harder. Heavy breathing serenaded us. Piña desperately searched for the zipper of my slacks. I wasn't going to help her. I wanted her to show me how badly she wanted me. For the first time in a long time, I felt needed the way a man should have been needed by a woman. The carnal pleasure that told a man he had a big ego that the woman in his life didn't mind stroking.

Piña found my zipper. Found that opening in my boxer briefs and pulled me out. Her hand was warm as she caressed me. Stroked slowly. Used her fingers to saturate the head of my dick with my pre-cum. I popped her breasts from the thin fabric that had been caging them in. Suckled on one while using my free hand to massage the other. I switched back and forth between the two, making sure to show both equal attention.

"Damn, that feels good, Rome. You feel so good," she praised me.

"You're so wet," I told her.

We were eye-to-eye as we spoke. Bated breaths showed how intense the moment was for us.

"You have no idea how badly I want you right now. I needed this," she moaned when I dipped two fingers inside of her.

Her head fell against the wall and her eyes rolled into the back of her head.

"Let me show you something," she crooned.

Piña dropped down to her knees and sucked me into her hot mouth like she'd been thinking about doing it all day. I placed both hands on the wall so my body was angled at a position to hide her, give her privacy, while she gave me super head.

"Jesus Christ," I mumbled.

The bass in the club thumped around us. People milled about, but they couldn't see us in the VIP area I was in. I saw the waitress coming back. Tried to pull Piña up, but she wouldn't budge. She kept sucking like my dick was her lifeline. The waitress smiled, then stopped abruptly. It was too late to try to hide anything. She'd seen an eyeful, but surprisingly, all she did was lay my card down next to the drinks on the table.

Piña had control of the moment. Her slobber coated my dick as she took me to the back of her throat. It felt too good for me to be ashamed of the moment. Piña moaned. Made that vibration tickle the head of my dick and almost took me to my knees. The waitress watched until a red light flashed on her waist. Somebody else in another VIP section needed her. She had to go but didn't want to.

I smiled at her as Piña stood. Piña turned to face the wall. Arched her ass back perfectly. I knew what she wanted. She'd told me taking dick from the back was her favorite position. I pulled a condom from my pocket. Ripped the golden foil off. Expertly slid the condom on. I pushed her dress up around her waist. Shook my head at how perfect her ass was.

This was no doubt what all the conversations between the two of us had been about ultimately. Our voyeur had disappeared. One could only hope she kept what she had seen to herself. I held my dick in my hand and rubbed the head of it up and down Piña's slit. She was anxious. Each time I got close to dipping inside of her, she moaned a little deeper, cooed a little sweeter. The only reason I didn't slip right in was because I wanted to pace myself, lest I come in four strokes and embarrass myself.

I took my time, touching her and teasing. Massaging each ass cheek, touching her breasts, pinching her nipples. And just when she thought she wouldn't be able to handle the wait any longer, I gave her what she wanted. The low, throaty sound she gave me was music to my ears. I stopped a moment to enjoy the vibrations of her song. Damn. Piña was hot, tight, and wet. It had been so long since I'd felt the insides of a woman. Too long since I'd made one moan my name.

"Shit, Rome … shit," she cried out. "Wait, don't make me come yet."

I heard her, but I didn't hear her. I was in a zone. Too caught up to even care that she was begging me not to make her tap out. There was nothing gentle about what I was doing to her. I handled her roughly. Handful of her hair. Deep, hard, penetrating thrusts had her nails scraping the wall. I slapped my hand against her ass as hard as I could, leaving prints I'm sure her husband would question if he saw them.

I needed this. I didn't think Sheila knew how much I, as a man, needed her to want me, but Piña did. Piña knew how to throw her ass back, catch those thrusts and throw them back to me just as good as I gave. As badly as I didn't want to, I knew we had to stop. We were in a crowded club. At any moment, the waitress could come back with security. Even with all that running through my head, I didn't care. The only people in the club at that moment were me and Piña.

I could feel my manhood swell. I was on the verge of release. Sweat beads coated my forehead as my throaty growls and lusty grunts joined in with Piña's purrs and seductive moans.

"I'm coming, Rome. Come with me, baby. Fuck this pussy and come with me," she egged me on.

My hand snaked around her neck. A firm grip in place to show that she had indeed awakened the beast in me.

"You like that?" I asked in a low, throaty growl.

"Yes. I like that shit. Harder," she aggressively whispered.

I gave her what she wanted. Dipped my hips and fucked her harder. I knew when I hit her spot. She quivered and her vaginal muscles contracted around me. It had been so long since I'd come inside of a woman. Why, Sheila? Why did she make do this? The more I thought about my wife, the harder I fucked Piña. The more I thought about the fact that Sheila had been neglecting me, the more my dick grew, the harder it became.

"Oh shit, Rome. Oh shit," Piña cried as my nails dug into her throat.

She threw her head back, bouncing her perfect brown ass back into my thrusts. She angled her head just enough to take my mouth. That simple move—a simple yet sloppy kiss—was the straw to break the camel's back. I let loose my pent-up aggression so hard that I was sure it probably blew a hole in the condom and her stomach.

All the Things I'm Missing at Home

***

The waitress came back just as we had adjusted our clothes and took a seat on the leather sofa. I wrapped the condom in a napkin and put it in my pocket. I would flush it later. The waitress looked disappointed that she'd missed the show. She would look at me, then eyeball Piña like she was jealous she couldn't get that kind of action. While they made small talk about random shit, my mind traveled back to my wife. I needed to get home. I knew that much.

Needed to wash away the sins of my betrayal. While in the thick of things, Piña had given me all that I'd been missing at home. But it made me question what exactly it was I had been missing at home. As crazy as it sounded, I'd begun to wonder what it would be like to leave my wife for Piña. It was a stupid, crazy thought I knew. But I didn't think people understood what neglect could do to men, especially when those men wanted like hell to be with their wives. Yet, their wives were too focused on other things to pay attention to them.

Don't get me wrong, I loved the fact my wife had a career and an education, but between those two things couldn't there be room for me? She used to make room for me. It made me question what I'd done to push her to the point that she no longer cared enough about home to make sure all was well within our four walls.

"You okay?" Piña asked me as the waitress walked away.

I nodded. "Yeah."

She studied me for a moment. "It gets easier. The first time is always awkward. You sit and you wonder how you're going to keep a straight face once you get back home. How you're going to react once your spouse looks you in the face and asks you what's wrong. You'll be angry at her. Angry that she pushed you this far. You'll blame her for not seeing what she was forcing you to become. An adulterous fornicator. That's what we are, Rome. Adulterous fornicators."

The more Piña talked, the more I started to see a reflection of myself. She forced me to look at myself head-on and it terrified me.

Chapter 4

"So you've done this before?" I asked Piña.

I noticed that she didn't appear to be fighting with her demons about the fact she had just cheated on her husband. And judging by the words she'd just spoken about how after the first time things would be easier, I already knew the answer to my question. I rolled my shoulders and took a good look at her.

"Once or twice," she answered.

She had poured herself a drink and watched me just as intently as I was watching her. I noticed she drank a lot.

"You're lying," I countered.

"Maybe."

She took a sip of her drink, then glanced down at the wedding band on her finger. It was the first time I'd noticed it. She looked back up at me. Saw me looking at her hand and gave a tight smile.

"Took it off while we were fucking," she told me like she knew what I had been thinking. "Didn't want to disrespect him that way."

Frowning, I quirked a brow. "And meeting men online then fucking them isn't disrespectful enough?"

In that moment, she wasn't Piña, she was my wife, Sheila. Piña's infidelity made me wonder if Sheila was off somewhere cheating on me. I felt pain in my chest. Yes, the sex between Piña and I had been amazing, but now that the moment was over, I was second guessing my decision. I'd gone in search of another woman to do what my wife wouldn't.

"I wear the ring for me more so than him. I do it to see if I still feel anything for him. I wonder if there is any hope left."

As the music blasted around the club, it started to annoy me. *What the fuck am I even doing in this club?* I asked myself.

"You told me you didn't love him anymore," I said.

"I don't love the man he's become. I love who he used to be."

I thumbed my nose and ran a hand through my locs. "How is this okay? How is what we just did okay, Piña?"

"I never said it was."

"But you're not saying it isn't either."

Turning her lips down, she shook her head. She was still ever the lady. She sat with poise and grace. Sipped her drink with finesse.

"Nope. He doesn't care what I do one way or the other," she spat.

There was hurt mixed with the venom in her voice.

I stood and walked to look over the railing down at the dance floor again. A sea of bodies moved like waves crashing against the shores.

I told Piña, "You don't know that. Have you talked to him?"

"Why does it matter to you? You sound more hurt than he would be. I told you he was cheating on me, and you try to make me feel bad about what we just did?"

Turning to look at her, I said, "Call me crazy, but no matter what my wife has done to me, I never cheated on her with another woman."

"You just did," she countered.

I sighed. "Okay, until now."

"With a woman you met online. A woman you had no idea what she looked like until now. How is what you did any different than what I've done?"

"I don't make it a habit."

"Neither do I."

"You're lying."

Piña shrugged, set her drink on the table, then stood.

"I'm not here for your conscience. Definitely not here to make you feel bad," she continued as she walked up closer to me.

Just a few moments before Piña had me feeling higher than camel's pussy. But just the thought of her going back home to kiss her husband with my dick on her breath unnerved me. How many times had Sheila come home with another man's dick on her breath? My guilt was getting to me, making me think things that were possibly untrue. Looking down at Piña now angered me. I couldn't front.

"You have no idea what it's like to have your husband reject you, look at you like you don't even exist," she confessed softly. "I'm lonely, Rome. I've been lonely for a long time. So please don't judge me for what I choose to do to remedy that."

"How did we get to this place?" I asked.

"I can't speak for my husband, but I'm here because he pushed me here. It's very possible that a significant other can be at fault for the other cheating. Forget that age old saying, screaming it's not the other person's fault they got cheated on. It is very much possible that a husband can push his wife into the arms of another man."

I stood wide legged and folded my arms across my broad chest. "Like my wife pushed me into your arms?"

Piña glanced down at her feet, then back up at me. "Did she push you away or were you looking for a way out?"

"Nah, she very much pushed me away. Yes, Piña, I know exactly what it's like to be rejected. My wife has made it her daily mantra for the last few years to ignore me. Work, school, friends, and everything else came before me. So yes, I know what it's like to be pushed away."

Piña stared at me for a long time. The look she gave me made the hairs on the back of my neck stand up. If I never knew the depth of a woman's pain and hurt before, I knew it in that moment. The mood around us chilled, and for brief seconds, Piña looked at me as if I was her husband. She looked at me as if I was the one who had put that pain in her eyes and that hurt in her voice. Her nose crinkled and her lips curled.

Then, like I'd never seen the murderous intent behind her eyelids at all, she smiled. She smiled like she remembered that a lady was never supposed to show her emotions in public. Smiled like all was well in her world.

"This is what married couples do, you know? They go through these phases where they fall in and out of love," she drawled, her Southern bell accent coming through.

That island accent she had from her voicemail fading in and out.

"Yeah."

That was the only answer I could give her.

"Why so sullen all of a sudden?" she wanted to know.

"How many men have you cheated on your husband with?"

"Why?"

The veins throbbed in my neck as my fists clenched at my sides. She'd made me feel as if I was the only one. Foolish of me to think so when I met the woman on a chat line. I needed to get out of here. Needed to get away from the madness I'd created. I could still smell Piña on me. Wondered if I could get home and wash away my sins before my wife could sniff them out. Then I wondered if Sheila had ever come home with the scent of another man on her and I was too far removed from my marriage to recognize it.

"I'm just curious to know what number I am," I responded, sarcastically so.

Piña chuckled low, letting the insult breeze by her.

"You know, you're the only man I've ever met that I felt truly got me. The way you responded in those emails let me know I'd found a man who was just as desperate as I was to feel something, anything. That's a shame, huh?"

I didn't know what else to say to this woman. One minute she was the Piña I'd met online, the next she was a woman scorned. It was funny how people could put on airs while online, but in person they were nothing like who they portrayed themselves to be. Piña was nothing more than a whore looking for an excuse to cheat on her husband. She was a fucking whore, and I had to get away from her. She was my mirror and I hated it.

Hated the fact that she and I were whores together, had become adulterous fornicators because we were too chicken shit to be faithful to those we'd taken vows to.

I jumped when Piña touched me. Jumped back like hot fish grease had assaulted me. She looked offended, taken aback.

"I'm sorry. Did I do something wrong?" she asked.

"Go home to your husband," I told her, coolly.

Her features frowned. "Fuck him to be honest. You go home to your wife."

"She isn't home. Probably out whoring."

"Like you?"

"No, like you. Tell me ..." I started as I walked up on Piña so that we would be face-to-face. She backed up. The more she did, the more I stalked her. "Are you going to go home and kiss your husband with my dick on your breath?"

She laughed. I mean a full-on cackle that almost drowned out the music thumping around us, and then, she shrugged. My upper lip twitched. Rage felt as if it was flowing through my veins. I stopped stalking her. When I imagined that she was Sheila and my hand was around her throat, I knew it was time for me to leave. But I didn't.

A Wife's Regret: Piña
Chapter 5

I walked into my home about a quarter to three. Normally, Donovan would leave the lights in the foyer on for me or something. I guess he'd decided to be a dick tonight because I told him I wouldn't be home by the time he got there. I knew he was home. His Jaguar was parked on the cobblestone driveway. We lived lavishly. There was nothing I wanted materialistically that Donovan wouldn't give to me. I wish I could have said the same about everything else in this hell for a marriage.

I kicked my heels off at the door, knowing it would annoy him when he walked out the next morning to find them there. My husband was a neat freak and hated for anything to be out of place. My thighs still hurt. Pussy thumped in remembrance of Rome being there. I snatched the ponytail holder from my hair and let the cold floor soothe the soles of my feet. I popped the lights on and made my way to the kitchen. It had been cleaned. All the dishes that I'd intentionally left about on the counters and the stove had been put away. The floor swept and mopped to spit shine perfection.

I grabbed a bottle of water from the subzero refrigerator, then leaned against the island to let the cool taste take away some of the heat I still felt from being with Rome. I smiled as I thought about the way he fucked me again before racing out to head home to his wife. After he had asked me about leaving the club with his dick on my breath to kiss my husband, he took me by the arm and practically dragged me from the club.

Instead of the elevator, we headed down the stairs, sometimes stopping to touch and kiss. Once down to the first floor, we rushed out through the back door. He kept a tight grip on my upper arm until we got to the darkest corner of the building. There had been another couple back there, but they were only kissing. Rome didn't care. He made me face the brick wall and fucked me from behind like I was his to do so. It had been rough and ragged, but the passion behind each of his thrusts was so real. The way he bit down on my shoulder sent shudders through me. The methodical way he let his fingers massage my clit while he dipped his hips and made me hit a falsetto as I orgasmed would always stick with me.

I watched the other couple as they watched us. Loved the way the woman gazed into my eyes while my face lightly scraped the wall. I connected with her. It was like every time Rome had hit my spot, I made sure she could feel it, too. By the time Rome had come, the chick was on her knees sucking her man off. The night had been good to me. Better than my day had been.

"Where have you been?"

I jumped. The bottle of water fell from my hand, and I abruptly spun around to find Donovan standing behind me. I'd been so caught up in the memories of my extracurricular activities that I hadn't even heard him walk up.

Tiredness was in his eyes. His drawstring pants hung low on his waist. The perfectly etched out V-cut played host to the silky trail of hair which played peekaboo over the waistline of his pajamas. Aesthetically, my husband was everything a woman could want, from the above average height to the broad shoulders, beautiful caramel skin, and copper-colored eyes. While he didn't have washboard abs, his stomach held not an ounce of fat.

My name stood out on his neck. It was good he ran his own business as things like the ink on his skin would probably give people the wrong impression of him. There had been a time when he wore my name proudly. He'd never given a fuck about what people had thought about a businessman wearing his wife's name on his neck. These days he hid it more than he showed it. Shit hurt my feelings most times to be honest.

Still, Donovan's deep rumbled question had taken away my escapades with Rome and that annoyed me.

"Out," I answered him defiantly.

He folded his muscled arms across his chiseled chest. His face told me he wasn't impressed with my answer.

He wanted to know, "Out where?"

Sighing, I rolled my eyes. "Does it really matter? Where did you go tonight?" Rome's questions plagued my mind. "Did you come home with the stench of your mistress's pussy on you tonight?"

Donovan smirked lightly. I couldn't stand him. Hated the fact that everywhere we went women found him so damn sexually appealing that they often showed their interest whether I was in the room or not.

He licked his lips. "You stumble in here, drunk I might add, and ask me my whereabouts?"

"Oh, so being drunk is a problem now, too?"

"It is when it comes to you. Add that to the fact you're driving."

I waved my hand with a frown. "Pete drove me home."

Pete was one of the best drivers Donovan had at his company. Customers always raved about his good customer service. He was a nice guy and kept his mouth shut. That was the one reason I always called him when I needed a ride to and from places.

"My drivers are paid to work for me, not to drive your drunk-ass home."

"I like the way you talk to me, Donovan. Is that the way you speak to Tara?" I asked sarcastically.

Anytime I mentioned her, he smirked. I wanted to smack that shit right off his face but knew better. Donovan would hit back, and while our marriage had never been perfect, physical violence wasn't a part of the equation. I found out in college that he had no problem with smacking me back if I hit him. Boundaries had been set after our first altercation.

"You're drunk. Go shower and get in the bed," he ordered me.

He walked over and picked up the bottle I'd dropped, poured the remaining water into the sink, then tossed the plastic bottle in the recycling bin. He brushed past me. No hugs. No I miss you. No nothing. There was no need for me to cry about what I knew wasn't coming. I tucked my tail between my legs and headed upstairs.

"Staci," he called me.

No, my name wasn't Piña like I'd told Rome. I turned around quickly, hopeful that he would show me some kind of affection. I craved anything Donovan would give me.

"Yeah," I answered.

Maybe … just maybe tonight would be different.

He looked up as he mopped the floor. Sultry eyes drawing me in, teasing me just as his very presence did.

"Take your shoes with you," was all he said.

I shook my head and turned back around to head upstairs.

"A'ight, those motherfuckers will be in the trash when you wake up," he yelled behind me.

I didn't give a shit. I'd just use his credit card to buy more like I always did. I didn't even bother to go into the bedroom we shared as husband and wife. I bypassed it, headed to the guest room down the hall and hopped into the shower. It didn't take me long to wash away my transgressions. I wondered what Rome was doing while I showered. Wondered if his walk of shame had been anything like mine. Was he thinking about me? I wasn't even sure he and I would hook up again. We left things out in the open when we parted. To be honest, since connecting with Rome on the chat line, I hadn't checked a message or email since.

I asked him if he would email me. He told me he wouldn't make any promises. I shrugged it off like it didn't matter when it did. I liked the connection he gave me, but I knew that I would probably never see him again. I would have to be okay with that.

I stopped the water, then dried off before exiting the shower. Donovan hated water to be left on the floor in the bathroom. He always told me it was best I dry off in the shower. He'd trained me to do so over the years as I got tired of hearing his mouth about it. Once done drying off, I stepped out. Grabbed the organic coconut oil and moisturized my skin. I pulled a headband on to my hair to keep it out my face. I finished in the bathroom, cleaned everything up.

Well … almost everything. I left a pair of my underwear on the floor just to fuck with Donovan. I turned the covers back on the bed then sat down. I inhaled and exhaled. I was so tired. More mentally than physically. I flexed my manicured toes on the lush, chocolate-colored carpet. My husband had decorated our home from top to bottom. I'd had no say in anything other than picking out the colors for the guest room I was in.

I heard Donovan walking up the stairs. He was on the phone. My ears perked up so I could hear him.

"I'm not coming back out tonight. I told you that. Staci's home," he told his mistress.

Yes, my husband had a mistress, and yes, I knew about her. I also knew that would be the only person he would be petty enough to talk to this time of night about coming back out. Still, that didn't mean I had to be disrespected in my own home. I jumped up from the bed, then stormed to snatch the room door open. My face gave a scowl that stopped my husband before he made it all the way up the stairs.

"Hang up," I demanded.

"Is that her?" I heard the voice on the other end of the phone ask.

He had her on speakerphone, and I knew he'd done it to annoy me. He knew everything about her annoyed me. That bitch made my ass itch. Everything about her made all of the Black women in my bloodline who came before me turn over in their graves. She was my polar opposite, not only in race but in everything. She was what Donovan would call domesticated. When I told him no, she always told him yes. He said jump, Tara asked how high and how long he needed her to stay in the air.

Donovan only smirked—that stupid, sexy motherfucking smirk—at me. "I have to go," he told Tara.

"No! You said you were coming over," she fussed.

"I lied."

"Please, Donovan. I need to see you."

"Can't do it," he told her as he kept his eyes on me.

She sighed, sucked her teeth, then told him, "I miss you, baby."

"I miss you more."

Snarling, I stalked closer to him on the stairs.

I was all set to smack the spit from his mouth. Him hitting me back be damned. I was sick of him disrespecting me and assuming I wouldn't do anything about it.

"You're a real asshole, Donovan. You're seriously going to stand in my face and speak to this bitch?" I spat at him.

He continued up the steps. "Nothing I ain't done before."

What he said was true. He'd spoken to Tara in front of me numerous times because this was Donovan's world, and we were all pawns. Donovan's world, Donovan's rules.

"Why doesn't she go drink herself to sleep like always?" Tara quipped.

"I can hear you, bitch," I yelled.

"Screw off," Tara shot back.

"Watch your fucking mouth, Tara," Donovan scolded her.

There was silence on the other end of his cell. She quieted down like the trained female dog she was. I tried to snatch his phone from his hand, but he easily pushed me to the side and walked into the guest room. I knew what he was looking for.

"You about to get in the bed?" he asked me.

"No."

"Then fix the fucking bed back," he snapped, then flipped the light on in the bathroom. "Pick your fucking underwear up, Staci."

I ignored his request. "Hang up the phone, Donovan."

His face was in a twisted frown as I knew his OCD was kicking in. I didn't care.

Tara spoke up, "Baby, are you—"

"If you ask me if I'm coming over again, you won't see me for the rest of the week," he barked at her.

"But … but, Daddy, you said you were coming to take me to dance rehearsal tomorrow," an angelic little voice came through on the other end of phone.

I swallowed the emotion that had welled up in my throat. My heart beat rapidly against my ribcage.

Donovan snatched my underwear from the floor, then took a deep inhale before tossing them in the laundry basket underneath the counter.

"I am, sweetie. Daddy never breaks promises to you, does he?" Donovan asked his four-year-old daughter.

"No, Daddy, but Mommy said you were coming tonight, too," Rebecca said.

"Rebecca, tell Mommy it's not nice to fib, and once you're done, ask Mommy why you're not in bed."

Rebecca giggled a bit. "Mommy, Daddy says it's not nice to tell fibs, and she let me stay up because we thought you were coming. I-I-I—"

"Slow down, Becka."

Little redheaded Rebecca had a stuttering problem. Anytime she got too excited, she stuttered a mile a minute before she could get what she was trying to say out.

"Okay," she replied breathlessly. "I did fall asleep for a little bit, but I got back up when I thought I heard you come in."

The smile that eased over my husband's face as he spoke to his child made bile rise in my throat. I couldn't compete with a little girl, and I wouldn't try. I left my pride behind as I rushed out of the guest room and slammed the door behind me. I stomped down the stairs, grabbed up a glass tumbler before I headed to Donovan's home office where he kept all the good Cuban rum. I turned all the pictures down of the biracial child smiling up at me from his desk and one of another child who I refused to look at. Grabbed the rum from its neat position on the top of his bookcase, popped the stopper, then poured a healthy helping.

I took the whole glass to the head. Confusing as the shit may have been to those on the outside looking in, it was my life. I had to live everyday knowing I couldn't give my husband anymore children. Unexplained infertility had been the diagnosis after I'd had repeated miscarriages early on in our marriage and later down the line as well. Every time I looked at little Rebecca, she reminded me of my failure as a woman. I wondered what was wrong with me. What had I done in past lives for this ailment to be bestowed upon me?

I picked up Rebecca's picture and stared at the dark tanned child with the red hair. She'd gotten that from Donovan, not her mother, Tara. Tara was a blonde-haired walking cunt. Donovan's friends used to call him Red back in high school and most of college. It wasn't until he became a respected businessman that he requested people call him by his government name.

My husband's trimmed beard and his lowcut fade were the beautiful color of a new penny. Rebecca was a replica of Donovan, only she had the face of an angel and her smile made my womb cry each time I saw her. The mistress had one upped me and I had to deal with that. I poured myself another drink and took it to the head. One more, and I had the feeling I needed to take me away from the pain. I looked at the glass of liquor and giggled as I'd drank it down to half. I put the glass stopper back in the rum bottle then set it back on the shelf.

When Donovan walked in, he would spot it. The fact the bottle was half empty and the pictures were turned down his desk would grate his nerves.

Chapter 6

The next morning, I woke up with a blanket thrown over me that I hadn't put there. I was balled in fetal position as I sat in the nook of the bay window in our sitting room. The smell of breakfast floated through the house. Bacon and freshly made biscuits called out to me. The sun wasn't shining as the rain had come in a few hours prior. It was a bit chilly because I'd opened the window on the other side of the room before I fell asleep.

I stood slowly and stretched my limbs while yawning. Folded the blanket and placed it back in the linen closet as I passed it on the way to the kitchen. I walked toward the kitchen expecting to see Donovan cooking breakfast. Instead, little Rebecca came rushing toward me. She was dressed in her Sunday's best; an all-white dress that flared down to her ankles. Her long, red hair was pulled back in a sleek ponytail. Shiny, black Mary Jane style shoes adorned her feet along with white ruffle socks.

Her ponytail bounced as she ran to me. "Staci," she greeted excitedly.

Like always, my body stiffened as soon as she wrapped her tiny, little arms around my waist. I couldn't help it and God knew I didn't want to hate the child because of her parents. I worked on my anger daily when it came to her. It was hard to flat out hate the child anyway. She was always so damn happy. Always cheery and bubbly, and for some reason, she'd taken a liking to me that I didn't understand. From the moment I found out about her when she was two years old, she wanted to be around me. Wanted to talk to me. Hold my hand. Ask me a thousand and one question, and she always wanted to comb my hair.

Donovan and I had fought many times about my dislike of the child, but for some reason, Rebecca hadn't noticed my aversion to her.

"I missed you so much, Staci. Why didn't you come to my last dance recital, huh? I looked for you. Daddy said you were sick and couldn't get out of bed. I got worried then."

She spoke so eloquently. She had her father to thank for that. By the time I'd met the child she was already trying to speak French. It had been at least three weeks since I'd last seen her. And I had to thank my dirty, cheating whore of a husband for lying for me. I hadn't been sick at all, but I couldn't stomach the stares and whispers anymore. I heard what all those people whispered whenever Donovan and I showed up to her recitals and school functions. It was the most awkward shit for me to wonder where I fit in when it was time for pictures.

As the wife, did I stand on the right side of my husband or in the middle of him and his mistress as they posed with their child for photos? But best believe Tara's trash box behind was all smiles. She posed for pictures with my husband and their child anytime she could. I was the odd man out.

I looked down at the little girl with a tightlipped smile. I noticed her face was a little redder on one side than the other. That made me think back to the times she'd had other bruises and such. Tara had told Donovan the school said Rebecca had fallen a few times. I didn't know, but something inside of me questioned it. Still, I brushed it off. Maybe it was just me wanting something to be wrong.

"How did you do?" I asked.

"I did great! I got to dance to 'Let it Go' from Frozen and it was so awesome for me," she bragged in that singsong, sweet little voice of hers.

Rebecca had me wrapped so tight in her embrace that I could barely move. She had my arms locked so I stood there stiff as a tree. I knew what she wanted. The little munchkin wasn't going to let me go until I picked her up. To get this not so happy reunion—for me anyway—over with, I scooped her into my arms and placed her on my waist.

She giggled softly and placed a big kiss on my cheek.

"Where's Daddy?" I asked.

"Outside. He's fussing at Mommy. She made a booboo."

For the first time, I genuinely smiled at the kid. Anytime Donovan cussed Tara's ass out was a happy time for me. I carried Rebecca into the kitchen, grabbed a piece of bacon from the plate sitting on the island, handed her a piece, and then walked to the back door. Tara stood like she was being scolded as Donovan spoke to her. I couldn't tell what he was saying but judging by the way he moved his hands and the expression on his face, I knew it wasn't nice.

Tara stood dressed in all black. The mini dress she had on stopped midthigh. Six-inch heels gave her long legs more definition. Her blonde hair laid against her head in a bone straight style, parted down the middle to give her a model-like look. The driver side door to her new model BMW was open, and she stood with one hand on the door and the other hanging at her side.

"What did Mommy do, Rebecca?" I questioned the kid.

Rebecca snacked on her bacon same as me as we watched on. "She left me at Grandpa Ryan's while she went to dance."

I shook my head. Now for as long as Tara had been doing the parenting thing with Donovan, she should have known leaving Rebecca in that trailer park would set him off. Especially, to go to a damn club. To be honest, I didn't trust the hillbilly rednecks, not enough to be leaving a mixed-race child in their care. Like Tara could feel me looking at her, she gazed over at the door to see me watching. I knew the sight of her daughter in my arms annoyed her. Smiling, I waved for the hell of it.

Donovan turned to look at Rebecca and me. He said something to Tara before he waved his hands dismissively. She looked dejected. She tried to say something to him, but he kept walking toward the house. He was in his Sunday's best, too. Gray dress pants tailored to fit his athletic frame, pink, long-sleeved dress shirt with cream cuffs and gold cufflinks. The gray vest he had on over the shirt brought attention to the muscular definition of his chest and the gray wing-tipped dress shoes finished off the ensemble.

"Good morning," he said to me as he walked in.

"Morning," I replied.

Wasn't shit good about my morning. He took his daughter from my arms.

"You should get dressed. Church is within the hour." With that, he headed to the kitchen so Rebecca could finish her breakfast.

That was all Donovan said to me. When I told Rome I was literally starved for attention, I meant it. It was very rare that Donovan gave me the affection I needed. Sometimes, it felt as if I was invisible to him. Every Sunday it was the same routine. We raised hell with one another most of the week, then come Sunday we smiled in church like we were the happy couple. Donovan reminded me of why I didn't like Christians. I wondered how it was that he could drag me to church with him every Sunday, praise the Lord, then fuck his mistress afterwards. I didn't like that shit, but I went to save face. Donovan needed to prove to his father that he could have a family regardless of the evidence of his adultery sitting between us.

While I had no mind to sit in the house of the Lord and pretend, yet again, that all was well in our world, after my escapade last night, I needed to have a talk with Jesus. I moved from the kitchen to get dressed without making a fuss. Took me forty-five minutes to do so. I pulled my hair back in a tight bun. Forewent the heavy makeup and settled for a natural lip gloss, minor eye liner, and a little cover powder.

I pulled on my best pearl set. Made sure my pink skirt suit had not one wrinkle. I slid on my gray pumps, grabbed the gray clutch, and headed downstairs where Donovan waited on me at the bottom of the stairs.

"Wow, Staci," Rebecca exclaimed. "Daddy, she looks like a beauty queen. I think beauty queens look like your wife, Daddy," she kept going.

Donovan didn't respond. No smile was on his face, but his eyes twinkled and that told me I had his approval as he watched me. I made me way down the stairs, and then followed my husband to church like the dutiful wife I was supposed to be.

Once at church, all eyes were on us as we made our way down the aisle to the front pew. That was where the bishop's son and son's wife were supposed to sit according to Donovan's parents. Just walking into the big church turned my stomach. Bunch of fucking hypocrites resided in this place. Donovan moved to the side and held his hand out for me to sit. Rebecca then nestled her little self close to me so she could be between her father and me.

As always, Donovan's father's church was packed to capacity. The organ was going. Drums banging. Praise team doing a routine I'd seen before. His mother's eyes cut a glare at us as we were a few minutes late. Deborah's café au lait skin glowed under the lights. Even though the woman was in her early sixties, she still had the body of a fit thirty-year-old. Her long, red hair flowed around her shoulders. She smiled as she waved at Rebecca. The little girl happily waved back at her grandmother.

Deborah Dixon nodded at her son. She didn't spare me a second glance though. I tsked and let it roll off my shoulders. Bishop Darryl Curtis Dixon bobbed his head and pat his feet as he sat behind the altar in his red and white bishop's robe. Donovan was the spitting image of the man, minus the red hair. It was as if his mother had only been an incubator. All she'd given him was his red hair because Donovan was every bit of his father all the way down to the copper-colored eyes.

If I were to be perfectly honest, I couldn't stand the bishop all that much either. He was a condescending asshole. The way he believed in gender roles sickened me. He took that whole thing way too seriously. To him a woman was only supposed to be heard when she was in the kitchen and the bedroom. I believe if he could have, he would have convinced Donovan to backhand me for fun every once and a while.

I sat through the whole service unmoved. While people jumped up and hollered, "Hallelujah!" and, "You better teach, Bishop," all I could do was shake my head. Black people and organized religion, especially Christianity, would forever be a conundrum to me. I didn't understand the whole fascination with being a part of the very religion that kept us enslaved for hundreds of years. Bishop Dixon made it his business to let his members know the reason they were so downtrodden was because they had turned their backs on the church. He wanted them to know that because they had become a modern-day Babylon, Sodom and Gomorra if you would, that God was going to rain down hellfire and brimstone.

While he preached, I kept my eyes on the man who was his second-in-command. The tall, dark-skinned man, slim in stature, was very in tune to what the bishop had to say. His suit fit him to the letter. Dimples were placed evenly on each side of his cheeks. His light brown eyes twinkled with delight as he yelled, "Teach, Bishop!" His wife was right there beside him. She, a white woman, was more crunk for Jesus than most of the sisters in the place. Sharon threw her hands in the air, yelped a scream, and caught the spirit as soon as the organ started going again.

As soon as I walked in, Sharon's husband stared me down as he always did. I could feel his eyes on me, trying to get my attention. Trying to get me to notice him in some way. However, I wasn't interested. I hadn't been interested in hearing what he had to say since I ended our relationship all those years back. Oh yeah, Pastor Reynaldo would try his damnedest to get me to even breathe in his direction these days, but as far as I was concerned, he could kiss the blackest part of my ass.

By the time service was over, I felt closer to hell than I felt to God. The whole sermon was about condemning folk who—God forbid—didn't think like they did to hell. As usual, when they passed the offering plate around, I let my husband do the honors for me and him. I'd be damned if I gave his father another red cent of my hard-earned money. I just didn't get it. Half the damn members in the church were below the poverty line, yet, Bishop Dixon had private jets and rode around in Phantoms. Hmph. Go figure.

"Did you enjoy the service today, Rebecca?" Deborah asked her granddaughter after service was over.

Like every Sunday, once church services were over, Deborah required the family eat dinner together at their home. This Sunday she had invited several church members over as well. While the church was in Stockbridge, the bishop and his wife lived lavishly in Fayetteville, Georgia. Lush, green grass and manicured hedges could be seen on every home in the exclusive neighborhood. Most sat behind intricately designed wrought iron gates while others sat openly. No matter the type or style of the home, I knew I had just driven into money.

Rebecca had changed out of her Sunday dress. Black tights and a purple tunic were her style of choice. She was barefoot with a bowl of grapes in her hand as she sat in her grandmother's arms.

She nodded happily. "I did, Nana. Poppop did very good today."

Deborah smiled with joy. "Did you feel the spirit in that place today, baby?"

Rebecca smiled wide. "Like fire shut up in my bones, Nana."

"Hallelujah! Praise God."

I had to look away to keep from rolling my damn eyes. It annoyed me how they forced religion on the child. I heard Donovan chuckling in the other room. He was happy. That was good to know. His happiness was always there. Didn't matter if I was happy or not. The first family's house was packed. I smelled barbeque and fried fish in the air. Spices from the other different foods were creating a mouthwatering scent throughout the place as well.

"How about you, Staci? Did you enjoy the service?" my mother-in-law turned to me and asked.

She'd pulled her hair back into a ponytail. A floral, loose fitting dress flowed softly over her curves.

"I did," I lied with a smile.

Judging by the nongenuine smile she had on her face, I could tell she knew I was being dishonest. "Well, that's good to know. We have to keep in mind that we get out of service what we put in."

"I understand that very well, but just because I'm not jumping up and down doesn't mean I don't hear what's being said."

"You can hear all you want but are you listening is the question." Deborah put Rebecca down. "Go play with your cousins, baby," she told her.

"Okay, Nana." Rebecca beamed up at her grandma. "I love you."

"Nana loves you, too, baby."

Rebecca walked over to me. "I love you, too, Staci."

My upper lip twitched as I gave a faux smile at the bright-eyed child. "That's nice, Rebecca. Thank you," I told her.

I wasn't about to lie to the child. I wasn't sure what I felt in my heart for her, but I knew for certain it wasn't love. Rebecca hugged me, and then I watched her run off. Looked back up to see Deborah staring at me.

"The child has done nothing to you," she told me.

"I've done nothing to her either."

"She's innocent. Your quibble is with Donovan and Tara. Don't you dare treat my grandchild like she has anything to do with how she was conceived."

I was used to this. Used to people trying to make me feel like shit because I wasn't as accepting of my husband's bastard child. I got so damn sick and tired of people expecting me to just get over it because I chose to stay with him. I had every damn right to feel how I felt. I didn't harm Rebecca at all. I fed the child. I clothed her. I bathed her, tucked her in sometimes. Held her, even the times when I wanted her nowhere near me. So, Deborah was not going to make me out to be some kind of damn monster because I wasn't ready to be all kumbaya with my husband's mistress's child. Furthermore, Deborah Dixon was a goddamned hypocrite!

"Deborah, I really don't want to get into this with you, okay? We do this every single time," I told her.

"And we'll keep doing it until you treat Rebecca like she's human," she spat.

"I do treat her like she's a damn human, and at least I acknowledge her freaking existence," I defended.

"Don't curse in my house!"

"Hold that same mirror up to your own face. What you won't do is make me out to be some kind of monster, Deborah, because I'm not. And before you come marching up to me all high and mighty, check the skeletons in your own damn closet!"

Deborah sat back like she had been shoved. She would do a whole lot better to leave me the hell alone, lest I started picking all the bones from that damned graveyard she and her husband were hiding.

"Just because you don't say it doesn't mean we all can't see it and feel it any time you look at her. You need some help, Staci. To see an innocent child as the enemy is pathetic," she scolded.

Deborah Dixon had just been added to the list of people who could kiss my ass. Call it childish, immature, or whatever, but I would not be made to feel as if I didn't have a right to my feelings. Just as I got ready to tell her about herself, Pastor Reynaldo walked into the reading room where we were.

"Everything okay?" he asked as he studied each of the angry looks adorning our faces.

Deborah smiled politely. "Yes, everything is fine, Pastor. Bishop needs me?" she wanted to know.

Pastor Reynaldo nodded. "He wanted you to come taste his barbeque sauce. You know it's not perfect unless you give your approval." He then chuckled.

"I better get on that. We got a house full of hungry people," she said with a laugh.

She cast a side long glance at me before she headed out the room.

Chapter 7

Why she had left me in the room with that man was beyond me. I knew as soon as she was out of ear shot, he would try to talk to me.

"How are you?" he asked.

He was smiling like all was well in the world. Smiled like I didn't know the real him and it sickened me.

My eye twitched as I looked at the man. "Fine," I answered.

"Is it okay if we talk?"

"You're going to try to talk to me whether I like it or not."

He carefully made his way across the room and sat in the chair adjacent to me.

"How's work going? Any new investments I should be looking into?"

By day I was a senior financial advisor for the Savoy International Group, which was one of the best and top-rated financial companies to work for in the south. I'd been with the company for over ten years and had worked my way up the corporate ladder without having to sleep with anyone to do it. Not that I felt I was any better than the women who had. Hey, it was a dog-eat-dog world, and I wouldn't fault anyone for doing what they had to do to survive.

I stood and walked over the big, floor-to-ceiling window with a loud sigh. "No, there isn't."

"Would you really tell me if there were?"

"No."

There was silence behind me. Without even turning around, I imagined Chris wringing his hands, then running them down his face. He always did that when he didn't know what else to say.

"Heard from Delilah lately?" he asked.

I turned to look at him, fire in my eyes. "Why do you care? How're Sharon and the children?"

I knew he could tell that wasn't a genuine question because I'd spat it out with such venom, I knew it chilled his veins.

Chris Reynaldo stood and walked closer to me.

I held out a hand to stop him from coming any closer. "Don't."

He looked pained. "How much longer are we going to do this, Staci?"

"Until you can explain why you left us."

"I didn't leave you, Staci. I left your mother."

I shook my head at the man who had donated his sperm to help create me. "No. You left *us*. Where were you?"

"I was in prison for three years, Staci."

"And the two before that?"

He frowned and took a deep breath. "Drugs had me, baby girl. Drugs and alcohol had a hold on me, baby. I was messed up. But I tried to make it right when I came home."

"You didn't try hard enough, Chris."

"I hate when you call me that."

"Get used to it. It won't change anytime soon."

He knew arguing with me about calling him his name was a no win for him. He changed the subject. "Is there any way I can ever make it up to you?"

I shook my head. "No. If it hadn't been for you leaving us, Mom wouldn't be where she is today."

"I didn't want to leave—"

"But you did."

"I had to, baby. That's what I needed you to understand. Your mother and I were going to kill one another eventually. I had to go. I loved her enough to leave. I loved you enough to leave."

"Do you know the night you left, the man you owed money kicked down our door looking for you? If Mom hadn't hidden me in that damn hole in the floor who knows what may have happened to me. They beat her until she couldn't stand. Then I had to watch them brutalize her over and over. So, pardon me, Chris, if I don't care to hear your sob story."

I saw my father's eyes watering. I wondered if Sharon knew my daddy still loved my mom. I saw it in his eyes. Every single time he tried to talk to me, a mention of my mother was slipped in there somewhere.

"I'm sorry," he whispered.

"They came back. Three nights in a row. Kept coming back until she couldn't hold her bowels anymore."

He yelled at me, "Stop! Stop it … I get it."

Chris said he had come back after getting out of prison and he did. But not much changed once he got out. He tried to do the straight and narrow thing, both he and my mother. But it didn't last long. It didn't take long for the needle to call them again. We went from a fake healthy family back to the real us. Dirty-ass house crawling with roaches, rats, and sometimes maggots. I tried to keep it clean best I could, but it was hard with junkies running in and out the house.

I didn't get how a star football player with so much potential and his cheerleader girlfriend who excelled in everything academically ended up being the most talked about junkies in their neighborhood. About six months after my father got out of prison, the police came and snatched him up again. After that, he was in and out of prison. Sometimes he'd show up and sometimes he wouldn't. Then one day he just disappeared altogether. I was around sixteen years old then. It wasn't until I'd graduated from college for the second time at the age of twenty-six that I saw him again.

He showed up outside of my graduation with a new wife and new kids in tow. That was the first time I met Sharon. I hadn't seen my father in a little over ten years before then. But there he was with a grinning white woman and two little girls who looked nothing like me. Donovan and I were already married. My husband's father and my father had been best friends through high school and college. Donovan and I had grown up together for the most part. He'd been the only boy to show genuine interest in me and try to be my friend. I held so much resentment in my heart for Christopher Reynaldo.

"I'm sorry, Staci, and I don't know how many more times I can say that. When I gave my life back over to God, I prayed and begged his forgiveness because I went against his word, left my family to fend for themselves, but he gave me a second chance. If I was as strong in my faith then as I am now, the Devil wouldn't have stood a chance," he pleaded his case. "I know I was wrong, and all I ask is that you give me a chance to make it right. It's been eight years since I've been blessed enough to have you back in my life and I won't give up on you. I know you don't want to forgive me now, but I know in my heart, in time, you will."

I grunted, then gave a light chuckle. "Seriously, Chris. Get a grip on reality. If God didn't tell you not to divorce Delilah, I—"

"Stop, Staci," he cut me off.

I frowned. "Why? Don't want to hear the truth?"

"That's not it. I don't want you speaking blasphemous of the Lord and his work."

"Oh, no worries. I was only going to speak ill of you. I want you to stay the fuck away from me. Stop trying to talk to me. Stop trying to reach out to me. I want nothing to do with you or that bitch you married. Stop trying to introduce me to those little heifers you call daughters, and for the love of God, stop calling my husband to ask how I'm doing," I spat.

"Staci," a thunderous voice called.

I glanced behind my father to see Donovan walking up the hall. There was a stern look on his handsome features that told me he'd heard more than half of what had happened. With his left hand in the pocket of his dress slacks, the sunlight in the room beamed off the expensive watch on his wrist.

"Excuse me, Pastor Reynaldo. May I speak to my wife in private for a moment?" Donovan asked.

My father gazed at me for a few more moments then nodded before leaving the room. Donovan gave my dad a pat on the back as he walked out then shut the door behind him.

He turned to look at me, then thumbed his nose. "Give me your purse," he demanded.

I scratched my head. Went to move to sit in one of the chairs in the room, then almost twisted my ankle in the heels I was wearing.

I righted myself, best I could, then shook my head. "No. What for?"

Sneering, Donovan looked down his nose at me. "Give. Me. Your. Purse," he demanded again, more sternly this time. "You went to the bathroom five times in one service. You think I wouldn't notice? Think I wouldn't pick up on why you're keeping your distance from me?"

"So what? I can't …" I sighed, caught my breath, then plopped down in the chair behind me, "I can't go take a piss while in church now?"

Before I could finish speaking, Donovan stormed over to me. Through a snarl, he snatched the clutch from my hand. "Give me the fucking purse!"

As soon as he snatched it from my hand, the contents went spilling across the Italian marble flooring. MAC cosmetics, my smart phone, a bottle of perfume, and a small flask of Southern Comfort. It wasn't the normal alcohol I'd drink, but I'd been in a rush when we stopped at the gas station. I grabbed what I could before Donovan would suspect I was paying for more than gas.

Donovan glanced at the flask, then snatched it up. He looked at it in his hand before casting his gaze over at me as he shook his head.

"You don't ever fucking stop, do you?" he asked. "When will enough be enough?"

"I only had a little."

"You're lying. Your eyes are bloodshot. You keep popping mints thinking it'll hide the smell of the liquor emanating from your breath. You can barely stand still. Not to mention Rebecca told me she saw you drinking your tea again."

"Y-You made her spy on me?"

"I didn't make her do a damn thing. She was coming to bring you cookies earlier and saw your ass in here drinking. You should be ashamed of your damn self."

"I'm no more ashamed of my drinking than you are of bringing your—"

Donovan walked up on me, and my words got caught in my throat. His tall, hulking frame towered over me. His anger forcing me to lean back in the chair. "Say it," he dared me. "Disrespect my child the way you do your father's daughters. I dare you. You took away one of the only things in my life that ever mattered to me. And now you're mad because I found it again. How many more barrels of liquor will you have to consume before enough is enough? How many more lives will you have to take, Staci? Huh? Get your drunk ass up so I can take you home. You won't embarrass me in my parents' home anymore today," he snapped.

Donovan walked toward the door, snatched it open, and then stormed from the room. I heard the music and light murmurs of the guests his parents had over. I was left alone with my alcoholic demons. The one thing my husband could have said to me to hurt me, he'd said it. It had been so long since he had thrown that tragic day in my face. Tears burned my eyelids as I watched his retreating back.

I stood slowly. Had to, lest all the alcohol I'd downed come rumbling up. I knew people were talking about me. Even as they tried to hide it while I walked through the front room to the kitchen so I could leave out through the back door since Donovan had parked our car back there, I knew they were talking. My father was standing near the walk-in pantry. Bishop Dixon and Sharon seemed to be consoling him. I scoffed at the notion. Just as I walked out the door, I heard that little girl calling my name.

"Staci! Staci, wait," she cried.

Taking a deep breath, I turned to the child. If I didn't sit back down soon, I would end up vomiting as I'd gone over my limit of alcohol intake. I swallowed back bile. "Yes, Rebecca," I answered, words slurring a bit.

"My friend told me to tell you—you can't see him, only I can—he said to tell you the first to apologize is the bravest, but the first to forgive is the strongest."

I frowned at her. I didn't have time for her or her imaginary friends to be honest. Besides, I was too drunk to even care what she was talking about. I felt beads of sweat form at my temples. All the pressure points I owned were on fire, and the more I stood in the tall heels, the more I threatened to tip over.

"Look, Rebecca, I need to get to the car to sit down, okay?"

"Why can't you just sit in the house?"

"I don't feel well so I have to leave, okay?"

"Do you want me to pray for you? Nana and PopPop always say a prayer over me when I'm sick, and then I wake up feeling better."

I closed my eyes to steady myself. I felt the world around me swaying. Once I opened my eyes, my vision was blurry due to the water clouding them. I squinted as I tried to focus my attention.

"No, Becka. I-I-I don't … I don't want you to pray for me, okay?"

"Are you sure? You look like it. You're sick, Staci—"

Before she could even finish, I lurched over and emptied the contents of my stomach. Chunks of the food I'd eaten along with the alcohol splashed on the pavement in front of me and on to Rebecca's feet and pants.

"Oh, for the love of God," I heard Donovan belt out.

My world tilted, and I fell to the ground. Everything around me went black.

I woke up hours later. The room was dark minus the moonlight shining through the window. It took me a minute to get my bearings about me. I'd been taken out of the skirt suit I'd worn to church. A silk pajama set had been put on in its place. The vomit had been washed away and I smelled like honey and lavender. The room was a bit chilly. I groggily sat up. Head was pounding. Phone was vibrating on the nightstand. I sat still until the room stopped spinning. Then I stood and headed downstairs.

There was no need for me to go looking for my husband. Our bedroom door was closed and more than likely locked. My husband always locked me out of our room whenever I had too much to drink. He must have taken Rebecca home since she had school the next day. Besides, I didn't see her in her room when I passed it. The stairs were cool underneath my feet as I made my way down to the kitchen.

Once there, I grabbed a bottle of water and downed it. The dimmers were on in certain areas of the house, giving it a mysterious kind of illumination. I could smell the scent of eucalyptus in the air which meant Donovan was burning a candle or had put some oil on one of the oil burners. The light hum of the central air was going, and I could hear the faint sounds of music coming from somewhere in the house.

"You took away one of the only things in my life that had ever mattered to me."

Donovan's words replayed over and over in my head. I tossed the empty bottle into the recycling bin, then headed to Donovan's office. I prayed he hadn't locked it down. I twisted the cold knob to find he hadn't. It was the only place in the house I could find what I was looking for. I walked over to the bookcase, pulled Donovan's chair up to stand in it, then grabbed what I was looking for. I stepped down from the chair.

"Put it down," I heard Donovan say.

I hadn't even heard him walk up. His booming voice scared me so badly, I damn near dropped what I was holding.

"I want to see it … him."

"For what?" he asked as he tilted his head to the side.

All he had on was his long, black robe and linen pajama pants.

"I needed to see him, Donovan. Can we please not do this tonight? Would it be so bad for you to not do this to me?"

"Do this to you? Do what to you exactly? Remind you of how your drinking killed our son? Or remind you of the fact that you were driving the car while piss drunk and wrapped it around a fucking tree, killing our son in process, Staci? Is that what you don't want me to remind you of?"

Tears flooded my eyes. "It was a mistake, Donovan!"

"It wasn't a fucking mistake. For years, I dealt with your damn drinking. I looked the other way. Even provided you with the damn alcohol at home, all so you wouldn't go out and drink then try to drive home. I did every fucking thing humanly possible to help you, Staci, and in the end, it cost me my fucking child!"

I yelled, "He was my son, too! I was his mother just as much as you were his father."

Donovan's whole face had turned colors with a ruddy undertone.

My husband's eyes watered, but he didn't shed a tear when he said to me, "God only knows how much I regret that shit. You killed my son, and then you proved just how much of a woman you weren't when you couldn't give me another child."

A loud gasp escaped my lips. His words socked me like an uppercut to the face, then a gut punch. Two miscarriages before we were able to conceive Donovan Malachi Dixon the Third. And three after … after …

I couldn't bring myself to say it. Didn't want to think about the fact that after our son died, my body wouldn't allow me to carry a child full term.

My face burned and my sobs got caught in my throat. I tried to speak but I couldn't. Each time I tried, no words came out and it sounded as if I was choking. For as much love as I used to see in my husband's eyes for me before, only hate, disdain, and utter resentment resided there now.

We tried so many times to have another child and each time, each time it ended in unexplained miscarriages. It was like God was punishing me for what I had done. After a while, Donovan and I just stopped trying altogether. Our marriage bed became cold. Small arguments turned to knock down, drag out fights. His words of comfort soon turned to soliloquies of hate. My regret and guilt soon manifested themselves in bitter angry words that I tossed at my husband in defense of myself.

I picked up alcohol again. Started drinking because it was the only way I could function. My husband didn't want me anymore, so I started to look for affection elsewhere. So, no, Rome hadn't been the first man I'd cheated on my husband with. Just as Tara wasn't the only woman my husband had on the side. She was once my best friend and now she meant nothing to me. I wouldn't piss on that whore if she was on fire.

I didn't know why God chose to punish me. Had no idea what I'd done that would warrant such a mess of a life. From the time I was a child, who'd been afflicted with junkie parents, to my life as an adult, it felt as if God was punishing me for something.

My husband walked over to me and snatched D-Three's—that's what we used to call him—picture from my hand. Red Junior was what family and friends had called him.

I was supposed to pick him up from band practice, but I was late. Had been at the bar drinking with Tara. I rushed out of the bar. Got in the car, ignoring that fact I'd had three beers and too many shots of Patron to count. I thought I could do it. I'd been drinking and driving since college.

That evening was the first time I drank and drove with my child in the car. We were five minutes away from home when I came around the curve too fast while it was raining. The rain had been coming down in sheets. I could barely see two feet in front of me. I could have sworn with everything in me that a truck was on the road with me. I swore that truck swerved into my lane and caused me to lose control of my car. I told people that, but no one believed a drunk. There were no other tire marks on the road, and with all the alcohol in my system, I guessed I'd imagined it all anyway

The only other thing I remembered clearly was my eight-year-old son screaming for me while the car spun out of control. I woke up hours later in the hospital to the news my son's head had almost been ripped from his shoulders on impact.

Unhappily Never After: Donovan

Chapter 8

Our son would have been fourteen last month. No matter how many times I tried to forgive my wife, she always did something to make me remember why I couldn't. I fought hard not to become this bitter, angry man, but over time, it just stuck with me. In 2009, I lost my only son because his mother didn't know when enough alcohol was more than enough, especially when it came to her.

As I sat in my office at work, I worked silently while in deep thought. On the flat screen computer mounted on the wall to the right of me, there were little red dots moving around like it was a Pac-Man game. The backdrop was a map of Metro

Atlanta and each dot represented one of my cars that were out on the road. I was the owner of one of the most prominent limousine and car services in the Metro Atlanta area. I started the company when I was twenty years old.

Started out just shuttling my father and his ministers around. From there, word of mouth got around about my punctuality, professionalism, and reliability. I went from three used limousines to a fleet of cars, trucks, limos, and SUVs in a matter of four years. Whether clients needed us to pick them up from the airport or transport their wedding party, Dixon's Elite Limousine & Car Service was who they called.

Yes, my wife had helped me build my company from the ground up. Yes, her money had been a part of the startup fund. Trust me, there had once been a time when we had lived that happily ever after fairytale life. That had all been shot to hell now.

I looked up just as Tara walked in. She had been trying to get me to stop by her place for a good week now. Normally, I would have been all for it, but lately my need to cheat on my wife hadn't been there. It went from a full fledge fire burning to a dull ache. I couldn't explain why. Tara and Staci had once been best friends. That was before she and I started sleeping around. The night it happened hadn't been planned. It just kind of happened. She had stopped by my office. It was one of those nights when Staci and I had been fighting about her drinking. Never mind the fact we both were still grieving over the loss of our son.

Tara had been there for me more than she had her best friend. That notion gave me pause at first, but after a while, it didn't really matter anymore. Did I love Tara? No. I cared for her. That still wasn't enough to make me want to leave my wife.

Tara's long, tanned legs were the first things I saw when she walked in. She was tall and thin. Typical Victoria Secrets model build. Not my typical type. Her blonde hair fell around her shoulders. She had on black, four-inch pumps which elongated her already tall physique. She kept herself up, stayed in the gym like her life depended on it. Nice C-cup breasts peeked out of the buttons of her cream, silk blouse. The red skirt she had on stopped midthigh. Most people told her she looked like Stacy Keibler.

"You haven't been answering my calls," she said as she took a seat in one of the wingback chairs in front of my desk.

It wasn't like I'd invited her to come see me. She took it upon herself to do so. My mood was already in the dump and having her show up unannounced soured it further.

"I've been busy," I replied.

"That's funny. You seem to be able to answer when Rebecca calls."

"I'm going to always answer when my child calls me."

I clasped my hands together on my desk as I watched her. Tara ran a hand through her hair. Her facial expression may have been blank, but her eyes held a bit of fire.

"So, tell me what's going on, Donnie. What does all this mean?"

"What does what mean?"

"You've been acting different. Acting funny lately. Why?"

I scratched between my eyes, then sighed. I wasn't in the mood to have that conversation with her. Yes, there had been a time where I'd spent as much time with Tara as I could. She was a great distraction from the fucked-up marriage I'd found myself in. These days, though, I drenched myself in work. If it didn't have anything to do with Rebecca, I wasn't interested.

"Tara, I'm not about to do this shit with you, okay? We're not married so I don't have to explain my actions to you," I told her, brows furrowed.

"So this is what we've come to? No, you're not married to me, but that doesn't stop you from fucking me anytime you want to."

I shrugged. "We fuck, so what?"

"We have a daughter, Donnie. For the last five years, we've been doing this thing. I've waited in the shadows while you still play house with that drunk bitch. Meanwhile, Rebecca and I have to sit and wait on the sidelines."

"First off, this has nothing to do with Rebecca. Even when I don't want you anymore, my daughter will always remain priority. Second of all, you know I don't like all this whining shit you're doing," I told her emphatically. "You knew what you were getting into before you offered pussy to me."

"Don't disrespect me, Donnie. Don't talk to me like I'm some random broad on the street." Tara's face turned red. Her eyes watered a bit as they always did when she was emotional or angry.

"Tara," I said, then sighed, "don't start this shit with me today, understand? You'll be wasting your fucking breath and time if you do. You can throw a temper tantrum all you want, but at the end of the day, all this shit you're complaining about will still be the same. Don't act like a petulant child because it's only going to piss me the fuck off," I snapped at her, voice rising at the end of my statement.

Her thin lips thinned out even further as I could tell she was itching at the chance to say something but knew better. Pissing me off had never worked out well for the other person. She knew that firsthand.

She stood and stormed toward the door. *Good. I don't have time for her shit today.* I had other things on my mind.

She yanked my office door open, then turned to look at me. "Are you coming for dinner tonight? Rebecca's expecting you," she said, ice in her voice.

"Do I ever miss a Monday dinner, Tara?"

"No, but what I mean is, will you be staying afterwards?"

"I don't know. Don't ask me again."

She slammed the door on her way out. Didn't bother me. I looked at the clock on the wall, stood, and grabbed navy blue jacket that matched the slacks I had on.

I pressed the red button on my phone and waited for my secretary to pick up.

"Yes, Mr. Dixon," Monet answered.

"I'll be out of the office for the rest of the day. Forward all my calls to my cell," I told her.

"Yes, sir. Anything else?"

"Yeah, radio Pete and tell him not to answer if my wife calls him drunk again."

"Mr. Dixon—"

"Do what I said, Monet. I'll handle her."

"Okay."

I pressed the end button, then made my way out. I was more stressed than normal. Had no idea where my marriage was headed and that scared me more than anything. Staci and I had been together for a long time. I knew all her secrets and she knew all of mine. I hated what we had become. I hopped in my car and made my way to my two o'clock meeting. Traffic wasn't as congested as it normally was on a Monday, so I was grateful for that. If I had to choose, I'd rather get stuck in traffic on I-75 instead of I-20. Being that I was in my main office near the airport there was always a possibility I would get stuck in either or.

Today was different. Maybe that should have been my first sign that something was wrong. I made it to 55 Allen Plaza in no time. I parked in the enclosed parking deck after getting a ticket. Because I'd left a little later than planned, I was fifteen minutes late. I walked in the office building and nodded at the security team at the front desk. They greeted me in return with various hellos. The floor-to-ceiling vision glass gave a stunning view from all floors.

People of all races and ethnicities milled about. Some in business suits. A few in attire that told me they were there to clean the building. I got on the elevator and made my way up to the sixth floor. The receptionist smiled as I soon as I stepped off the elevator.

"Mr. Dixon, good to see you," she greeted. "Your wife is already in with Dr. Thibodeaux so you can step right in as well."

I smiled. "Thank you, Lauren."

"No problem."

I took a deep breath before walking in. I heard the soft chuckle of the two women in the room already. Dr. Sheila Thibodeaux had been our therapist for a few years now. She was a beautiful woman. Dark skin, natural auburn colored hair, dark brown eyes, and bowed lips gave her a look that made it seem as if she was always smiling seductively at you. She was a plus-sized woman who carried her weight well. She was curvy. The teal pantsuit she had on complemented her figure perfectly.

She sat where she normally did, in a chair across from the small, Tudor style sofa Staci and I always sat on. Her right leg was crossed on the left one. Her feet were clad in black ballet style flats.

"Good afternoon, Donovan," she greeted.

Staci said nothing. She was decked out in cream-colored, wide-legged slacks. Black platform styled heels on her feet. The black sheer blouse she had on fit her plentiful breasts. She sat with her head high, shoulders down so her delicate throat was displayed. Her eyes weren't red which I was grateful for. That meant she wasn't drunk. She had her arms folded across her chest. She was sitting in a defensive posture which told me this session wasn't going to be a cake walk. Her manicured pointed nails were painted red and sat out in stark contrast to the black blouse she had on. I adjusted my slacks then took a seat.

"Good afternoon, Dr. Thibodeaux."

"We should go ahead and get started since we're behind already. Which one of you wants to start first?"

Anytime we came to our sessions, Staci never wanted to speak up first. Today was different.

"He continues to let his mistress disrespect me and our home. She gets to come and go as she pleases—"

I interrupted, "She's lying."

Staci continued. "He talks to her in front of me, and I have to deal with his illegitimate spawn—"

"You better watch your fucking mouth," I snapped as I looked at her.

Staci was staring straight ahead. She didn't flinch or spare me a glance.

"Is this true, Donovan?" Dr. Thibodeaux asked me.

"No, it's not true."

"So you don't allow Tara to come to your home?"

I frowned as I gazed at the doctor. Sometimes, I felt as if we'd told her a little bit too much. She knew shit that my own family and friends didn't know. I mean, yeah, they knew about Tara because, hey, we had a kid. But the doctor knew everything from the last time I sniffed my wife's pussy to the last time I stuck my dick in Tara.

"She does come by, but only to drop off my daughter," I defended.

"I came home one day to find her coming out of our bedroom," Staci spoke up again, then turned slowly to look me in my eyes. "The same one he locks me out of."

"I told you she walked in there when I was in the shower. I had no idea she was in the room. And I lock you out when you're drunk, Staci. You're not the same person when you're drunk. Sometimes I don't want to deal with you. You came home the other night, drunk out of your mind. You smelled like you had been dancing in a distillery."

"I went to a club … with friends. That's what people do at clubs. They drink."

"And what about Sunday, Staci? You took several trips to the bathroom and I'm sure each time you had a drink. You were at my parents' house, while they were fellowshipping with other church members, drunk," I scolded her.

Dr. Thibodeaux sat there and watched us like a spectator as always.

There was fire in Staci's eyes when she asked, "Why does your mother have to always get in my face, Donovan? Always. She always has something snide to say to me."

"Probably for the same reason you have something snide to say about my daughter."

"You can't force me to accept her," she spat out bitterly.

I knew what I'd done to Staci—having an affair with her best friend and producing a child—had hurt her tremendously, but nothing I'd done could compare to losing our son because of her addiction.

"Staci, do you think the reason you can't accept Rebecca is because you resent what she represents?" Dr. Thibodeaux cut in to ask.

Unfolding her arms, Staci inhaled and exhaled loudly. "I don't understand what you mean."

"Do you resent the fact that another woman has given Donovan what you snatched away from him? Rebecca represents the child you feel you stole from your husband. Do you resent her?"

Staci was quiet for a moment. She was visibly uncomfortable with the question. I'd always thought she didn't like Rebecca because she was a constant reminder that her husband and best friend had betrayed her.

"I don't … I-I don't …" She couldn't find her words. "I just don't like the fact that I have a constant reminder of my husband's infidelity."

"Is that all?" the doctor questioned again as she tilted her head and studied my wife.

"Yes."

"Are you sure? This would be the perfect time to tell Donovan how you really feel, Staci."

"He knows how I feel. He just doesn't care."

Dr. Thibodeaux turned her gaze to me. She looked at me as a parent would gaze at their child when they expected them to speak up about something.

"Donovan, how does this make you feel? Do you care how your wife feels in this situation?" she asked.

It wasn't that I didn't care. I couldn't care. I couldn't bring myself to care about the woman who didn't care enough about me, our son, or our lives. She didn't seem to care when she decided to drive drunk with our son in the car. The severity of the crash was so bad, RJ's head had almost been ripped from his body. She walked away with only a broken leg and a few scars.

"How do you care for someone who doesn't care for themselves?" I answered the doctor, a question for her question. "Killing our son hasn't made her care enough to put the bottle down."

I could see Staci's chest heavily heave up and down. My words had cut her as I'd intended them to do.

"You son of a bitch," she spat lowly.

"I'll be that. I'd be anything you needed me to be if it would bring back our son."

"I can't … bring him back, Donovan. If I could, I would."

Her voice shook. She was emotional. Good. It wasn't fair that she got to drink away her pain and I had to live with mine every day. Every time I looked into her eyes, I saw RJ staring back at me. Every time she smiled, I saw his dimpled, cheeky grin. I turned to see she had tears slowly easing down her cheeks. Fuck her tears.

As the session continued, Staci and I went at one another like we were combatants on opposite sides of a battlefield. Dr. Thibodeaux only cut in to ask the standard 'and how does this make you feel?' to either one of us. By the time we were done, Staci stormed out the office and I felt no better than I had when I first walked in there.

Chapter 9

"Daddy, when will you and Staci have another baby? Mommy said Staci killed your first son, my brother," Rebecca commented while chewing on the end of a piece of her steamed asparagus.

I cut my eyes at Tara. Lately, she had gotten beside herself. She had been more disrespectful toward Staci than she had been before. I cast a gentle glance at my daughter. She had on a Doc McStuffins shirt with matching pants. Dora the Explorer sat in a highchair next to her while Barbie was sitting in a maid's uniform on the floor. There was a bun atop her small head. Her oval face was turned to me like she was indeed expecting a legitimate answer. Sometimes Rebecca was too smart for her own good and was able to comprehend far too much at her young age.

"The dinner table isn't the place to discuss loss of life, Rebecca," I answered.

"Okay, but … but, did Staci kill my brother, Daddy?" she queried again. "Just say yes or no and I'll be quiet for the rest of dinner."

I laid the fork down on my plate of half-eaten food. I wasn't hungry to begin with.

"There was an accident. Staci lost control of the car she and RJ were in. He passed away."

Rebecca nodded. "That's why she's always so sad, Daddy? I'd be sad, too. We should pray for her. She needs us, Daddy. She does. Mommy doesn't pray, but we do, Daddy. We should pray for her. Can we say a prayer for Staci tonight, Daddy?"

I was about to say something but stopped. I cleared my throat. Rebecca's words brought heat to my eyes. Talking about the loss of my son had always brought out the emotions I tried to hide.

"Need to say a prayer for her to stop drinking," I heard Tara mumble.

My patience was wearing thin where she was concerned, but I would never disrespect my daughter's mother in her presence.

"We'll say a prayer for her, baby girl. Finish your dinner," I told Rebecca.

My answer made her happy as she bounced around in her seat while humming. I smiled. "Amazing Grace" was her song of choice. I kept the conversation pretty light around her for the rest of dinner. She wanted me to know about her new imaginary friend. I nodded when I was supposed to.

Asked the right questions at the right time. Rebecca was never too hard to please. She was a simple child who would be happier with a doll from the dollar store more so than an expensive one.

Once she had brushed her teeth and I knelt beside her, I told her she could lead the prayer.

"Dear God," she started. "Please be with Staci. She's in a lot of pain and I really hate that. If I could, I would take it all away from her, but I can't. You can though, God, because you're awesome like that. Oh, and watch over Daddy, too. His eyes were sad today. So he might be in pain, too. And, if my brother is near you, watching down, right now, tell him hi for me. I'd like to meet him one day, but not before you want me to. Okay, now, God. Next time I'll say more prayers for Daddy and his wife. But I'm too sleepy now. Amen. Oh, wait, one more thing, please let Mommy not be so angry all the time and fuss at me so much. Okay, amen now."

Rebecca bounced up. I stood with a smile. Sometimes all it took were a few words from her to make me realize how blessed I was. I pulled her Doc McStuffins comforter back and watched her crawl in bed. Once settled in, she smiled up at me.

"What story do you want tonight?" I asked.

"None tonight, Daddy. I'm too tired. I just want to sleep," she said, then yawned.

That shocked me. Usually, Rebecca would throw a fit if I didn't read to her.

"You sure?"

"I am. I love you, Daddy."

"I love you, too, baby. Rest well."

She closed her eyes while holding her doll tight. After walking out, I found Tara in her room. She was coming out the bathroom, towel wrapped around her wet body, hair wet, smile on her face.

"Why does Rebecca think you're angry all the time?" I asked.

That part of her prayer wasn't lost on me. Tara sighed and waved her hand as if she was fanning off a fly.

"Becka thinks every time I raise my voice I'm angry. She's spoiled, Donnie. Anytime I fuss, she thinks I'm being mean or something," Tara explained.

Rebecca was spoiled, and maybe that was my fault, but if I found out Tara was taking any of her anger toward me out on my daughter, we would have a problem. I sat on the edge of the bed. I was tired and wanted to sleep. Going home wasn't in my plans though. I knew there was a fight waiting for me in between those walls. I didn't have it in me to fight tonight.

The weight of the bed shifted behind me. A few seconds later, Tara's long, slender arms wrapped around my waist. Her wet hair fell over my shoulders. She smelled of honeysuckle. Probably something frivolous she'd spent my money on. The house we were in, car she drove, all courtesy of me. Staci ran through my mind. I shook the guilty feeling off as I turned my head to kiss Tara on the lips.

"I've missed you," she crooned softly in my ear.

"I've missed you, too," I replied by rote. "But do me a favor, keep my son and Staci out of your conversations with Rebecca, understand?"

Tara smacked her lips, and although I couldn't see her face, I knew she rolled her eyes. "Fine, Donnie. I swear, one minute I think you hate her and then other times you act as if you still love her."

I did still love my wife, but I wouldn't tell Tara that.

"You heard what I said," I told her.

She huffed. "Anyway, back to you missing me …"

I wasn't really sure if I missed her or if I just missed what she represented. I hadn't really spent that much time with her as of late. My focus had been on work and the deterioration of my marriage. I felt the end was nearing, and to be honest, that scared me. The other day I was doing laundry and smelled cologne on Staci's dress she'd worn out that night. It wouldn't be the first time I had. When I confronted her about it before, she told me it was from colleagues at work.

Staci worked in a male dominated arena so it wasn't too farfetched that she would come home with those kinds of scents on her. Still, she'd told me she had been out with friends at a club and yet, all I smelled on her dress was the scent of another man. Nothing in me wanted to believe that Staci would step out on me. *She didn't have the balls, did she?*

Yeah, I'd made it a habit to cheat on Staci these days. Was Tara the only one? Hell no. While she was the main side chick—if there was even such thing—she wasn't enough to feed the hunger inside of me. I needed more than one woman to make up for what Staci could no longer be.

I looked around the bedroom. Not a single thing was out of place. Unlike Staci, Tara didn't intentionally try to trigger my OCD. Everything was where it was supposed to be. Bed fixed. Pillows neatly arranged. The orange and red colors perfectly blended. No dust was anywhere in sight. I was willing to bet that bathroom had been cleaned before she walked out as well. Tara always went above and beyond to please me. Still, she wasn't enough.

I looked down at Tara as she moved from the bed to kneel between my thighs. She took my shoes off, then my socks before taking the time to place my shoes on the rack beside the door with the socks stuffed in them. She came back, then urged me to stand. I did. She undressed me with care, taking the time to hang my slacks and shirt. All I was left in was my gray boxer briefs, and soon, she eased those off me as well.

"Hmmm," she moaned while admiring my body. "You look so tense. What can I do to help ease some of this tension, baby?"

"You already know what I need," was my response.

Tara knew I had never been one to beat around the bush. When I wanted, more like needed something, I had no problem outright asking for it.

She smiled seductively up at me. Always so willing and ready to please, she was. In that moment, I hated that Staci had taken that away from me. I imagined it was her on her knees, looking up at me with eager eyes. She used to be the one for me. Staci used to be the only woman who could please me the way I wanted ... needed. Now there were more. Sometimes two or three in a day to get me the satisfaction I needed to be satiated.

Tara moaned low and stroked my dick the way I liked. "Baby, I need a little bump in my finances. Got some things I'm trying to take care of. Think you can give me a little extra?"

Normally, I'd ask her what she needed it for. Right now, I didn't care. I needed to get today's counseling session out of my head. Needed to get Staci's tears out my memory. Truth be told, I hated to see my wife cry. I truly did. But fuck her for putting her habit over me. Staci always liked to throw in my face how I'd broken our vows. But to be honest, she'd stepped out on me first. She started cheating on me with that damn bottle long before I started to stick my dick in other women.

I often wondered why she never loved me enough to let go. I wanted to know why she never loved me and our son enough to say no to alcohol. Yes, I drank occasionally for special reasons. Staci was a functioning alcoholic, and she couldn't even start her day without some kind of liquor in her system. It sickened me. Angered me every day I woke to the fact I'd never be to her what her alcohol was. *Fuck her.*

Even as those words left my mental psyche, I knew they were a lie.

"Let my dick tap the back of your throat," I told Tara, my right hand roughly grabbing a handful of her hair. "Then we talk about you getting more money."

I urged her down on her knees. Took my dick in my left hand and placed her mouth where I wanted it to be. She wasted no time getting down to the deed. Tara's head was sloppy. Most times my OCD wanted me to stop and wash my dick off, but the part of me that made me a male refused to deny her. I was well endowed, there was no doubt about that, but Tara managed to swallow my whole dick, no problem. I loved to see her pink lips against the brown skin of my manhood. Something about the way she eagerly wanted to please me always made me harder.

"That's right, baby. Get Daddy off the way I like," I encouraged her. "Move your hands," I demanded.

She obeyed. I grabbed the other side of her hair and face fucked her to my liking. My pace aggressive, with no regards to her gag reflexes. The more she gagged, the more her face reddened and eyes watered, the harder I fucked her mouth. I imagined it was Staci I was choking with my dick. Maybe if I drank enough liquor, she would swallow my seed as it would taste like the beverage she loved so much.

Damn it, Staci, why did you make me hate you? I loved you ... still do if I were to be honest. But I hate you. I hate you so fucking much, my mind screamed as if my wife could hear me. *Why, Staci? Why after all this time, even after killing our son, why won't you let this shit go?*

Slobber, mucus like in texture, hung from Tara's bottom lip.

"Don't let that shit touch my feet," I barked.

She cupped her hands, caught the saliva, and then used it to finger her clit. I felt my balls tighten. The muscles in my ass clenched with the need for release. My dick head swelled. Staci—no, Tara—Tara knew what to do. She gripped my balls, then the shaft of my dick. She knew I hated to come too quick. Staci had spoiled me. She knew how to keep me from ejaculating too soon. Taught me that when we were in college.

While most niggas were out cheating on their girls, Staci had me locked in her dorm room doing all kinds of nasty shit to me. I had no reason to cheat on her back then. If Tara wanted to keep me, she needed to learn how to suck my dick like my wife used to. So I taught her. I taught Tara how to grip my balls first, then my shaft to make the mounting pleasure more intense. I liked for my toes to curl in a need to release so strong that it almost blinded me.

Staci had fucking spoiled me. I had to teach one mistress how to suck dick like my wife, another how to make her kegel muscles so strong that I'd know if she was fucking somebody else, another how to take all my manhood up her ass, and another just to pamper me the way my wife had once done. The rest of them were there simply for fun. They were like toys to me.

I grabbed both sides of Tara's face. Pushed my dick so far to the back of her throat that I swore I was going to strangle her. But she was used to it. I threw my head back. The muscles in my back coiled and rolled. Thighs were on fire. I felt that nut travel from the base of my abdomen, up my spine, then back down again and I came so hard, Tara was clawing at my hands because it was difficult for her to breathe.

"Fuck," I yelled out, then calmed myself remembering my daughter was in the next room.

My eyes watered as I looked down at Tara. The euphoric feeling I had quickly dissipated when I saw my come running from the sides of her mouth. I groaned and grunted as I kept releasing, then frowned. Staci had never wasted not one drop of my semen. Never. No matter how hard I came or how much there was, she never wasted one single drop.

Tara looked up at me and saw my displeasure. I yanked my dick from her mouth. She cupped her hand, still trying to swallow.

Once she did, she spurted out, "I'm sorry, baby. I'm sorry. It was a lot. I wasn't expecting that much. I'm sorry," she apologized quickly.

She knew me well enough to know why I wasn't pleased with her. "Get on the bed," I ordered.

She did so quickly. Her blonde hair bounced around her face. I didn't want to look into her face right now. It was hard to look at one woman while envisioning another.

"On your knees."

She quickly turned over and assumed the position. I grabbed a condom from the drawer, ripped the wrapper, and sheathed my semi hardened dick. Tara was wet. Her pink pussy glistened with sticky arousal that invited me in. I grabbed her hips, snatched her back while I roughly entered her.

She hissed, hands gripped the comforter. "Sssss, damn, Donnie, baby. Shit."

Most times, Tara needed a few minutes to adjust to my size and length. I didn't give her the time. I fucked her hard and long. Wrapped her long, blonde hair around my hand and rocked my hips into her barely-there ass. I spanked her hard. Left my big handprint on her ass. She grunted and moaned. Whimpered and hissed as she coated the condom with her satisfaction. She glazed my dick like a Krispy Kreme donut. Pussy was tight and warm. She was throwing it back just as good as I gave. Said the right amount of nasty shit. Gave me everything she had and still … still she wasn't Staci, and she never would be.

***

A few hours later, after I'd showered and made Tara shower as well—and changed the covers on the bed—I laid with her in my arms. She liked to sleep there. Said it made her feel safe when I wrapped her in my arms. She was sleeping soundly. I was awake, phone in my hand, texting my wife.

Where are you? I wanted to know.

When I'd initially sent the text, it was a little after midnight. She didn't respond until a quarter to one.

At the office, she replied.

I picked up the cell I used for work to text Pete and asked him if Staci was at her office. His reply made me get up. Pete had been one of my best friends since college. For a while he had a promising career in the NFL, but bad decisions, fast women, money problems, and a gambling habit took him out the game. He spent five years in prison for a rape, a crime he adamantly denied. I believed him being that Pete had never hidden anything from me. He told me the story of how that night went. Even went as far as to have private investigators try to clear his name.

But of course, he fell into the proverbial "white woman screams rape after being caught with the big, Black man" trap. Her husband came home before he was supposed to. Pete was into having white women call him the N-word while he was screwing them. He liked to play the big, Black man coming to assault the timid, pure, white woman role-play and it came back to bite him in the ass in the end. But that was another story for another time.

Pete just told me Staci wasn't at work, that she had met some man at a bar near Phipps Plaza. She lied to me.

Dark skin, long locs. Stocky build. Dressed nice. If I'm not mistaken, this cat used to play for the Falcons, Pete sent me.

I quickly pulled my clothes on. Tara moaned softly as I moved around the room. When I turned to put my tie on, I saw her reaching for me to find I wasn't there. She opened her eyes. It took her a minute to adjust to the dim lighting in the room.

"I'm leaving," I told her.

"What … why? I thought you were staying the whole night," her husky voice inquired.

"Something came up."

"What came up, Donnie? You promised."

"Don't question me, Tara. I said I have to go. Let that be that," I snapped while sliding my feet into my shoes.

Tara gave a slight pout, then her eyes shot daggers into me. "What about when Becka wakes up in the morning? She's going to be expecting Daddy."

I hated when Tara did that shit. When she couldn't get her way with me, she always tried to bring my daughter into the equation.

"Rebecca is smarter than you give her credit for. She'll understand why I'm gone."

Tara sat up fully in the bed. Her breasts, not as firm as they once were, but still nice to look at, were barely covered by the sheet. Running a hand through her hair, she sighed.

"Donnie, don't keep doing this to me. I feel like I'm barely hanging on by a thread here. I hardly get time with you anymore," she whined.

"Don't do that. Don't whine. I hate that shit. You don't need to be laid up under me all the time anyway. I come over here a few nights out of the week as is."

"To spend time with Becka. If you're not screwing me then I don't get any time. I'm about sick of this shit, Donnie."

I finished adjusting my clothes. Grabbed my wallet, cuff links, and watch from the nightstand. Put the watch on and my wallet in my back pocket.

I then turned to coolly stare at her. "You're sick of what, Tara? Living in this house? Driving that brand new BMW out there? Tired of the credit cards? Thousands of dollars in your bank account? Exactly what are you tired of?" I asked her with ice in my voice.

She stared me down, something she didn't do often. She was pissed. She threw the covers off, jumped from the bed, grabbed the peach, silk robe that had been neatly lying across the ottoman, and slid her arms through before roughly tying the sash at the waist.

Tara stopped short of getting in my face when she spat, "I'm sick of you treating me like a piece of ass. You say you love me, right? Then act like it."

"I care for you because you have my child. Nothing more," I clarified.

Tara recoiled like she had been slapped. "Excuse me?"

"You heard me. Now get out of my face before we have a problem."

As bad as I wanted to feel about the way I spoke to Tara, I didn't feel bad at all. She knew I was married. Shit, I was married to her ex-best friend. So I had no idea why she kept expecting more of me than I was willing to give. Yes, part of that was my fault as when we first started hooking up, I did spend a lot of time with her. Spent so much time that one night I slipped up and said fuck the condom. Fucked her raw, and as a result, Rebecca was born. That would never happen again. The expression on Staci's face when she found out I had been cheating with her best friend was heartbreaking. The way she cried and shut herself off from me when she found out Tara had my child was something else altogether. For a while I stopped having sex with Tara. Tried to bring some normalcy back into my home. But, once again, Staci picked her bottle of choice over me, and I was left to look for solace elsewhere.

Tara's eyes watered and reddened with intense heat. My phone vibrated with a message from Pete.

It read, **They're leaving together.**

"You're so full of shit, Donnie. Get out. Get the hell out. And when she's too drunk to recognize what a good man you claim to be, don't come running back to me," she shouted.

I closed the gap between us and damn near yanked her off the floor when I grabbed her chin. She gasped and tensed up. Her hands gripped my wrist.

"Get your hands off of me," I snapped. She quickly removed her hands from my wrist. "Watch the way you speak to me, understand? Don't ever get so beside yourself that you think you can run me, Tara. I come and I go as I please. You don't get the right to dictate that, get me? Now, I want you to get back in the bed and relax. Get some rest. Make sure my daughter has breakfast in the morning and send her off to school like a good mother should. Are we clear?"

When she didn't respond, I gripped her chin tighter.

"Ow, Donnie," she whimpered.

"I said, are we clear?"

"Yes," she spat out so venomously it almost stung.

I gave her a quick kiss to the lips then let her go. She stumbled back a bit, rubbing her chin. I shut her bedroom door behind me as I walked out then walked across the hall to kiss a sleeping Rebecca one more time before leaving. I had been gone for about ten minutes when Tara texted me.

I hate you, her text read.

Tossing the phone on the passenger seat, I grunted. Thought about the state of my marriage. Sometimes I hated me, too.

Where Did We Go Wrong?: Sheila

Chapter 10

I sat home nursing a drink I'd poured myself about an hour ago. Candles were lit around the room. Ken Ford played softly in the background. His favorite meal, which was cool now, sat on the dinner table in the dining room. The purple lingerie I had on was starting to feel uncomfortable as it was crawling up crevices I didn't know I had. I suppose it was my fault that I was alone on our anniversary.

Jerome Thibodeaux, one of the Atlanta Falcons all-time rushing running backs, and now one of the top sports agents in the south, was in a league of his own. Not because of the sports accolades, but because of who he was as a husband. Jerome was the best thing that had ever happened to me, but trust issues had gotten in the way of our love. Trust issues and my eagerness to create my own path in life.

My father ran off and left my mother with seven of us to raise alone. A house full of women. Daddy decided he just didn't want to be a husband or father anymore, so we had to fend for ourselves. Because of that, Mama had always told us girls never to depend on a man for shit. Always have your own was what she had instilled into us starting the day Daddy left.

I was all of ten when Mama came home with pain in her eyes.

"Where's Daddy?" Michaela, who had been named after him, asked.

Daddy's name was Michael. She was the oldest, fourteen at the time. Mama, a hefty, but beautiful woman, had tears in her eyes. Her deep dimples showed even when she was sad. We'd grown up in a little, three-bedroom house on Highway 17 in Lexington, Mississippi. The shit-green house stood out, and often times we got made fun of because of its color, but Mama and Daddy had made that little house a home … or so we'd thought.

The rest of my sisters and I had been sitting on a blanket on the floor eating the bacon and rice Michaela had cooked for us. We had no kitchen table. The one we'd had, finally gave out on us and Mama could no longer put enough nails in it to hold it together. We had to eat on the floor for the time being. Michaela was the oldest at fourteen with the rest of us falling in right behind her from the ages of thirteen to eight.

"Daddy's not coming home tonight," Mama said.

As always, when Mama went to get Daddy from work, she was dressed in her best. Red lipstick on her plush, pink lips. Hair always done in some fancy do. That time it was in a long, sleek ponytail. She had on yellow jeans that contoured to her shapely hips. Blouse complemented her hefty chest. And her makeup was flawless.

"Where he at?" Delilah had wanted to know.

"Not 'where he at', " Michaela corrected. "It's where is he?"

She swore she was our mother, too, and was always correcting the way we would sometimes speak. She pushed her long, wavy hair over her shoulder and put a hand on her round hips. Then, she was the perfect blend of Mama and Daddy. Light skin, pretty eyes, and long, wavy hair. Every boy in the neighborhood wanted her, but Michaela wasn't into boys. She was into girls. Nobody knew but me and Mama though. Oh, and Daddy. When he found out, he damn near beat Michaela to death. Since the day he caught her kissing the little, white girl a few houses up from us and beat her so bad she wasn't able to sit, Michaela hadn't looked at another girl or boy for that matter.

"So where is he, Mama?" she asked.

Mama's face did all kinds of strange things. One minute it looked like she was going to laugh, then another it looked like she was sick. Then she made a face that said she was going to cry. Michaela made all of us get up so we could go eat in the kitchen.

"Spread the cover on the floor, Demetri," she ordered my thirteen-year-old sister who looked like she wanted to cry, too. "Then sit them in there to eat. Don't come out until I say so."

Demetri cried so easily. She'd always been the sensitive one in the family. She was one who would literally cry because she spilled milk. But Demetri rushed us into the kitchen. I pretended I had to use the bathroom just so I could be nosy. The bathroom was right down the hall from the front room, so I left the door cracked. I could hear and see well from my vantage point. When Mama thought we were all out the way, she dropped to the floor and started sobbing. I'd never seen my mama cry a day before, so the sight saddened me.

"Oh God, Mama, what's wrong?" Michaela rushed in to hug her.

"He's gone, Kayla," Mama cried.

She always called her Kayla.

"Who's gone? Daddy?"

Mama nodded as she cupped her mouth.

"Gone where? Daddy's dead?" my sister asked with wide eyes.

Mama shook her head. "No, but I wish that motherfucker was dead. How could he do this to us?"

"What, Mama? How could he do what?"

"He quit his job, baby. He quit his job and he ran off with Tony. Mr. Elroy said Michael ain't been to work

since about a week ago. He'd only been pretending to go. Would wait for me at the store so I would think he had worked."

Michaela shook her head with a deep frown etched on her features. "What? I don't understand."

Ran off with Tony where? *I thought. I knew who Tony was. He was Mama Jean's nineteen-year-old son who everybody had said was funny. Now I'd known Tony for a long time and there hadn't been anything that he'd ever said or done that I found funny. But all the older folk swore he was funny. He was a little on the flimsy side, and sometimes had female like mannerisms, but never ever had he made me laugh. Michaela sat eyes widened and jaws slack.*

She shook her head. "I don't … I don't understand, Mama. Daddy's ga— "

Before she could get the words out, I accidently knocked the soap dish off the small sink, and they jumped. Michaela left Mama's side and came barging down the hall to the bathroom. I quickly hopped on the toilet like I had been there the whole time. I had on a dress so it was easy for me to pull my panties down and hop up there.

"Were you eavesdropping?" Michaela yelled as she snatched me by my arm.

I shook my head fervently. "No. I wasn't. I swear," I lied.

"You hear anything Mama just said?"

"No. I don't know what she said, Michaela, I swear."

She had water in her eyes, too. I didn't know why at the time. "You better not be lying to me."

"I'm not. Promise. Please let my arm go. It hurts."

Michaela had always been heavy handed and could throw hands with the best of them. No girl wanted to fight her, and few boys were crazy enough to.

She let me go, then ran a hand through her hair. "Hurry up, Sheila, and go finish eating," she ordered before she closed the bathroom door on her way out.

That night, Mama stayed locked away in her room. Michaela ran the roost for the next few days. She told us Mama had gotten really sick. After about two weeks, Mama miraculously healed and none of us saw Daddy again until we were all adults. Life as we knew it changed for a while. We barely had enough food to eat. The car broke down. Mama was hardly home before daybreak as she was working three jobs. She developed diabetes and high blood pressure and had gout because she always walked to and from work. Sometimes neighbors would take pity and offer her rides. Michaela worked for the white lady up the street, the mother of the girl she got caught kissing. We had to move from that house into a two-bedroom trailer that was more like a shack. For a while, it was tough, but Mama and Michaela, with the rest of us doing our parts, made it work.

All seven of us graduated top of our class from high school and college. Two months after

Jacole, who was the youngest, graduated from college, Mama passed on. For a long time, she had been sick. For so long she held on. Michaela and I, who were the health nuts in the family, begged Mama to change her diet and to exercise more, but she refused. We foolishly assumed that because of Daddy she didn't care too much about her health anymore. We'd been so wrong.

On her dying bed, Mama told us the truth. She had contracted the Acquired Immune Deficiency Syndrome, the last stage of the HIV disease. Michaela, Demetri, Rochelle, Clara, and I were the last ones to know. Mila and Jacole knew because once Mama found out she had HIV, the doctor told her it would be best if she brought all of us in to be tested just to be sure. She had never lain with another man other than Daddy, so it was no guess to where she had contracted the disease from. Back when she took us to the doctor, we thought it was for a routine checkup. House full of women got those kinds of checkups every year.

Once Mama got the results for the tests, she told us she was devastated to find out she had passed the virus on to our younger sisters. They were born with it. Back then medicine and testing wasn't as advanced, so Mama hadn't been able to be tested beforehand for HIV. We sat in that hospital room and cried like babies when we learned the truth. The rest of us had been so angry at Mila and

Jacole for keeping that secret for so long. But Mama had made them. It all made sense then why she babied them so. It also made sense as to why Mila and Jacole refused to date anybody throughout school. They both went on to create a dating website for people with HIV and AIDS—a reputable site, not one of those sites that were used for tawdry hookups and sexual escapades.

I was very proud of my sisters and my mother. We'd fought so hard to remain intact and sane after Daddy left. It was because of Daddy I didn't know how to depend on my husband. Jerome was a good man, a damn good man. And I was afraid that I'd pushed him away because for the life of me, I didn't know how to let go and let him love me. I didn't want to end up like Mama. She loved Daddy her whole life, and in the end, it had cost her, her life.

My home phone rang, jarring me from my thoughts. I picked it up without thinking to check the caller identification screen first.

"H-Hello?" I answered, a bit groggy.

"He didn't come home, did he?" a sultry voice inquired on the other end.

I inhaled and exhaled hard. "No."

I stood from the chair I'd been sitting in and walked over to my floor-to-ceiling window. I saw cars passing up and down the street and wondered if any one of those cars held my husband. Was he coming home? I thought back to my clients earlier and wondered if my husband would become like Staci Dixon's husband. Would he not care that I knew he was cheating? Would he disrespect me the way Donovan did his wife?

Unlike Mrs. Dixon, I would deserve it. Mr. Dixon had pushed his wife so far that she had confided in me she had been playing around on chat lines just to get some kind of attention. My job wasn't to judge her, but I told her several reasons why she should have chosen another avenue to search out companionship. The dangers of meeting men online being a few of those reasons.

Michaela tsked. "I knew this was going to happen, Sheila. I told you it would."

I downed the rest of the amber-colored liquor in my glass. "I know. You did. But I've been trying, Kayla. I really have."

"No, you haven't. I told you your work at the hospital was enough, but then you went ahead and reopened your private practice. Jerome is and has always been a good man, sis. He's not Daddy and you shouldn't make him pay for what Daddy did to us."

Tears burned my eyelids. "I think I've lost my husband. He's never forgotten our anniversary. Never. Even when I was working late, he would show up with flowers and gifts."

"Has he called?"

"No. Not even a text."

There was once a time when Jerome would text me throughout the day. Even those times when I was "too busy" to respond, he would still call and text. For the past few days, that hadn't been the case.

"Have you tried calling him?" she asked.

"Yes. He isn't answering."

She was about to respond, but a smooth, silk-like voice in her background stopped her. I listened to Jillian ask her if everything was okay. Jillian had been the little, white girl Daddy had damn near beaten Michaela to death for kissing. They were a weird couple sometimes with the way they behaved with one another. On again. Off again. Jillian had even gotten married and had children. And still she always found her way back to my sister. That was why I also thought they were a beautiful couple. Jillian was a psychologist while my sister was one of the most popular celebrity fitness instructors in the world.

She even had international superstar clients. That was her day job. Her job on the side was that of a private investigator. With a PhD in criminal justice, she worked for the police department when called, attorneys, and had even done work for the FBI.

I listened as she told Jillian everything was fine. She cleared her throat, then I heard covers rustle in the background.

"I've followed him for the last couple of days and he hasn't done anything out of the norm. He's gone to his office, went to a bar a few times. To the park to jog. There was some woman there he jogged with. She flirted with him, but all he did was laugh and brush her off. They jogged together for a few miles, but then she ran off after he showed her the wedding band on his finger. He's been sleeping at his office most nights, and there was one night he was at the W, but he was alone. Went in alone, checked in alone. And no one came to his hotel room throughout the night. I've found no signs he's cheating, sis. None."

I sighed. "That's a relief," I said.

"Not if he's planning on leaving you it isn't. You need to fight for your marriage, sis. Jerome has put up with your shit when I didn't even want to. You're a goddamn handful and you know it."

We both chuckled a bit as she was right. I was Ms. Independent. The only thing I boasted I needed a man for was security and dick. Those were the exact words I'd told Jerome when we first met on the campus of Georgia State. That was the first time a man had ever laughed at me to my face. Most times, men—especially Black men—got the hell on when those words came from my mouth. Not Jerome. He laughed so hard his eyes watered.

For the first time in my entire existence, he made me feel foolish for those words leaving my mouth. I'd been so embarrassed that I stormed off. When I saw him the next day, he cracked a smile as soon as he saw me.

"Can I buy Ms. Independent Don't Need No Man For Shit a cup of coffee or would that be imposing too much on her independent status?" he asked me in jest.

I'd twisted my mouth up trying not to laugh, then rolled my eyes. "Fine," I snapped. "But it has to be the most expensive, best cup of coffee around."

"And if it isn't?" he challenged with a tilt of his head and a twinkle in his eyes.

"Then I don't need it. I can be mediocre on my own."

I thought for sure that would have run him off, but he smiled and nodded. "Fair enough," he said.

From that day forth, Jerome and I were inseparable. Things were good at first, and then one day, after marriage and taking a year off from school, I woke up and realized I was becoming too dependent on him. He was the most popular rookie in the NFL and I was becoming a football wife. That was unacceptable in my book. I needed my own identity, lest I become Mama all over again.

I'd been trying to hold back my tears, but when I picked up my cell to see that there had been no text and no calls from my husband, I broke down. Years and years of putting him on the backburner were now coming back to haunt me. Seeing so many dysfunctional married couples throughout the day showed me how lucky I was to be married to Jerome.

"Oh no, Sheila, I'm coming over," my sister said once she heard my sobs.

"I'm coming, too," Jillian yelled in the background.

She had been a good friend to me over the years as well, and at this point, I needed all the comfort I could get.

Chapter 11

The next night . . .

"Where have you been?" I asked Jerome when he walked into the house at midnight.

There was a smile on his face, and he had been on the phone until he saw me. He took one look at me, his smile faded, and he ended the call without saying good-bye to whomever had been on the other end. I'd left work early just so I could be home. No matter Jerome's work schedule, he had always tried to make it home before eight at night. It hadn't been that way for over a week now.

"Was at the office," he lied.

I knew he was lying because I'd stopped by his office, and the look on his partner's face told me all I'd needed to know. Jerome's locs were pulled back by a plastic band. He had on attire that looked as if he had been to the gym. He smelled fresh. Fresh like he had just stepped out of the shower.

"You're lying," I told him. "I know you, Jerome. Where have you been?"

He dropped his gym bag in the hall closet. Took his jacket off and hung it in the closet in the foyer. His sneakers squeaked on the wood grain floor as he walked toward me.

"I told you I was at the office," he said.

"No you weren't. I went there and only Clark was there."

I folded my arms across my chest. I had on biking shorts and a sports bra as I'd done an aggressive bout of cardio while I waited for him to get home.

Jerome frowned. "You, you stopped by my office?" he asked as if it was unbelievable that I did so.

"Yes, Jerome, I stopped by your office, and you weren't there, so please don't lie to me again. Where the hell were you?"

For a moment, he only stood there and watched me. He watched with a look on his face that said he was amused and wasn't quite sure what to make of my attitude at the moment.

He scratched his ear, then dropped his phone in his basketball shorts' pocket.

"So tonight, because you've come home early for a change, you want to inquire my whereabouts? To what do I owe the pleasure?" he asked with a sarcastic flare that grated my nerves.

Jerome brushed past me and walked into the kitchen. I slowly followed him and watched as he opened the black fridge and grabbed a bottle of water. My husband was fine to look at. That could never be denied. I'd seen many women throw themselves at him. Tall, athletically built, pencil thin locs, beautiful burnt cinnamon skin, and a smile that could melt the sun. His eyes always held a sparkle, one that drew women in like moths to a flame.

Just envisioning another person getting what I knew he was capable of giving when it came to the physical saddened, angered, and humbled me. I didn't want to lose my husband. All those doubts and fears I had … I was wondering if I'd just made them up.

"Look, I know I haven't been the best wife to you. I've made so many mistakes and I'm sorry," I apologized.

He frowned. "Sheila, what is this about? Is this a joke or something? You get fired from your job? Lose your practice? What could make my wonderful wife want to apologize to me?"

"Don't make this harder than it is. You weren't in your office, so please, just tell me where you were," I practically pleaded.

Quirking a brow, he set the water bottle on the granite countertop. From the outside looking in, people would assume we had the perfect life. Between my husband signing the top players in the NFL to his roster to my thriving private practice and administrative position, people would envy us. Nice houses, even nicer cars. Banks accounts never lacking. We could be the picture-perfect couple.

"If my very apologetic wife had been paying attention to me over the last few months then she would have known that I'm in the process of opening another office in Smyrna near the Falcons football camp. That is where I've been. So you want to tell me I'm lying again?"

I knew he could see when I breathed a visible sigh of relief. Jerome had told me early on that if he started to cheat or even got the notion to cheat on me then he would just up and leave. He said our relationship would be over and there would be nothing we could do to fix it. That was why I was so hell-bent on trying to find out if he was cheating or not.

He stormed out of the kitchen and made his way upstairs. The one thing he hated was to be accused of anything. His father had always called him a liar. Never believed in him. So when Jerome gave his word, it was his bond. I felt bad for accusing him with no hard evidence, but my gut was telling me something was off between us. If that was the case, I had no one to blame but myself.

I slowly followed suit. My husband was lying in bed. One leg propped up with a remote in his hand. He was watching an interview, of which his client was the star. I eased down on the bed, my back turned to him.

"Do you know what yesterday was?" I asked.

"Tuesday?" he answered.

My heart dropped. "Our anniversary. We were married fourteen years ago yesterday."

I looked over my shoulder at him. He muted the TV, then stroked his chin.

"I didn't forget," he said solemnly. "I just didn't think you cared. You haven't cared in the last five or six years. I finally got the hint and stopped thinking you would."

I watched Jerome slide off the bed. He walked into one of our closets, pushed the clothes to the side, and tapped the panel on the side wall.

"What are you doing?" I asked.

He opened the wall safe and inside were three gift boxes. Jerome picked each one up and brought them back to me on the bed.

"For the last five years, our anniversary has been just another day for you. For the last three, you haven't even bothered to look for gifts or ask for one. So I put them all in here for safe keeping. You're so busy working you don't even pay attention to our home anymore. If you had, you would have seen the new platinum set heart necklace hanging on your necklace hanger."

I turned to see what he was speaking of. Now that I was looking, the necklace was like a beacon. A half of a heart etched in gold and diamonds. I walked over to the dresser and picked it up.

"It's beautiful," I told him.

"I know. Remember when we first got together? You told me you liked to collect hearts. All kinds of hearts. No matter if it was gold, platinum, sterling silver, plastic, paper. Didn't matter to you. You had a thing for hearts."

I nodded. "I do. I remember that."

"Remember what I did?"

Jerome's brother was a cardiologist who thought his brother was nuts for going all out for a girl the way Jerome had done.

I kept nodding as tears rolled down my cheeks. "You went to have an echocardiogram, and then handed me the ultrasound. Had your brother do it for you. He thought you were fucking nuts, but you did it. You framed it and gave it to me on our six-month anniversary."

Jerome watched me as I spoke. "I figured, if my girl was collecting hearts, I may as well throw mine into the ring as well."

As crazy as what he'd done was, it had moved me to the point of tears and laughter. Jerome had always had that effect on me. He made me laugh when I wanted to cry. Made me cry when I was laughing.

"I thought you were nuts to go through that just to give me a visual of your heart."

"I was nuts. I was crazy in love with this beautiful, independent woman who showed me how to love. She taught me how to love. I wanted the love my parents had, but you, you came in and gave me a love of my own, our own."

"I remember—"

"Tell me something," he said. "Where is that photo?"

I frowned a bit. "It's umm … it's …"

Damn. Where did I put it?

Jerome stood, waiting patiently. The fact I couldn't remember where I had placed that photo reverberated around the room in surround sound.

After a while, Jerome chuckled. "There was a time you kept my heart close to you. Now you don't even remember where you put it. Funny how art imitates life, huh?" was all he said before he laid the other three gift boxes on the bed. "Your anniversary gifts from the last three years. I would always leave them places where I thought you would look; your car, your office, our bedroom. You never cared enough to see what was right in front of you though. So, no, I didn't forget our anniversary. I never have. Too bad you just started to remember them."

***

Over the next few days, life at home was in a shambles. Jerome started coming home later and later. My sister was still following him, so there was nobody else. I tried to talk to him, but he was unwilling to talk to me. I knew some of this was my fault, that was a given, but the more Jerome went out of his way to ignore me, the angrier I became.

"Don't force it, sis. He's angry right now," Michaela said as we shared a bowl of spinach dip.

"Yeah, but how much more of this am I supposed to take?"

"That's your problem, Sheila, you're trying to force him to come around on your terms. It doesn't work that way," Jillian added.

I cast a side long glance at her. I guess this month she was going through her Ellen DeGeneres phase. She'd cut her blonde hair to a pageboy haircut. She was rocking slim fitting, blue dress slacks and baby blue loafers to match the button-down shirt. Jillian was slim in stature. I'm sure she could have been a super model if she so wanted to. During these phases, she was what the world called androgynous. Total opposite of my sister.

Michaela had so many curves, sometimes I envied her. She kept her hair long, and make up always done like she was going to a photo shoot every day. She had on a black cat suit that left little to the imagination, a black leather jacket that matched the black calf-length combat boots she had on. Her light, catlike eyes always drew attention to her. She looked just like Daddy with a little bit of Mama mixed in.

"He's a prideful man. He's always been, Sheila," Michaela added. "For as big of a star as he is, he's always taken a backseat to you. He could have been like these other cats out here—"

"I know. I know," I said cutting her off.

I didn't need another reminder of how different Jerome was to his counterparts.

"I'm just saying, he's always sat in the background waiting on you," she added.

"And you're sure he's not cheating?"

"Why do you want him to be cheating so badly?" she asked.

"Because she can't fathom that Jerome would be treating her this way because of how she's treated him. She needs to believe that there is another woman to justify the fact her husband is about to walk out on her," Jillian added.

"Don't psychoanalyze me, Jillian," I snapped.

She didn't look as if the tone in my voice bothered her. "It's the truth. Don't be mad at me."

"Whatever."

Jillian shrugged, then sipped from her cup of coffee. We often argued and psychoanalyzed one another being that we were in the same field. Today just annoyed me more so than other times.

"I saw your father today," she said after an uncomfortable silence.

Dropping the chip she had in her hand, Michaela sat back in her chair. Her spine went stiff, and she looked away like something stunk to her.

I sat forward. "How is he?"

"Needs a kidney," Jillian told me.

"Did you tell him I'm going to stop by soon?"

She nodded. "I did. He wants to see you, too, Michaela."

"Fuck him," my oldest sister spat. "Don't talk to me about him. Anything you have to say about that man, tell Sheila. Don't tell me."

I was the only one of Daddy's daughters who would speak to him, which was ironic since I judged men based on what he had done to our family.

"You have to forgive him at some point, Michaela," I told my sister.

"Says the woman who made her husband pay for what our sperm donor did to us."

"I still can't believe Daddy moved to Atlanta," I said.

Jillian added, "And I can't believe he's one of my patients."

Jillian worked heavily in the gay community. She was one of the well-respected doctors who specialized in therapy for the LGBTx community as well. It took me well into my teenage years to accept the fact Daddy had left Mama for another man. Once that fact settled in, it made me even angrier. But Mama told us we couldn't hate the man. She said we had to understand that things had happened to Daddy when he was a child that shouldn't have happened to little kids. It didn't take rocket science to figure out what she had meant. She told us Daddy had demons that he had to come to terms with.

"Don't hate him," she said to us on her death bed. "He never got help for what happened to him. Pray for him, and not because he's bisexual. Pray for him because he's been hurt, severely, by those who were supposed to protect him and they didn't. It's hard for a man to admit certain things, baby. If he had admitted he'd been raped by women, folk would have clowned him. If he had admitted he'd been raped by men, they would have ostracized him. So, pray for his mental wellbeing that one day, one day he'll be able to heal because until that happens … hurt people, hurt people. Get me?"

I didn't understand her then. Didn't understand how she could want us to pray for the man who had fucked up our whole lives. I told her as much.

"Sheila, yes, we were poor, baby, but look at you girls. You all turned out very well. All these accolades in this room. Daddy leaving may have interrupted the show, but it didn't stop it. Be grateful. Don't hate the man. He'll come to his senses. Let's just hope it's not too late …"

I was jarred back to reality by Michaela leaving the table. Jillian shook her head. She pulled out her wallet and left a hundred dollars on the table.

"Sorry," she said as she stood. "You know Michael is a sore spot for her. But he's looking forward to your meeting this week. He needs those, so please keep them up." She kissed my jaw. "Talk soon. Love you," she said to me as she rushed behind my sister.

There was no need for me to leave a tip since Jillian had done more than take care of the bill and tip. I no longer had an appetite anyway. I soon left, too. The day was bright. A little windy, so a light jacket was needed. I thought back to my sister. Any time we mentioned Daddy, her reaction was always the same. She never forgave Daddy for beating her the way he did when he found out she was gay, when he, too, was bisexual himself. I could understand her angst when it came to that.

I pulled into a gated apartment community known as Windsor Landing. I didn't know why it was gated. There was nothing worth stealing from the outside looking in. As many times as I'd offered to move Daddy out of this place, he would never take me up on it. I wished he would have. Kids scattered back and forth out of the street as I drove through. The buildings needed to be pressure washed as caked on dirt had taken residence on the outside paneling. It was no longer the once cream color it had been. It looked more brown now. The lawn needed to be tended to.

The scent of barbeque filled the air. Some women—well, I wouldn't really call them that being that they looked like the now outdated term, transvestites, of old—eyeballed me as I cruised through. I drove all the way around the back until I got to building 'O'. I hoped nobody tried to steal my shit while I was here. Daddy always assured me nobody would, but I was never too sure. I got out and hit the alarm behind me. The wind had picked up, so I pulled my jacket tighter. I waved at a few of my dad's neighbors as I walked around to door number three.

His door was open, but he had one of those snap-on screen door things. I could hear his TV playing. I knocked on the side panel.

"Daddy?" I called out.

He was frying something. I could smell it.

"Come on in, baby girl. Knew I'd see you sometime this week. Didn't think it would be today," he yelled from the kitchen.

I walked in with a smile. Daddy's house was so clean I could eat off the floor. That was the way he had always been. He'd taught all of us to be the same way. Cleanliness was next to Godliness he would often preach. He and Mama even used to joke about the fact he cleaned and cooked more than she did. I could never understand why he walked off and left us. He and Mama had seemed to be so in love. I never saw Daddy raise a hand to Mama. Never heard him raise his voice. Since I had been old enough to remember, he was always touching on Mama, kissing on her, telling her how beautiful she was. She got flowers every Friday and Sunday. I didn't understand why he'd done what he did.

I always visited my father, but today I visited for one reason alone; I needed closure. For so long I'd run away from asking Daddy why. I didn't want to hear him say he loved another man more than he loved us. It wasn't until Mama's funeral that we saw him again. Michaela had flipped her lid. Told Daddy he wasn't welcomed, and he never would be as far as she was concerned. No matter how many times I tried to talk to her, how many times I tried to get her to remember Mama's words, she wouldn't budge. None of my sisters were as forgiving as I was.

While the rest of them would at least answer when he called, Michaela wouldn't. I didn't know why I so eagerly forgave Daddy. Or had I? How could I forgive him if I hadn't allowed him to give me his version of the truth?

Daddy walked from the kitchen with a warm smile. It was hard for me to take in the sight of him. He had HIV and he still looked as if there wasn't a thing wrong with him. He had raw honey-colored eyes, stocky in build, no fat on his body. He was in good shape, that couldn't be denied. His long, black hair cascaded around his shoulders. I often envied his hair. While mine sat wild and unruly most times, Daddy's, Mama's, and Michaela's hair never had a strand out of place. Michaela had some of Mama's features, but she looked every bit of our father.

That wasn't to say she looked like a man. That was because Daddy had … lady-like facial features. He was pretty per say. They used to call him Pretty Boy back home. Mama told us that was why the perverts targeted him, male and female. Daddy's voice was deep though. His baritone molasses thick. The man was sixty-two and still looked thirty.

He was dressed in linen drawstring pants. No shirt. His tattoos visible. Mama's face over his heart. All his daughters' names, including mine, on the other side of his chest. Chains tatted on his triceps to make them look as if they coiled around his arms. Abs constricted each step he took. He walked like there was power in his strides. I saw why any man or woman would be drawn to him. But if ever they looked long enough, deep enough, they'd see the pain and horror behind his eyes. They'd see there was a man in there they didn't want to trifle with. All the abuse he'd suffered, left a man who would break their necks at the snap of his finger if they disrespected him.

I smiled and greeted, "Hey, Daddy."

"Hello, baby girl," he responded and wrapped me in a warm embrace.

Daddy easily towered over me. I had to stand on my toes to get a good grip on him.

"Daddy, you know you shouldn't be eating all that fried food," I fussed.

He chuckled as he pulled back, then ushered me to sit on the black sofa next to his recliner. "Don't come over here fussing at me. I eat what I want. I'm healthy as a horse. I work out, too, so there's that," he defended.

He plopped down in his recliner then muted the TV. He was watching *Roots*.

"So how are you? Jillian said you need a kidney."

He nodded. "Docs say I do. Say one of mine is failing."

"How soon?"

Quirking a brow, Daddy studied me and smirked a bit. "I'll just keep that tad bit of info to myself since I can see you're thinking of doing something crazy like getting tested to see if yours would be a match."

"It couldn't hurt to check."

"No."

"Daddy—"

"I said no. I took enough from all of you. Won't take anymore."

He spoke his words with finality. I knew there was no sense in arguing with him about it. Daddy had always been one to say what he meant and mean what he says.

"How's Ricky?" I asked, changing the subject.

Ricky was a man he had been dating.

Daddy shrugged. "Don't know. Not seeing him anymore."

"Are you seeing anybody?"

He nodded, and a slow smile eased over his face. "Seeing this chick I met on your sisters' site. She kind of reminds me of your mother."

"She looks like Mama?" I asked with a smile.

Daddy's smile widened. "Kind of, but that's not why she reminds me of her. She reminds me of her because she knows what happened to me."

"You told her?"

He nodded once as he got up to head back to the kitchen. I assumed to check on his food.

"Told her on the third or fourth date. I knew she was special because she didn't shy away from me after that," he spoke loudly from the kitchen. "You know your mama was the only woman who ever knew what happened to me back then and she didn't run away from me."

He came back from the kitchen. In his hand were two Coronas. He popped the top and gave me one then took a seat. I put my purse on the couch and relaxed a bit. Daddy sat back down.

"Thank you," I said.

"Welcome. Did I ever tell you about how your mama and I met?"

I shook my head. "No."

He took a sip of his Corona before speaking. "She found me one day. I was hiding in the back of your grandfather's pickup truck. I was a bloody mess. Had been beaten and violated too many times to stick around my folks' place. So, I ran. Had run away before, but they always found me. I ran to the one place I knew nobody was fool enough to come looking for me. Grandpop Nook was nothing to play with. My folks, for as evil as they were, weren't crazy enough to come on his property and find me. Was thirteen years old. The man who donated sperm to me to had found me trying to kill myself and before he would allow me to off myself, he tried to do it for me. Make a long story short, your mama found me. Ran to get her daddy. From that day forward, I never had to leave her. Nook took me in. Nook was different than other folk. For one, he was a single father. Your mama was his only child, but he wasn't one of those crazed fools, you know.

"Let me stay with him and your mama. Only thing I had to do was heal and help around the house. Crazy-ass old man told me he didn't want no fag shit outta me. Even though he knew what had happened to me." Daddy chuckled. "Times were different back then, but Nook said he knew how boys like me turned out and he wouldn't stand for no fag shit around him. I didn't blame the old man, and, at the time, I didn't want no fag shit around me either. Nook was a man's man. Didn't understand my folks. A couple days later, word got out about how my old man ended up with both his legs broken. Nook had gone to see him. Best damn news I'd ever heard as a child. He broke my mama's jaw, too. Said he hadn't ever in his life hit a woman but said he didn't consider the piece of pussy who birthed me a woman. His words, not mine."

"Damn, Granddaddy," I said, thinking of the old man.

Daddy kept talking. "He set fire to a shed on their farm where they let stuff happen to me and my sisters. Shot a couple of my uncles. Nook was a one-man army. Didn't stop until everybody had paid for what they had done to me, my brothers, and my sisters. I never had a problem out of my folks since. Your mama had always been nice to me, but the day she found me in the back of that truck, I think was the day I fell in love with her."

As I sat and listened to my father speak of my mother with such fondness, it just didn't add up. It didn't make sense that he loved this woman so and leave us the way he did.

"Then why you leave her, Daddy? Why did you leave us?" I wanted to know.

Leaning forward, Daddy ran a big hand down his unusually pretty face. "I was wondering when and if one of you would ask me that. Out of all my daughters, I somehow figured it would be you. I'm going to give you my answer, but once I'm done, I want you to answer a question for me. Deal?"

I wanted to ask him what question, but Daddy's face had frowned. It almost looked as if he was in pain. I just nodded and remained quiet.

"Okay," he said. "I'm going to tell you this in hopes that you don't think this is all an excuse. A week before I left, the doctor called me and told me I had HIV. Back then, around '87-'88, HIV was still relatively new to the scene. But I knew what it was, and it scared me. I'd been doing shit that I shouldn't have been, baby. Couldn't tell your mother about it because I knew it would hurt her. Did you know your mother wrote me a letter every day from the day I left her? Didn't get them until after she died. She knew what I was doing. Told me in one of those letters, she wished I would have just come to her and she would have let me go. Said while she didn't understand my sexuality, she loved me enough to let me go, to live and be free. Something she felt I'd never done."

Tears lined my father's eyes. I stood, grabbed some Kleenex, and handed one to him. Daddy took the tissue, then my hand as I sat back down. I had some tissue of my own. I wiped at my eyes.

"I ran away because I didn't want to face the music. I felt sick to my stomach. I couldn't get away from the very thing that used to disgust me when I was being forced to have sex with adults. I hated myself after each time I laid with a man. Doc wanted me to bring my whole family in to test them. I panicked. Asked the doc if it was possible I passed this on to my wife and kids. When he told me it was very possible, I couldn't deal. I ran, but I didn't run away for Tony. Tony, the boy was gay and knew he couldn't stay in our hometown. He worked in the doctor's office, so he knew my secret. Asked me what I was going to do. I told him I was leaving, and he decided I was his way out, too."

"So you weren't cheating on Mama with Tony?" I asked.

I needed to know. Needed to clarify that Daddy never ran off with the other man.

Daddy looked up at me, eyes red, water leaking from them. "I didn't say that," he answered honestly.

I eased my hand away from his. Daddy looked like I'd just stabbed a dagger through his heart by doing so. Hearing the truth hurt like hell. No matter how Daddy tried to dress it up, in the end, he left us. He ran off with the boy he was cheating with which added even more insult to injury.

"People talked, Daddy. You have any idea how hard it is for little girls to go to school in the South, in Mississippi—in the country hick town of Lexington—when whispers of their daddy being a 'faggot' are so loud? Any idea the shame Mama felt? Any idea how many times she had to defend us against the rumors?" I asked.

My voice came out harsher than I'd intended, but I couldn't help it. I stood and paced around his front room. Looked at the pictures of me and my sisters that lined his wall. There were no pictures of Mama because they were all in his second bedroom. Daddy had built like this shrine dedicated to her. Nobody was allowed in that room, I'd seen it once, but only because he had unintentionally left the door open my first time at his place.

"No, baby, I have no idea what that's like," he answered solemnly.

"You left seven daughters and a grief-stricken wife."

"I know."

"Mama carried the weight of the world on her shoulders. Sometimes I think she only kept going to make sure we made it out alive. You took everything, Daddy, and you left us with nothing. Know what it's like to take everything from a poor person? We never had much to begin with, but you and Mama made us feel rich. We never knew just how much we didn't have until you left, Daddy. We lived in a trailer on someone else's property. There were no doors or windows for a long time," I told him, trying to get control of my sobs. "Ever see a woman so scared something would happen to her daughters she slept with a gun and a machete sitting upright in a chair? That's how you left us, Daddy."

I remembered Mama having to cook on an open fire outside because we didn't have gas in that trailer. Recalled sleeping in layers upon layers of clothes when it was cold. We all had to pile in one bed to stay warm. In the summertime, the mosquitoes would eat us alive. Sometimes a snake or two would get in and have us all running scared, but not Mama. She was afraid of maggots, but a snake didn't bother her. She'd cut that sucker up with the quickness and toss it back outside. Daddy had broken us to the core, but Mama didn't let the outside world know, and after a while, we stopped dwelling on it as well. We had to in order to push on. I told Daddy as much. He stood and rushed over to hug me.

"You were my baby. Followed me around like my shadow," Daddy said while he held me close to his chest.

And he was right. I was Daddy's right-hand girl. He gardened, I gardened. He went to pick plums and blackberries, I went to pick plums and blackberries. He went fishing, I went fishing.

By the time I got finished talking, we were both sobbing. I didn't think I could be any harder on the man than he had been on himself. I thought the reason I so eagerly forgave my father was because I needed to. I needed him. I'd always needed my father. That didn't take away anything from Mama, because she was a woman of strength and resilience. None of my other sisters understood me. But I needed my daddy. We stood in his front room, hugged up that way for a long time.

Chapter 12

After eating with Daddy and getting in some more daddy/daughter healing time, I headed home. Took me an hour to get there because somebody on I-20 decided it would be fun to speed in the rain and cause a three-car accident.

I felt good after my conversation with Daddy even after he asked me a question about my marriage I wasn't ready to answer. Felt like I could tackle the world. The world being my marriage. I was optimistic.

Daddy gave me some sage advice. Told me I was too much like him and needed to be more like my mother. Told me I should actually show my husband why I loved him. Said I should show him why I wanted to spend the rest of my life with him. Daddy said my mistake was growing away from Jerome instead of growing with him. I had to make it right.

"You gotta be willing to lose some battles in order to keep the peace, baby girl," he told me.

I got in the house and headed to the shower. Once done, I cleaned and cooked Jerome's favorite meal. I called him but got no answer. It was six in the evening, so he was probably closing up shop.

"He would call me back," I said to myself.

When eight rolled around I sent him a text asking him what time he would be home. I got no response. My heart beat heavily against my ribcage. At nine he sent a text telling me he would be late. I guess being home late meant all the way into the next day. Jerome, my husband, didn't come home.

Secret Lovers: Rome
Chapter 13

She laid resting peacefully in my arms. We'd danced and drank until we could barely stand. No, we didn't go out. We stayed locked away in my hotel room the whole time we were together. I didn't think that I would see her again. Had no intentions of ever reaching out to Piña again, ever. I'd felt so guilty after fucking the beautiful stranger in the club, then behind the building once again before I left, that I drove home praying my wife wasn't there.

I didn't think I'd be able to face her after what I had done. For as mad as I was at her, she didn't deserve to be cheated on, I'd admonished myself on the drive home. To be honest, I felt more disappointed in myself than anything. I'd never been with another woman other than my wife before Piña. I'd been the brunt of jokes during the height of my career. When my teammates were swimming in any woman with a hole, I was itching to get back home to Sheila, my wife. No woman I'd seen in the clubs, on the streets, anywhere was better than what I had at home.

I gazed down at Piña … Damn, how things had changed. The night I got home after the club, Sheila was nowhere to be found. I couldn't sleep. Tossed and turned most of the night. My guilt was eating me alive. After the first few days, I was so guilt stricken I was ready to fall on my sword and confess.

At least that had been my plan. But every time I tried to talk to my wife, she brushed me off. From the moment she walked in the house, she was in no mood to talk, she'd said. Pushed me to the side for whatever she was doing in that moment. The days that followed, she would lock herself in her office. Would leave a note on the door telling me she was busy and didn't want to be bothered. *What the fuck?* I'd thought. A note, seriously? Why was she treating me like I was one of her interns? She was busy? Didn't want to be bothered?

I banged on her office door, set to kick that motherfucker down when she snatched it open. A bored expression was on her face. One that said she didn't want to be bothered. I knew that look. I'd seen it many times over the years. The fight that had ensued afterwards was one I was all too familiar with. She needed time away from work to finish her new book. Needed a few hours of alone time after she was done so she could rest. That rest turned into her sleeping in her office or in the front room. I couldn't count how many nights I'd slept alone.

Once I saw that shit was never going to change between me and Sheila, I gave up hope in that moment. If she didn't give a fuck, then why should I? The next day, I sent Piña an email with my phone number. That was all I'd sent in the email. I figured she was smart enough to get the message. It took her a few days to call, but when she did, all was well in my world.

The first day, we met up at the park. Pretended as if we'd never met before. We ran a few miles together before I showed her my ring to let her know I was a faithful man. She giggled and then ran off to her car. A few minutes later, I headed to mine. I sent her a text asking if she could get some time away from home for a few hours. Gave her the name of the hotel and room number. Told her to be there waiting for me when I got there. I'd already left her name and an extra key for her at the front desk. Yes, I'd been presumptuous, but the fact that she was there waiting on me let me know I'd been right.

That had been our routine for the last three weeks. She would make it to the hotel before I would. We knew what we were doing was wrong, but we often ignored the wrongness of it. We just needed comfort. Secret lovers we had become. Although I doubted there was any love shared between us. We were just two ships passing in the night, as the adage went.

"Did she find the gift?"

I glanced down to find Piña's eyes open. "Thought you were sleeping," I said.

"I was for a moment," she responded, then turned onto her back.

The coldness I felt when she moved her head from my chest bothered me. I sat up. Threw my legs over the side of bed. The plush carpet underneath my feet tickled my toes. I was as naked as the day I'd come into the world and so was Piña. Her body was amazing. Even the stretch marks that decorated the lower part of her abdomen didn't take away from the breathtaking image. The sheets rustled behind me. Piña got up and walked across the suite to check her vibrating phone lying on the dresser. The shades were open just enough for the moonlight to shine through. The skyline of Atlanta was amazing this time of night, but it was Piña's silhouette that made my dick jump to life.

"She thought I'd forgotten," I told Piña.

"You did."

I grunted with a slight nod. "I did."

If I hadn't been discussing the many times my wife and I had fought about little things in our marriage, from her not coming home from work at decent hours to her forgetting our anniversary three years in a row, Piña wouldn't have been able to remind me that it was the date of my anniversary.

Piña finished texting on her phone, probably lying to her husband about where she was again. She scratched her backside. The sound was loud because of the silence in the room. Sounded as if she was scratching sandpaper. It made me chuckle since her skin was so soft to the touch.

She turned to look at me, her phone still in her hand. "What are you laughing at?"

I shook my head. "Nothing."

"First time you forgot your anniversary. You should thank me."

I had to piss. My balls were aching, and my bladder was having a fit. "I did thank you," I told her, referring to the sex we had right after she reminded me and just before I left to go get Sheila an anniversary gift.

"So what did she say?"

She cast a glance down at her phone. I told her she asked too many damn questions sometimes. It annoyed me. Piña picked up a bottle of wine, poured herself some, then almost downed the glass in one swallow.

"You drink a lot," I told her.

She looked at the glass, then sniffed. "Helps with the guilt. So, what did your wife say?"

When she mentioned guilt, I assumed she was talking about her infidelity. "I don't know. Left her in the room crying trying to figure out where she had placed my heart."

Piña looked confused, so I gave her a rundown of what happened. Told her about the photo, the echocardiogram of my heart and what it had meant to me and my wife so long ago. As I talked, I walked to the bathroom. Didn't bother turning the light on. Took a piss. The urine hitting the water laid soundtrack to our conversation.

"Wipe the tip of your dick off," she yelled. "I hate when guys piss and don't wipe the tip. You'll have yellow piss stains in front of your boxers."

"My boxer briefs are black. It won't show."

She giggled. "Ew, Rome."

I chuckled. I found we often did that. Made silly conversations to stave off the awkwardness of us cheating.

"Don't forget your ring," I told her as I washed my hands.

I stared at the symbol of her vow to another man lying on the cream granite countertop next to mine. Anytime we got together we took our rings off. We'd decided we didn't want the weight of them on us while we committed adulterous sins. I finished up in the bathroom and walked out to find she had opened the shades more. She was standing in front of the bay window naked. She didn't care that if someone from the office buildings across from us was working late, all they had to do was look across and get an eyeful.

I eased up behind her, my manhood resting against the top of her ass since I was taller than she was. My locs draped around my shoulders, swaying against hers. I let my hands slip from her waist down to her toned thighs. The Eye of Horus tattoo had always held my curiosity. I let my hand trace it absentmindedly until I felt abrasions or something that felt like a keloid. My mind went back to a day I'd rather forget.

"What happened here?" I asked.

I felt when her body tensed. She laid her hand over mine and eased it away from the tattoo before moving away from the window and me. For a long while she was quiet as she sat at the foot of the bed. I thought maybe I had broached a subject that I shouldn't have. Her head hung like she was too tired of holding it up.

"Car accident," she said softly. "I was driving home in the rain. Roads were slick. I lost control of the car …"

Her voice trailed off like there was more to the story that she wasn't willing to tell. I dropped my head, something akin to guilt overtaking me. I'd never been one to force anyone to talk when they didn't want to. So, I turned to look back out the window, gazing out over the city like a voyeur. Fog hung low, creating a dark atmosphere that seemed to hover over Atlanta. Tops of the tallest buildings had disappeared into the clouds it seemed. Down below, the faint sound of horns blaring could be heard. Headlights from different vehicles made me wonder if anyone inside of them were doing what we were … cheating, breaking vows that we had sworn to upheld.

Piña and I always met under the guise of anonymity. We never said too much. Just enough for us to feel close but distant at the same time. It worked for us and didn't complicate the situation we had placed ourselves in.

"Are you hungry?" I asked.

"No, not right now."

There was silence between us again before she asked, "How long do you think we can keep this up? I'm getting used to running to you when things go to shit at home."

I turned to look at her. Piña was so beautiful, but I could tell she had demons. The fact that she got up and picked up the wine bottle again told me that. I knew when a person was drinking to chase their demons away. I'd dealt with an alcoholic father. I wasn't calling Piña an alcoholic as she didn't seem to not be able to handle her liquor, but anytime she picked up her phone to call her husband or respond to text from him, she drank.

I walked over and sat next to her on the bed. I took the wine bottle from her, then took a healthy swallow.

"No change at home?" I asked.

She shook her head and ran her hands through her hair. "No. I think … I think it may be over for him and me."

"Why do you say that?"

Shrugging, she licked her plush lips. "Just a feeling I have deep in my gut. Never felt this before, but, yeah, I feel the time is near."

I was about to respond until I felt her shivering beside me. It wasn't cold in the room, so I figured it had to be emotions. I put the wine bottle down, then took her hand. I didn't have to see her face to know she was crying. Crazy game we were playing. There we were in love with two other people. Had just finished fucking to our hearts' content, but both emotionally torn because we genuinely loved the people we had at home.

Love was fucked up like that. Our version was at least. So many people lived with the notion that if you loved someone you wouldn't hurt them. When they said that shit, though, it was normally because one person had cheated on another. But what about those in marriages and relationships who hurt their significant others and spouses without cheating? What about neglect? What about that alienation of affection?

As a man, I'd run out of fucking options. I'd talked, begged, pleaded … shit, I'd pretty much given Sheila my manhood all in an effort to save my marriage and nothing had worked. Just like reality, love was based on perception. Everybody had a different view of what love was supposed to be. Most times, though, we had a fairytale idea of love and how it was supposed to be shown. Shit, for the first few years of my marriage I was under the impression I'd had the perfect love … how wrong I'd been.

Men got a bad rep for being the dogs in the relationship, but what could be said for men like me? Men who went out of their way to be a good husband and still found it wasn't enough? What about those men like me who sat back and watched their wives put work, school, and everything else before them? And, again, don't get me wrong, I absolutely loved the fact my wife was her own woman. I just didn't understand why there couldn't be room for me in her life like it used to be.

No matter what was going on in my life as far as my career, I never made Sheila take a back seat. I couldn't say the same for her though.

I hooked a finger under Piña's chin and turned her face to mine. "Do you still love him?" I asked.

I'd asked her that once before and she told me she missed the man her husband used to be. I felt that was a lie though. Looking at her red eyes and the way her emotions were written across her face, I could see the love she still had for him.

Tears led a stream over her lips. "I'll always love him. I never stopped. It's just … some things happened …"

Her lips quivered like she was fighting with whether she wanted to fully open up to me. I understood her hesitation and wouldn't force her to. Sometimes, words weren't needed to comfort a woman. Sometimes all she needed was a shoulder to cry on, someone to listen to her without judgment, or someone to give her the right touch at the right moment. I chose to give Piña all three. I hooked my pointing finger underneath her chin, then tilted her head up to kiss her. Soft and slow kisses to let her know she controlled the show.

Piña leaned into the kisses, moaning softly anytime my tongue touched hers. I felt it, too … that tug in the gut whenever we decided to take things further. There was no doubt in our minds that we were living out fantasies. We hadn't even been bold enough to tell the other our real names yet. Well, I'd been more truthful with my name than she was hers, I was sure. I could tell Piña wasn't her real name by the way she sometimes didn't answer when I called her that. I would call her two or three times before she remembered her name was supposed to be Piña.

The fact that she didn't know my face told me she wasn't a sports fan like she'd told me she was when we first started exchanging emails. Anybody who was an avid sports fan would have known my face off top. Piña didn't though and I found I liked that.

I pulled her on top of me as we fell back on the bed. There was nothing like when a woman who knew what she was doing took control. She straddled my hips as we kissed. My hands roamed over her back and plump ass. She was so fucking beautiful. While she stretched over to the nightstand to grab a condom, my mouth latched on to one of her breasts. Her nipples were the size of dimes and when hardened they made the perfect chocolate morsels. Sometimes I got so caught up in Piña that I wished we could forgo the condoms altogether, but we were both old and smart enough to know better.

"Oh shit," I growled when she used her mouth to slide the condom on my rigid shaft.

When she came back up and climbed on top of me, euphoria settled into my body. I bit down on my bottom lip while sending a heady gaze up at her. Piña was always so into the act of sex. She hissed and moaned. Grabbed her own breasts with one hand while strumming her clit with the other.

Whatever had happened between her and her husband to make her cheat had to be his loss. There was no doubt in my mind that if that man knew his good pussy was being stroked by another man, he'd flip his shit. Piña's pussy could make the president go to war. Never felt a pussy as hot, tight, and wet as hers.

Don't get me wrong, my wife had good sex, too, but Piña? Good God, this woman was heaven on earth. Her muscles sucked me in and wouldn't let go until she was ready. She made me dig my nails into her hips, grit my teeth, bite my lips, grunt, and all those other things some men would never publicly admit to doing during sex. Yeah, she even made me come before I was ready. All the things I'd forgotten my wife could do to me as well …

Chapter 14

A few hours later, after showering, I headed down to my car while Piña ordered room service. As always, she was hungry after sex. I needed to grab my other gym bag since we planned to stay most of the night. I had an extra pep in my step as I walked. Hadn't felt this good in years. I signed a few autographs when sports fans spotted me. Took a few photos, too. It was eight in the evening. Daylight savings time had rolled around a week before so there was still a little bit of light out.

I'd left my phone in the car. There was no need to keep it on me. I had no plans on answering it while I was with Piña. I'd called Clark and told him not to tell Sheila I wasn't at the office. I would never forget the look of disappointment on my friend's face when he asked me if I was cheating on Sheila the week before. While I didn't answer him, he could put two and two together. We had been friends since college. He knew me sometimes better than I knew myself. He was disappointed in me he had said.

He was no more disillusioned with me than I was with myself. Still, what was done, was done. I had twelve missed calls from Sheila. No surprise there. I weighed the options of calling her or letting her wonder, stew in her guilty conscience for the evening.

I opted to call her. She answered on the first ring.

"Hey," she said softly.

"Hey," I responded.

There was an awkward silence on the other end of the phone. I sat in my car. One leg in the car, one leg outside.

"Where are you?" she asked.

"Still at the office," I lied with ease.

I actually felt bad about that, but not bad enough to leave Piña naked in the hotel room to go back home just yet.

"Are you coming home?"

I sighed. "Going to be working late on some last-minute things for the new office."

"Are we ever going to talk about this?"

"What this?"

"Our marriage, Jerome."

"It will never amaze me how you expect me to jump now that you want to talk. For years, I've been doing this same song and dance. What's changed from then to now?"

Sheila sniffed, then I heard stuff moving around. Had no idea what it was. She finally exhaled loudly. "Lots has changed, Jerome. One being I realized I was making you pay for something you had no control over." She sighed. "Can we please talk about this when you get home? I'd like for us to do this face-to-face. Will you come home?"

"Not tonight. Got too much to do."

I had a moment of déjà vu. Only it was of her telling me those same words.

"What's their name?" she asked out the blue.

I sat up. Nerves made me lick my lips as my heart started to beat harder than it was before. "What's whose name?"

"Are you cheating on me, Jerome?"

"Why would you ask me that? Were you cheating on me all the times you were out working late?"

"You've changed."

"How so?"

"I don't know. You're just different. Not the same anymore. You don't call. You don't text. You're always *working* . . ." She said working as if she had put air quotes around the word. "I took some vacation time off."

I had to laugh at that shit. I couldn't remember that last time my wife had volunteered to take a day off.

"I want us to work, Jerome. I don't want to lose you. I can't lose you. I realized I messed up. I messed us up," she said, her voice cracking as she spoke.

I turned my eyes skyward. I didn't want to hear my wife crying. Didn't want her to know the hurt I knew. "Sheila, stop—"

"I know you're cheating on me. I can feel it."

"I'm not cheating on you. I'm working."

"I know you … sometimes more than I care to admit. You're lying, and I at least deserve to know the truth!"

I got out of the car, then slammed the door. "I don't know what you want me to say. I don't."

"I want you to say you still love me. I want you to say we have a chance to make this right. I want you to say you're coming home so we can talk."

If I didn't get off the phone, I knew we would do that same song and dance over and over. For as bad as I wanted to stay the night with Piña, I knew I couldn't. I had to really think about if I wanted to become that man. Did I want to become that man who made cheating on his wife a habit? Did I really want to be that no good son of a bitch who stayed out all night loving between another woman's thighs?

I was already trekking down that road, and I knew that I if I kept going, sooner or later I'd be at the point of no return.

"I-I gotta go. I'll be home soon." I hung up.

Soon never came.

When the Funk Hits the Fan: Staci

Chapter 15

"I'm going to get some fresh air," I told Rome.

He was laid out across the bed. We'd eaten, had sex, eaten again, and then had more sex. That was what we did. We made no qualms about it. We weren't in love, I knew that. But when I was with Rome, all seemed right in my world. Even when we were discussing the spouses we had at home, there was never any judgement on his end, and I appreciated that. In the days after the incident at Donovan's parents' house, we had become more distant. While he came home every night, it was still like he wasn't there.

When he wasn't in his office locked away, he was locked away in our bedroom. I'd been locked out of our lives, and as I'd confided in Rome, I felt like the end was near. That was a crushing thought. Like waves overtaking me and I was fighting for just a gulp air that never came.

From hooded lids, Rome gave me a slow once over. He looked drunk off sex. Once he had come back in, I didn't give him time to talk. I could tell by the expression on his face that he had spoken to his wife. I knew he was going to leave me in that hotel room. But I didn't want to be alone. I couldn't be alone. Not when my demons were haunting me. So I made sure that he thought twice about leaving me. Made sure his dick was so hard he wouldn't have been able function on the drive home if he did decide to leave.

Rome was a man who needed to be wanted. It was good for his pride and ego for a woman to show she wanted him. I'd crawled on that bed on all fours, arched my back so my ass made the perfect heart shape before him. The moment he groaned out my name and I heard his gym bag hit the floor, I knew I had him. Now he laid back, one leg straight, the other bent so they made the number four in the tangled sheets; one hand was on his dick and the other behind his head. He didn't look as if he would be going anywhere, anytime soon.

"I can't go home tonight," he said.

"What?" I asked as I hadn't said anything to him about going home.

"I can't go home tonight. If I do, she's going to know another woman has had me."

I almost felt sorry for him. Not because of what he had said, but the way he said it. Rome sounded like a wounded animal. He sounded like a man who was having regrets. While the notion pricked at something within me, I would be a fool to be mad at the man for having a conscience. He'd told me plenty of times that he loved his wife. I heard him loud and clear each time.

"Then stay here," I said with a shrug.

There was silence. He knew he couldn't go home, but he also knew he couldn't stay here. Yes, there had been plenty of hotel sessions, but normally at around two or three in the morning, we went our separate ways. I knew the times he didn't go home, though, because he would call and tell me he was going to his office. He would always tell me he didn't want to go home to an empty house anyway. I knew the feeling.

I also knew that I had started to crave to know what it would feel like to spend the night in his arms. I hadn't been held all night by a man in so long. I didn't even remember what it was like to be held by Donovan anymore. I barely remembered anything about our marital bed. I didn't remember what his lips felt like on mine. Couldn't recall the way his breath would catch when I kissed certain parts on his neck. Donovan could be rough at times. I missed the way he would bite, scratch, spank, and outright fuck me to sleep. I missed knowing the comfort of my man.

Mistakenly, I took Rome's silence for rejection. Judging by the way he turned his gaze away from me, I knew I wouldn't know what it felt to be held by a man throughout the night again anytime soon.

I grabbed up the hotel room key and my phone, then headed toward the door.

"I'll stay if you stay," Rome said just as I turned the handle.

I smiled in the low light setting. I didn't turn around to face him as I didn't want him to know what that simple declaration meant to me.

All I said was, "I'll stay if you stay."

"Okay. I'll be waiting when you get back."

There was an extra bounce in my step as I bopped through the lobby. The place was abuzz with life, but I noticed none of it. Was it so bad that I was excited about being held all night by someone who didn't loathe me or wish me dead anytime he laid eyes on me? I walked through the automatic sliding doors and a gust of cool air washed over me. The weather was perfect. I had no other care in the moment.

"Nice out here, huh?"

I turned to look beside me. A white woman who reminded me of Ellen DeGeneres was smiling at me. She had on black. skinny jeans, a V-neck tee-shirt, and a red blazer. She was smiling, hands in her pockets as if the night was too cool for her but it was just right for me.

"Yes, it is. Perfect weather for me," I replied.

She nodded. "I'm so iffy about the weather. Sometimes I like the cold, sometimes I like the heat. You staying here, too?" she asked while she pulled a pack of Virginia Slims from her pocket.

I nodded. "Yeah, for the night anyway."

I didn't know why this woman was talking to me, but being that I was from the south, it wasn't abnormal. Southern people tended to be very friendly. We'd strike up a conversation with anybody anywhere if the mood was right.

"They have good customer service here?" she asked after firing up her cancerous vice. She blew out smoke. "In town visiting my girlfriend, wanted to make sure this place was nice. I wanted a suite but booked too late. I want things to be good for her, you know. Hadn't seen her in a while. Been away for work and all."

"I haven't had any issues since I've been coming here for the last few weeks or so."

"You visiting, too?"

I shook my head. "No."

That was all I said on the matter. After all, she was a stranger. I didn't want to divulge too much info. Her phone beeped before she could ask whatever it was she was about to. She blew out smoke, then text something back quickly on her iPhone. I pulled out my phone to see texts from Donovan. There were missed calls as well.

Just as I was about to respond to one of his texts, he called.

I answered, "Yes, Donovan."

"Where the fuck are you?" was his response.

I frowned. "I'm out."

There was silence on the other end of the phone. "Staci, I'm going to ask you again, where are you?"

In that moment, something heavy settled in the pit of my stomach. I got a feeling that I couldn't explain; something akin to paranoia settled within me. I knew Donovan, and he had a tone in his voice that said he wasn't in the mood to play around. Any other time that tone in his voice would make me do or say whatever it was he wanted, but tonight was different.

"And I said, I'm out. Do you need something?" I asked.

"Excuse me?"

"Do you need something, Donovan? If not, I'm out with friends. I don't want to be rude."

"I've been calling and texting you all damn day and all night, Staci. This game you're playing, don't do it."

His words made me uneasy. *Did he know I was cheating on him? Did he know about Rome?*

No, how could he? I rationalized. This was just Donovan's way of trying to keep control of me and I was in no mood to be controlled.

"Where's Tara and your little minion?" I asked.

There was silence on the other end of the phone. "You sure this is the game you want to play?" Donovan asked.

I wasn't sure of what I wanted anymore. I'd fought for my marriage for so long that I didn't have any fight left. Donovan would never forgive me for causing the death of our son. Quiet as kept, I'd never forgive me either. So why were we still married? Why did Donovan care about where I was or who I was with? He for damn sure didn't want me. We were strangers. Years and years of marriage had been thrown away.

"Good-bye, Donovan," I said before pressing the button to end the call.

A gust of smoke came wafting my way. I turned to see the Ellen lookalike watching me. She gazed at me the way a woman sized up someone she was attracted to. I didn't consider myself a lesbian or bisexual even though Donovan and I had fucked a few women together back before marriage. We had been wild in college. But we lived in Atlanta. The land of the gays. It wasn't too farfetched that the woman was attracted to me.

"Sounds like trouble in paradise," she said as she blew out another gust of smoke.

I gave a faux smile. "You know how it is," I said.

"Ah. Man trouble?"

"Something like that."

"I know how that is. Was married myself. Kids and all. Got divorced after my husband cheated on me."

"Sorry to hear that."

"Don't be. Best thing that ever happened to me. Now the bitch he screwed me over for is giving him the same hell he gave me. Karma, right?" The woman's eyes darkened like her words were meant for me more so than for her.

"Guess so," I said.

She nodded, inhaled, and then took a long pull of her cigarette. She blew out smoke the way smokers did. Tossed the rest of the cancer vice to the ground, then stomped it out. She slid her hands in her pocket, then looked behind me.

"Aw shit," she murmured.

I turned to see what she was looking at. There was a woman coming toward us—long, beautiful hair, light skin, light eyes, and a body that would make Jesus tell his father to go to hell. Homegirl walked with her shoulders back, chest forward like she was on a mission. The heels on her buckled booties made her already statuesque frame even more appealing.

I didn't want any shit. Didn't need her thinking I was trying to come on to her woman. The woman walking toward us looked like she was ready to fight. The woman I called 'Ellen', since she had never revealed her name, moved swiftly. She rushed over to the other woman and stopped her. I couldn't hear what they were talking about, but I could pick up on tension when I saw it.

I looked at my vibrating phone again. Donovan had texted me.

Don't fuck with me, his text read.

I responded, **Fuck off, Donovan.**

A few seconds later, he called. I sent his call to voicemail.

"I was just talking to her," I heard behind me.

'Ellen' was trying to keep her girl from walking over to me. I didn't have time for that bullshit. I was already dealing with a jealous husband. My phone rang again. I looked down to see Rome was calling.

"Hello," I answered.

"Where are you?"

I glanced at the lesbian couple again, then walked back into the hotel.

"I'm coming up. Just needed some air."

"Hurry up," he said.

His voice was low and calm, sexy even. Listening to him made me wish he was mine. Made me wish we could share more than a stolen night. Rome's voice lured me like he wanted me, needed me. I smiled while walking to the elevator. Just as the golden doors closed, the Black woman from the lesbian relationship stuck her foot between the doors to stop them. I moved over to the other side when she stepped on. The expression on her face told me she wasn't in a good mood.

She stared me down as the elevator crawled to the top floor. It made me uncomfortable. The space was small. I could smell the sweet scent of her lotion and perfume. She smelled good enough to eat, but her eyes told me she wasn't in the mood to be ogled. I didn't know her. Didn't know why she was staring me down either, but I wasn't going to be punked.

"Is ... there a problem?" I asked.

She didn't answer, just gave a slow blink. Shaking my head, I rolled my eyes. Could it be that she wasn't a lesbian at all? Maybe she was one of Donovan's whores. Wouldn't be the first time I'd run into one of them. I tsked. Then he had the nerve to call and question my whereabouts. *Screw him!*

Once the doors dinged, I stepped off. The woman stepped off behind me. I was happy when she went the opposite way. Had she followed me, I would have had to get a bit hood.

Donovan rang my phone again. I knew he wouldn't stop. I had a good mind to turn that motherfucker off, but something told me not to.

I angrily pressed the phone against my ear after tapping the button for answer on the touch screen.

"What, Donovan?" I snapped.

"I'm ten minutes away. If a nigga is in the room with you when I get there, all hell is going to break loose."

"Are you following me?"

"No."

"Do you have Pete following me?" I asked, panic taking residence inside of me.

I put nothing past Donovan, nothing. Pete was known to do Donovan's dirty work so it wasn't so farfetched that he would be following me.

"Ten minutes, Staci," he repeated as if he was warning me, giving me time to get rid of all my adulterous evidence.

Before I could even fix my mouth to respond, someone tapped me on my right shoulder. I turned to look to find no one there, then turned left. A fist seemed to materialize out of thin air. For the first five seconds, it was as if my head played tilt-a-whirl. Did Donovan hit me? Was he here already and called me to throw me off? The first hit rocked me. The next hit sent me flying backwards on my ass.

I heard ringing in my ears. My right eye stung and my head was throbbing. I got snatched up by my hair. Tried to angle my body to see my attacker but couldn't. A forearm clasped around my neck. I couldn't breathe, couldn't scream. I threw my hands backwards. I grabbed hair first, a handful of it. I knew it wasn't Donovan. That scared me more. A complete stranger was attacking me. I couldn't scream. There was no one else in the hall who could help me. My eyes watered, head got lighter. All I could think about was my son, the one I'd all but murdered.

Oh, dear God, help me, my mind screamed.

I kept clawing until I grabbed my attacker's face. I dug my nails deep until I was sure I drew blood. That forced them to shove me forward. I hit the wall hard, but turned to see who it was. My eyes widened seeing the woman from the elevator. She ran for me. I screamed, then kicked my feet to keep her away from me.

She went stumbling backwards. I swung out. Almost connected with her jaw, but that Amazonian bitch was quicker than I was. She moved and dodged like she had been trained by Bruce Lee. There was a madness in that woman's eyes that I wasn't familiar with. I had to wonder if she was Rome's wife. Could she have followed him to the hotel or had him followed?

"Get away from me," I yelled, backing away but still trying to defend myself.

She rushed toward me again. Her fist came for my face. I ducked underneath her arm, but her left hand caught me by the back of my hair and threw me face first into the wall. I almost fell, but knew if I did, she would stomp me just as sure as she was kicking my ass. I got my footing and rushed that Xena-built bitch. She sent her elbow into my back, taking me down to one knee. I grabbed her leg and moved forward until her back hit the wall.

For the first time, she yelled out. I sent a flurry of fists to her face. She dodged most of them. My hair was working against me as she grabbed it again, did a spin move that lifted me from the floor and sent me flying backwards over my head. The unmitigated look of murderous intent on the woman's face rattled me so badly that I saw my life flash before my eyes.

I screamed so loud, it scared me. She was coming for me again until hotel room doors opened. A few people stuck their heads out.

The woman looked around nervously. Her face had my claw marks. She didn't seem to be bothered by it. "Stay away from him," she warned.

After glancing around, she backed away. Without another word, she turned and jogged off.

"Are you alright, ma'am?" I heard someone ask.

I slowly pulled myself up and rushed to my hotel room door. A few people kept asking me if I was okay or if I needed the police to be called. I ignored them all. Put the key card in the slot and pushed the door open. I heard the shower going, which explained why Rome didn't hear my scream. I rushed over to the mirror on the wall to look at my face.

My eye was swelling, and I had a busted lip. The left side of my face was bruised. I really looked like I got my ass whupped. I lifted my neck to see the bruising there as well. That bitch was strong. Had almost lifted me from the floor when she was choking me. I was so caught up in what had just happened, that I never heard the shower go off or Rome come out the bathroom.

He was all smiles until he saw my face. "What the hell happened to you?" he asked in a low monotone.

Tears were still falling from my eyes when I turned to look at him. He walked over and cupped my face in his hands. He looked me over with concern in his eyes. Water drizzled down his chest. A white towel was draped around his waist. Anytime he inhaled and exhaled, his abs constricted. His locs swayed around his broad shoulders. Not even his aesthetics could take my mind off what had just happened.

"Some woman attacked me in the hall."

He frowned. "What? You need to call the cops. All the damn money I'm paying for this room, and they can't get good security around here?"

I took a deep breath. "Does your wife know where you are?"

His head jerked back like he had been slapped and his frowned deepened. "What? No. And even if she did, she wouldn't have attacked you. She isn't a fighter, not like that."

"That's funny. The woman who attacked me said 'stay away from him' as she was kicking my ass," I said. "The only him she could be talking about is you."

"What did she look like?" he asked before he grabbed a washcloth from the bathroom, filled it with ice from the bucket for the wine we had earlier, and then placed it to my lip.

I'd all but forgotten I was bleeding.

I told him what the woman looked like. He twisted his lips and made a face that said he was thinking. He scratched his ear. "My wife doesn't look like that," he said.

"But you know someone who does?" He didn't answer. "Rome, please don't tell me you have other women running around out here who would be crazy enough to do this to me."

"No, I don't … never been with another woman but my wife before now."

Rome gave me a hard glare before he moved around the room. He didn't even bother drying off. He pulled on a tee-shirt and some black gym shorts. He quickly pulled his locs back into a ponytail, then picked up his ringing phone.

"Hello?" he belted out, then tossed the phone on the bed.

He always talked on speakerphone around me unless it was his wife. So that let me know it wasn't her.

"You're a lying sack of shit," the voice on the other end of the phone spat out venomously. "You tell my sister you're not fucking around—"

"Michaela?" he asked, head tilting to the side.

"Who the fuck is she? And is that the best you could do? I can't believe you would do some shit like this, Jerome. I would expect this from anybody but you."

"What the fuck, Michaela? You following me?" he asked.

"You better believe it. On my way to tell my sister what a piece of shit she married."

Rome's spine stiffened. A look of uncertainty and panic crossed his features. He snatched the phone off the bed, took it off speaker. "Michaela, mind your business," he said through clenched teeth.

Whatever was being said on the other end of his phone had his face contorted.

"Mind your fucking business," he spat again. "Hello? Hello?" Rome slapped a hand against his forehead, then yelled, *"Fuck!"*

Chapter 16

"I have to go."

Those were the only words Rome said to me as he rushed around the room grabbing his things. There was no more concern about my assault or who had done it. He had to rush out, rush home to save his marriage. He needed to beat his sister-in-law home before she could tell his wife he was in a hotel room with another woman.

Once his bag was packed, he picked it up and looked at me. Rome walked to stand in front of me. He dipped his head, then kissed my lips.

"I'm sorry," was all he said before he rushed from the room.

I didn't know where my head was. All I knew was I'd just gotten my ass handed to me. I wanted to run, jump, kick, scream. Something. Anything. Rome's sister-in-law had just attacked me like a mad woman, and I couldn't fight back. She caught me off guard. Funky bitch waited until I turned my back and attacked me. Mama always said there were no rules in fighting, but shit, I didn't know a fight was coming. Why had she attacked me?

I mean, yeah, the obvious reason would have been she knew I was fucking Rome, but how did she find out? How long had she known? Rome and I had been doing our little routine for weeks. I went to the bathroom to rinse the towel. My lip was still bleeding but my mind was all over the place.

There was rapid knocking on the door.

"Police, ma'am. Could you open the door for us?" I heard a male voice say.

"Shit," I mumbled.

I hated the cops. Had never had a good run in with them that I could remember. From having the police raid my parents' home to the way they treated me after the car accident, cops and I had never had a good rapport. I walked to the door. I opened it to find hotel management and two police officers there. They asked me to step out of the room. I did. Two Black officers who looked like they bench pressed iron for fun, or it could have been the bulletproof vests making them appear bigger than they were, stood looking at me. One was light, the other dark. I blinked a few times as the eye I had been punched in was watering and had me seeing double.

"We got reports that someone assaulted you?" the light one said.

"You want to tell us what happened?" the other one asked.

"It's, um …" I started then stopped.

Looked around to see people passing up and down the hall. Most being nosy because no one was around when that woman attacked me. I was just about to tell them what happened when I saw him. The expression on his face said he wasn't to be fucked with. Dark denim jeans, black loafers, a collarless, black shirt that hugged the muscles in his chest and arms. iPhone on his hip. Keys jingling from his fingers.

He walked like the world belonged to him. Red hair and light, copper-colored eyes made him stand out. It was the "don't fuck with me" look on his face that made people part like the Red Sea. My heart started beating rapidly. I got the shivers. I'd forgotten about Donovan's phone call during the melee.

Now, I was happy Rome had gotten the hell on. If he had been here with Donovan showing up, who knew what would have happened.

"Ma'am, were you attacked?" the officer asked, bringing my attention back to him.

"Y-Yeah."

"Can you tell us who it was?"

I shook my head, then ran a hand through my hair. "I don't know. I didn't see her face."

"If you didn't see a face, how do you know it was a 'her'?" He gave me a skeptical look.

"What's going on?" Donovan's deep baritone voice cut in as he slid his keys into his pocket.

"Sir, could you please take a step back?" the other cop asked Donovan.

The cop had one hand on his gun, the other hand was stretched out toward my husband. Donovan eyed the man's outstretched hand, then looked back at the officer.

"That's my wife," he said coolly.

"I don't care. You need to stay back."

Donovan tilted his head to the side, took a deep breath, and then looked back at me. "Staci, are you okay?" he asked.

My eyes darted between the officers and my husband. The way I was behaving, they probably thought Donovan had done something to me when that wasn't the case at all. I was just so shaken up, I couldn't function.

"I'm—"

"Sir, I won't ask you again to step back," the other officer said again. The aggression in his voice told me things were about to go from sugar to shit.

"You'd better get the fuck up out my face," Donovan snarled.

The officer bristled. I stepped in front of my husband. Donovan's temper was nothing to sneeze at. I'd seen him beat men unconscious. The last thing I needed was for him to go at it with trigger happy police.

"Please," I said. "I'm okay. Yes, I was attacked, but I don't know by who. I didn't see their face. So, I can't tell you much."

"You have to tell us something if you want us to help you."

"Can't you watch the surveillance cameras?"

The officer looked at me as if he was annoyed. "It would be better if you told us what happened."

"I don't know. All I remember is someone tapping me on the shoulder. I turned around and they punched me in the face."

"Looks like they did more than punch you in the face."

"Everything happened so fast … I-I-I don't know, okay?"

The officer huffed like he was becoming impatient. "Fine. Can you at least fill out a police report?"

I shook my head. "I just want to go home."

"So you rented a hotel a room, got assaulted, but now you want to go home?"

"Yes, I got the room before I knew some psycho was going to attack me."

The officer put his little notepad away, then sighed while holding his hands out as if to say he gave up. After a few more minutes of fluff, the hotel manager answering questions about security cameras, and the dark-skinned cop staring my husband down, I walked back into the hotel room with Donovan behind me.

That presented another dilemma, another kind of nervousness. I walked around the room, snatching up my things. I heard Donovan breathing behind me. His angry energy swarmed around the room. It made it feel as if the walls were closing in on me. His eyes were on me; I could feel it. I had to wonder if he could smell sex in the air. Was scared shitless at the notion he could see all the things Rome and I had done on the bed.

I did any and everything to keep from looking at him. I couldn't bring my eyes to his. I'd cheated on Donovan before, but this felt different. Maybe that was because Rome and I had started to bond on a different level. I'd only fucked the other guys. Never saw them again after that. All I'd wanted was instant gratification. They provide that and then they were of no more use to me.

"Who was in this room with you?" Donovan finally asked.

I stopped putting clothes into my bag. I swallowed, then stood up to my full height. I took a deep breath, open and closed my eyes. "No one, Donovan," I lied.

I turned to look at him. His eyes had gone to slits, shoulders squared. If I didn't know any better, I'd think my husband wanted to fight me.

The left corner of his upper lip twitched. "Stop lying to me," he said coolly.

I averted my eyes, ran a hand through my hair. All I wanted to do was pop two pills, have a glass of something stronger than wine, and get into bed.

"I'm not."

"You are. At least I respected you enough to tell you the truth when you asked me about my affairs."

My brows furrowed. "That has to be like some kind of oxymoron, right? My husband respecting me enough to tell me he was fucking other women? One being my best friend who gave birth to your child two years before you told me? So when my best friend brought her daughter around, I had no idea it was my husband's kid for a whole damn two years? Oh," I said, sarcasm lacing my tongue.

Donovan swallowed. His Adam's apple bobbed up and down while his eyes bored holes through me. "Staci, was there a man in here with you?" he asked like nothing I'd just said mattered.

I was a lot of things, but a damn fool I wasn't. No matter what Donovan had done or how many rancid cunts he had fucked, me telling him I'd been with another man would send him over the edge. My husband was my first. We taught one another a lot of things about sex.

I watched as Donovan's big hands fisted by side. His face held a scowl like something stunk or he was in pain.

"No."

I turned back around to finish picking up my clothes. I picked up the wine bottle. The moonlight cast a glare off something on the floor near the foot of the bed when I moved. My heart raced. Rome's watch. He'd tossed it on the floor when it got tangled in my hair during one of our sex sessions. I walked over to the bed at a pace that wouldn't alarm Donovan, then kicked the watch underneath it. That made me remember the wedding bands Rome and I left in the bathroom.

I said a silent prayer that Donovan hadn't noticed I wasn't wearing mine. His nostrils flared as he watched me. He rolled the sleeves of his shirt up.

"I smell your sex in the air. I know the sweet scent of my wife's twat. Your lips are swollen and not just from that punch to the mouth. I smell another man in this room," he said through bared teeth.

His chest heaved up and down slowly like it was hard for him to breathe. He stepped closer to me, face getting redder. I took a step back.

"You got some fucking nerve, Donovan. Some goddamn fucking nerve. So what? So what if I fucked somebody else?" I boldly asked.

Donovan closed in on me so quickly, I lost my footing, tripped over something, and fell backwards. I landed on my elbows. Tears stung my eyes as I backed away from my husband. He swarmed on me like a madman. Donovan snatched me up by my hair. I screamed out when his hand closed around my neck.

"I'll fucking kill you, Staci, you hear me?" he snarled while holding my face to his.

Donovan had damn near snatched me off the floor. His face was so close to mine, I could count the tiny hairs in the five o'clock shadow on his face. My tears slipped down my cheeks over his hand. Dear God, how did we end up here? How did we go from having everything so well put together to this? My sobs got stuck in my throat, and when I tried to take a deep breath, it strangled me.

The vein in the center of Donovan's forehead protruded.

"Hypocrite," I whispered. "Y-You don't wa-want me."

Slobber stitched my lips together, but pain was breaking my heart. Donovan's eyes watered, but no tears fell. There we were, locked in a room full of demons. Donovan loosened his grip, then all but threw me on the floor. I dropped down like a sack of potatoes. Any other night, I'd put up a fight, but I had none left in me. So I sat there, sobbing, crying like a baby.

I always knew this was how I would turn out. God ain't ever given me shit he didn't take away. He took my parents. Took my son. Taking my marriage, my husband. I didn't even know why he let my mother birth me. In the end, I'd ended up just like her.

I was so undone that when I heard the door close behind Donovan, I still didn't move.

We both knew what time it was … Time to face the truth.

Time to let go.

Time to move on.

Shame: Donovam

Chapter 17

I was ashamed of me. Wish I had never put my hands on my wife the way I'd done. Staci was right. I didn't want her. I didn't want the woman she had become. But that didn't mean I didn't miss the woman she used to be. We were done. I knew that much. My marriage was over. I tried. The Lord knew I tried, but my best wasn't good enough.

The thought of another man touching, kissing, loving, holding … fucking my wife did something to me I didn't think was possible. It made me remember how much I loved my wife, how much I missed her. None of that mattered though. In my mind, we were broken beyond repair.

"You alright, son?"

I glanced over at my father. Staci hadn't been home in two days. I couldn't get the sounds of her sobs out my mind as I left her in that hotel room.

"I don't know, Pop. I don't know," I answered honestly.

"Here," he said.

I looked up, took the tumbler of amber liquid from his hand. "Thank you."

He nodded, then took a seat in the chair across from the leather sofa I was sitting on in his home office. His office gave off a very masculine feel. Everything was dark brown and wooden from the floor-to-ceiling bookcase to the big, oak desk. He had the window open so fresh air was spilling through. On his desk were several opened bibles, thesauruses, dictionaries, pens, pencils, note pads, and a laptop.

He'd been preparing for bible study and his sermon for Sunday when I called and asked him if I could stop by.

"Talk to me," he said. "Tell me what's going on."

"My marriage is over," I said.

He grunted. "Well tell me something I don't know."

I took a sip of the rum, then glanced at my dad. "For real this time. Staci's been with another man."

"Like you've been with other women."

I ran my tongue over my teeth. "Yeah."

"That's what got you ready to end it?"

"Yeah."

"So, killing your son wasn't the straw that broke the camel's back, but her committing adultery is?"

I eyed my pops. It was no secret he never wanted me to marry Staci to begin with. Whether her father had been one of his best friends or not, Pops didn't want me involved with no junky's daughter. Those had been his words when I told him and my mother Staci and I were getting married.

"A lot of shit I can handle, Pop, but that ain't one. Not to mention, lots of shit just compounded."

"Told you not to marry that gal no how. You ain't want to listen to your old man though. She come with too many demons. You see what happened to her mama."

"Staci is nothing like Delilah," I defended.

"Why? 'Cus it's a bottle of liquor instead of a pipe or a needle? Same damn difference, son. An addict ain't that much different than an alcoholic."

"She was fine for a while—"

"So was her mama. So was Chris, but you see how that worked out. I told him from the beginning to leave that Delilah alone. Always thought she was better than folk. Chris got clean because he came back to the Lord. Delilah still out there. Don't nobody know where she is, what she doing. Hell, we don't even know if the woman is alive. Drugs gone kill her like alcohol killed your son, my grandson. And you best let Staci go before she kills you."

"Doesn't God frown on divorce?" I asked.

My pops finished his drink, then set his tumbler on the small, round table next to his chair.

"Ain't nowhere in the bible where God said stay somewhere it ain't healthy for you to be. So many nice, single women in my congregation would be good for you, son. And they'd accept little Rebecca without contempt."

I stared into my father's eyes. Those secrets our family never spoke about swam around the room.

I bet they would, I thought. "They'd accept all my money, houses, and cars, too."

"Prenup, son. That's trivial in the grand scheme of things."

"You know Mama wouldn't agree with you encouraging me to do this, don't you?"

"She don't even like the gal."

"Still, she would have a problem with this."

Pops chuckled. "She'll be alright. You need to worry about saving yourself. You can't save Staci, like Chris couldn't save her mama. In the end, you gotta save ya'self. Delilah always thought she was better than everybody. Came from a damn shack in Augusta, but swore she was too good for—"

Pops cleared his throat. He had been talking like he forgot I was in the room, like he was thinking back to things that he didn't really want me to know about. That was why he caught himself … which made me wonder just what the hell he had been about to say.

"Like I said, son, save yourself. Staci ain't worth it. Like her mama wasn't in the end."

"That's pretty harsh, Pops," I said, brows furrowed.

"Ain't no harsher than them drugs she on. No more harsh than Staci killing my grandson."

I gave a tightlipped smile and nodded once. I stared at the liquor in the clear glass. My mind was all over the place. I'd thought talking to my pops would help me clear my head, but it hadn't. It only made things less clear.

Staci was heavy on my mind. Neither one of us had made an attempt to reach out to the other. I knew she had gone to work though. She'd left the hotel that same night. Went to one of our houses over in Stockbridge. Pete had been trailing her for me.

My pops and I chatted for a few more minutes before I left. I had more work to do at my office. So I headed there after leaving my parents' house. My mother was out doing whatever charity work she was into for the month. Probably sending water to Flint or helping on someone's campaign trail. She was very active. Always in the community doing something.

I cleared my throat as I walked into my office. I was trying to think of something, anything to take my mind off my hand around Staci's throat. Her words echoed in my mind. She'd called me a hypocrite. Said I didn't want her as if she was blaming me for her stepping outside of our marriage.

Okay, so maybe I hadn't been the most faithful of husbands, but damn it, she pushed me. She fucking took me there. All she ever had to do was choose me over that goddamned bottle. I thought back to when we were kids. Back when I found out she'd lied to me about drinking again. We had been walking from school. The sun had been shining, but clouds were rolling in. Staci didn't want to go home.

"Why?" I asked.

"Mama is probably high again. Don't feel like cleaning her or her mess up. No food in the house either. Tired of cereal," she said.

Staci had always been beautiful. Her long hair was slicked back into a ponytail. I'd taken her to a beauty supply store a few days before. All she got was some gel, a comb, brush, some hair ties, and some Blue Magic hair grease. Her face was dry, and her lips chapped a bit. That annoyed me. I took my Chapstick and handed it to her. She took it. Looked embarrassed before she put some on her lips.

She handed it back to me. I held up a hand and shook my head. "Keep it."

"Thank you," she all but whispered.

"You look like you're losing weight again," I told her.

"Just told you wasn't no food in the house, Donnie."

I had her books in my hand. All AP classes she took. Smart as hell. That was one of the reasons I liked her so much. I could have had my pick of any girl at Henry County High School, but none of them stood out to me the way Staci did. Yes, our parents had been best friends at one time, but none of the other girls could hold a candle to Staci. Even when her clothes were a bit dingy or her eyes looked tired, she was still a cut above the rest.

"Want to come by my crib and grab something to eat?" I asked.

"No. Your daddy doesn't like me."

I chuckled. "He does, too."

"No, he doesn't, and you know he doesn't. He doesn't say a word to me when I do come over. Always looking at me like I stink and I know I don't stink. I may not have the best, but I keep soap and a wash rag to keep my tail clean."

I threw my head back and laughed.

Staci rolled her eyes. "Whatever, Donnie."

She called me Donnie back then. I missed hearing her call me that.

"You want Mickey D's or something then?"

She frowned. "Nah. But can I borrow like twenty bucks? I can get some chicken, some rice, eggs, and stuff. It'll last longer than McDonalds."

"You already owe me sixty bucks," I reminded her.

We stopped walking when we were in front of her house. She cast a glance down at the ground and twisted her lips.

"I know," she mumbled. "I wouldn't have to ask if Mama hadn't gotten me fired."

Staci had been working at the corner store until the owner caught Delilah stealing and since she was Staci's mama, that meant Staci had to go. I hooked my finger and lifted her chin to bring her eyes back up to mine. She had tears in her eyes that weren't there before. I dipped my head to kiss her but stopped. I sniffed her breath.

"What is that?" I asked.

She swallowed, then moved her chin before stepping back a bit. "What is what?"

I told her, "You smell like you've been drinking something."

She ran a hand through her hair like she always did when she was about to lie. "I-I had a soda earlier," she said.

"You can barely afford to buy a pencil, but you had money for soda? One that smells like Boone's Farm?"

"I gotta go," she quipped before turning to rush toward the steps of her house.

"Staci," I yelled, "you lied to me. You promised me you wouldn't do it again."

She stopped, then turned around. "I had a sip. One drink, okay?"

My eyes went to the oversized jacket she had on. I rushed up to her. Dropped her books on top of an old car that was sitting in the yard.

"No, stop, Donovan," she cried as I snatched her jacket open.

She tried to fight but I was stronger than she was. There, the inner pocket of her jacket was a soda bottle filled with a red liquid that I knew wasn't soda. I snatched the bottle, twisted the cap off. I sniffed the insides, then frowned.

She was crying. Tried to snatch the bottle away from me.

"Move," I snapped at her. "You fucking lied to me," I snarled.

"I need it, Donnie. You don't know what it's like being in that damn house with her," she cried.

For the first time, I noticed the redness in her eyes probably didn't come from being tired like she'd said earlier.

"You want to end up just like her?"

"It's just a little—"

"This now, something else later. The fuck you going to do when you need something stronger, Staci. Huh? Going to share a pipe with your crackhead-ass mama next?"

As soon as the words left my mouth, I regretted it. Staci stepped back like she had been slapped. The tears cascading down her face simmered my anger a bit.

I sighed. "I'm sorry. I didn't mean that."

I didn't even realize people had been looking at us. Everybody always stared at us. Star high school football player hanging around with the neighborhood's crackhead's daughter. Staci's lips trembled as she backed away from me. Just then, the front door to Staci's house opened and the raggedy screen door.

"Staci," Delilah's croaky voice called out. "You a'ight, baby?" she asked.

I looked at Delilah. There was once a time her brown skin shone with a golden glow. Once a time her cheeks weren't sullen, eyes weren't sunk in. There had been a time when she didn't look fragile like if the wind blew the wrong way, she would break in half. She had on a house robe that wasn't closed all the way. Her breasts and bushy pubic hair could be seen.

Staci quickly slapped tears away from her face and rushed up the stairs. She closed her mama's robe. "Mama, you shouldn't be out here," she said, her voice gentle as if she was the adult and her mother the child.

Delilah's eyes fluttered. Her dry lips looked like they were scabbed over. Her fragile arms had open sores. "I heard yelling," Delilah said.

"It's okay, Mama. Some kids probably."

"You brang anything home for me? Get the twenty dollars like I asked you?"

Staci hid her faces in her hands. I ran a hand through my hair this time. She wasn't going to buy food with the money she asked me for. She was going to give it to her mother. I didn't know the feelings that shot through me at that bit of revealed truth. Something akin to betrayal.

Staci's voice was shaky when she said, "Not yet, Mama ..."

"You gotta get it for me, baby. Mama needs a hit or tonight gone be another long night."

Staci nodded. "Okay, Mama. Go back inside, alright?"

"What'chu crying for?" Delilah asked like she had just noticed Staci's tears. "Somebody hurt you?"

"No."

Delilah looked around. Saw people staring. She jerked her head to the side. "The hell is all y'all looking at? Nosy ma'fuckers. Stop staring at my gotdamn, baby," she yelled. "One of dem hurt you, Staci? I'll fuck 'em—"

"No, Mama."

Delilah was trying to walk off the porch, but Staci stopped her.

"I'm alright. Just tired."

"Well you can get some shut eye once you get Mama what she need, a'ight? Get that for me and we can both be okay."

By now, half the damn neighborhood was out. Staci was trembling when she finally got her mother to go back inside. She stood there for a minute, hands over her eyes. Her back expanded and shoulders shook as she cried. I knew she was embarrassed. Hell, who wouldn't be? She knew people were gawking at her, too. So when she turned around, she

216

rushed back down the stairs, grabbed her books I'd put on the car.

I touched her arm, and she jerked away.

"I'm sorry," I said to her.

"Just go home, Donovan. Just go home and leave me alone," she said before she ran into the house.

Later that night, I stole gin from my father's stash in his study. I stuffed it in my backpack, then asked my pops to let me use the car.

That was the night I became an enabler to my wife's drinking problem.

Chapter 18

"Daddy, are you coming over tonight?" Rebecca asked.

I was still in my office. The phone had jarred me from my thoughts.

"No, baby. Not tonight," I said.

"Can Mommy bring me over?"

"I'm not home yet, baby girl. Daddy is still at work."

"Oh, well … okay then. Is Staci home? She can watch me until you get off, Daddy. I really want to see you."

I opened my desk drawer. Pulled out a bottle of Tylenol. "Daddy will get you this weekend, baby. I've got a lot going on right now, okay?"

"Mommy says you and Staci are deee-vouching. What's that, Daddy?"

I frowned. "She said what?"

"She said you and Staci are deee-vouching and that when Staci moves out, me and Mommy can move in."

I swore I had a good mind to put my foot up Tara's ass. "Rebecca—"

"I-I-I don't want Staci to go away, Daddy. And my friend doesn't want her to go away either. He says you two can't split up, Daddy," she whined.

"What friend?"

"You can't s-s-s-see him."

"Slow down when speaking, Rebecca."

"Okay, but we don't want her to go, and you can't deevouch Staci either."

I wanted to tell my child it was pronounced divorce but caught myself. Tara shouldn't have been discussing such things with her anyway.

"Honey, Daddy will call you back once I leave work, okay?"

"Okay, Daddy. We love you, Daddy. And Mommy loves you, too."

"I love you, Rebecca."

"And my friend, too, Daddy?"

"Yes, and your imaginary friend, too."

She giggled and handed the phone to Tara. I hung up before she could say anything to me. Tara called me a few times. When I wouldn't answer my cell, she called my work line. I sent her to voicemail no matter what line she called. I had other things on my mind.

A hard rap of knuckles on my door forced me to look up while taking two Tylenol. Pete was there. I swallowed the pills down with no water.

"Come in," I told him once I was done.

"Got time to talk?"

"Yeah, have a seat," I said.

I motioned to the chair in front of my desk. Pete was dressed in the black Italian suit that I required all my drivers to wear. His low haircut had been lined to perfection. Midnight black skin often made women ogle over him. His eyes were dark and held a mysterious glare.

"Looks like we got a problem," he said.

"Talk to me."

"I'm not the only one following Staci."

I sat forward. "What does that mean?"

"Someone else, a woman, is following Staci. Probably the same one who attacked her at the hotel since I remember seeing her there."

None of it made sense to me. "Why would she be following Staci?"

"Best I can call it is that she's either ole boy's wife or girlfriend."

"Would make sense if she was the one who attacked Staci ..."

I was quiet for a few. Didn't like to think about Staci fucking another man.

"Tell me what you know about this dude again."

Sitting back, Pete folded his arms across his big chest.

"Jerome Thibodeaux. Played for the Falcons a while ago. Took them to the Super Bowl twice. Always played in the Pro Bowl. Was MVP in the Super Bowl both times they went. Owns a PR firm that's pretty popular. Got a lot of A-list players on his roster …"

I listened to Pete talk. I knew who the man was. Anybody who was or had been a sports fan knew who he was. I heard Pete when he gave me the rundown on who some of the man's clients were. From Cam Newton to Mike Vick, the man was good at picking the best of the best. Pete talked about how Staci had been meeting the man for weeks now. Pete said if he wasn't mistaken, he saw Jerome Thibodeaux at the club with Staci that night he brought her home, too. And the night he'd seen her at Phipps. By the time I made it out that way, Pete had gone to the bathroom, and when he got back, the man was gone and Staci was sitting alone at the bar.

I heard Pete, but I didn't really hear him. My mind was on my wife. She hadn't called me, and I hadn't called her. I didn't know which fucked with me more. Nah. I was lying. The fact that Staci hadn't called me bothered me.

I picked up my ringing cell, interrupting whatever Pete was telling me.

"What, Tara?" I snapped into the phone.

"Wow. What's wrong with you?"

I took a deep breath. "I'm busy. Does Rebecca need something?"

"I'm so sick of this," she huffed.

"Sick of what?"

"Lately, every time you get mad at that bitch you're married to, you take it out on me," she said.

I ran a hand over my head. "That bitch, as you call her, was once your best friend, Tara."

"So? Staci doesn't give a damn about anyone but herself. She's proved it over and over. And why do you seem to care all of a sudden?"

This was the part of Tara I hated. She assumed that I should have given her the same attention I gave my daughter or that she should have had some special place in line before Staci. I admit, part of that was my fault, but on the other hand, it wasn't. That shit probably came from the fact her father never paid her much attention but was always willing to fuck her mother when she would call. I remembered the stories she used to share with Staci. Sometimes I felt like shit for coming between Staci and Tara. For a long while, Tara was the only real friend Staci had. Or had she been?

"I'm busy, Tara. If there is nothing wrong with Rebecca, please don't call me back tonight."

She chuckled, the kind that told she found nothing funny. "I can't believe you."

I hung up. Dialed Staci. She didn't answer. I tried again and again and again. Each time I got sent to voicemail.

"You need me to tail her again after she leaves work?" Pete asked.

I shook my head. "No. I'm going to see her. You can take the rest of the day off but keep your cell on just in case we need an extra driver."

Pete nodded and then left my office. After giving Monet the schedule for the day and telling her to make sure each driver got to his or her route on time, I headed out. If my wife wouldn't take my phone calls, she would have to see me face-to-face. She owed me an explanation.

Getting to the Buckhead Tower at Lenox Square took me no time at all. Traffic didn't bother me at all today. I got on I85 North, took Exit 2 from Georgia 400, followed that until I got to Lenox Road. I got to 3339 Peachtree Road in no time. Fancy-ass building had valet parking. I handed my keys to the valet, then took my ticket.

The place reeked of money and prestige. The automatic sliding doors were trimmed in platinum. Italian marble flooring greeted me as soon as I walked into the doors. The place was intricately designed to be state of the art. Floor-to-ceiling glass windows allowed me a panoramic view of the surrounding area. Meticulous care had blended office, hotel, and retail components to create the Lenox Square complex.

I headed to the elevators, then up to the 17th floor to Suite 1750. I stepped off the elevator to a smiling receptionist. Her blonde hair fell over her slender shoulders. The modest red business suit she had on clung to her barely-there hips and brought out the golden undertones to her skin. Her eyes twinkled when she saw me. Her nametag read Amber. I already knew her name though. Just like I already knew her mouth could work wonders in the art of oral sex.

"Hello, Mr. Dixon. Is Staci expecting you?" she asked.

I gave a curt smile, nodded. "No, but she will see me anyway."

She put on that businesslike smile receptionists gave when they were about to do their job. You know, the 'I'm sorry but she isn't available' face?

"I'm sorry, Mr. Dixon. Her schedule is quite booked today, and she isn't open for—"

I rolled my eyes and started down the hall.

"Mr. Dixon!" Amber called me. "She's in a meeting with her top bosses and investors," she yelled.

I didn't give a shit. I kept walking down the hall, bypassed Staci's office and headed toward the conference room. I could hear Staci's voice. She sounded vibrant with life, like us not speaking for two days was perfectly okay with her. I wondered what her bosses and investors thought about the bruises she had on her face and neck. Wondered what lie she told them to cover up the fact some strange woman had kicked her ass.

"Our company is committed to a high-quality and transparent system of corporate governance which would work out quite well for your company's portfolio," she was saying when I pushed the door open.

My wife was in a room full of white men who were giving her their full attention. She was in a white suit. Wide legged pants that hugged her rounded hips. The jacket and blouse pushed her perfect breasts to attention while also remaining businesslike. She had on red pumps that screamed she meant business. She stopped with the laser pointer, then cast a glance at me that would castrate any other man.

I shot her a gaze back just as lethal.

"Um, if you would excuse me for a moment," she said to men the table.

All the men nodded.

"Jason," she called to the white man who looked like he belonged more so in a wrestling ring than a corporate office.

He looked like Jack Swagger and was built like him, too.

"Yes, Mrs. Dixon," he said as he stood.

"Will you take over for me while I'm away?" she asked.

Jason nodded happily.

Staci turned to smile at the men. "No worries. I assure you Jason is just about as good as I am."

"Just about?" one of the men inquired.

Staci put on a dick hardening smile. "No one can be as good as me, but I do have people on my team who can fool you into thinking they are. Jason is that guy."

The men around the table chuckled. I growled low in my throat at the way she handled them. I was jealous in a sense, but also proud of the way she held her own in a boardroom. As a functioning alcoholic, she still handled business like any sober businesswoman or man would. I could tell she hadn't been drinking today though. Her eyes nor her face were red. She was more than alert and walked like she had something to prove.

Once she made sure the men in the room were comfortable with her leaving them in the hands of Jason, she walked out. Staci brushed past me without even a glance. Treated me like I was an assistant who had interrupted her instead of her husband. She strutted forward like there wasn't a bruise decorating the side of her face or there wasn't a split in her lip.

Staci moved like she hadn't been worried about who attacked her two days before, like she didn't give a damn we had fought in a hotel room. My heart drummed against my ribcage at what I suspected she had been doing at that hotel. I pushed that emotion away though. Didn't want to think on what I suspected to be true. Call me a hypocrite. Call me whatever. I didn't give a damn. No man had the right to touch my wife. None. I'd put my foot in anyone's ass who said differently.

People around her office watched us as we passed them. Probably thought the big, angry Black man had abused his wife. Amber saw her boss coming and stood. The expression on her face said she was scared. Staci cut a look at the woman that made her appear to cower.

"I tried to stop him," Amber all but whispered.

"Try harder next time. We have security," Staci snapped as she passed the woman and shoved her office door open.

Amber plopped down in her desk chair, a look of apprehension on her face. I wished a motherfucker would call security on me while my wife was in this building. I'd turn this place on its head. Staci knew it. Her partners knew it. Amber did, too. Which is probably why she didn't attempt it.

I walked in behind Staci, closed the door, and locked it.

"I'm at work, Donovan. This couldn't wait until later?" she asked as soon as I turned around.

She stood by her desk. Far enough away from me so I couldn't reach out and touch her. That was how she always behaved after we'd had a physical altercation.

"If you had answered your phone then maybe," I said.

She folded her arms across her chest and took a deep breath. "What is it?"

"So you think it's okay to not say anything to me for two days? No phone call? No text? Not even an email?"

"You choked me and then left me there, crying, like it was nothing."

"You fucked a man in that room."

"You have no proof of this."

"That doesn't mean the shit isn't true."

"You want to show your ass about the possibility of me fucking someone else, meanwhile I have more than enough proof of your adultery."

"Your righteous indignation does nothing for me right now."

"Screw you, Donovan, okay? Screw you."

"I would, but since you're out whoring—"

Before the words could leave my mouth, Staci flew across the room. The slap she gave me was enough to make the people in the hall pretending not to eavesdrop, whistle, hiss, and let out low howls. Staci was breathing like fire was coming from her nostrils. Her fists shook, feet planted shoulder width apart as if she was gearing up to fight.

"You can hit me, but some random woman fucked you up in a hotel hallway. Got you out here looking like you went a couple rounds with Rhonda Rousey who then tagged in Layla Ali."

The slap angered me. Made me want to smack her back, but I still felt like shit for choking her in that hotel room. Her words still haunted me, so I absorbed the hit. Sucked my bottom lip into my mouth and bit down on it. A sheen of sweat had broken out on her forehead. She was expecting a fight, wanted one. She smacked me again, this time her open palm catching me across the middle of my face.

"That make you feel better?" I taunted her.

"Get the hell out of my office, Donovan."

I stepped closer to her. Got right up in her face as I glared down at her. "Make me, Staci."

She didn't back down. "So you came here to be an asshole? Came here to fight? All those nights at home when I would beg you to talk to me, you ignored me. But the minute you think another man is slanging dick my way you start acting like an immature teenager?"

I lowered my head, my face closer to hers, breaths deepened. I asked her, "Are you telling me you're fucking somebody else?"

She didn't answer. I didn't know, couldn't tell if she was fucking with me or not. Her refusal to answer me made me think about choking her again. This time, I wouldn't let go, not until her faced turned red, eyes widened with the life leaving them. This time I wouldn't let go until she stopped breathing. Then I would find the motherfucker who she had been cheating on me with. I'd kill him, too. Throw my whole damn life away because my wife had cheated on me. Staci had already taken my soul when she took my son from me. May as well hand my life over, too.

Staci shoved me. She caught me off guard, so when she pushed me, I stumbled back a bit. "Get the hell out of my damn office," she yelled.

Not loud enough to cause alarm, but loud enough to make Amber knock on the door and rattle the knob.

"Mrs. Dixon, are you okay?" Amber asked.

"I'm fine, Amber."

Getting my footing, I snatched my wife by the arm. She tried to pull away, and I ripped the sleeve of her blouse. That didn't stop me. Staci's eyes held so much hatred. One that I hadn't seen before … or had I just not recognized it? My face stung. Staci had slapped me again. This time she was like a wild banshee. She kept swinging over and over and over.

In that moment, I hated her. Hated what she had made me become. Hated her for making me love her, then making me regret it. Hated her for stealing our son, my son away from me. I hated her so much that when I used my right leg to take her feet from under her, I didn't give a damn how hard she hit the floor.

And she did hit the floor … hard. So hard I heard a few of her bones curse me out. I no longer gave a shit that she was at her job. All sanity left me. Staci looked up at me from the floor. The gleam in her eyes was the one Black women gave men just before they had to kill a nigga. Staci was no longer afraid of me. What I saw in her eyes told me she no longer gave a damn about me or our marriage.

I kept thinking about her legs on another man's shoulder. Kept seeing another nigga moving his hips, pounding against her backside. Imagined her throwing that pretty, round mound of all-men-joy back into his groin. I hadn't come to her office to do any of this. I really didn't know why I had come. I was lying. I had to make sure she was at work. Had to make sure that she hadn't disappeared since Pete stopped trailing her.

Staci sprang to her feet. Came for me with her fists balled, but then she stopped. Whatever she saw in my eyes stopped her dead in her tracks. Too late. I met her halfway. She backed away, her tall heels causing her to stumble, twist her ankle. She had always been a fighter. That was why I was surprised some woman had kicked her ass in a hotel hallway. If Staci could do nothing else, she could fight.

But even the best fighter would be a fool to go up against me. I reached out to grab her. I caught her hair. She screamed out. Amber started beating on the door, yelling Staci's name. I didn't give a shit. Staci fell backwards. I fell with her. She landed on the sofa behind her. It did a dance as it moved across the floor.

We tussled. She kept trying to knee me in places that would hurt like hell. I was too smart for that move though. I grunted as if she had kneed me in those places. Call it a natural reaction to my body barely escaping impact.

"Donovan," she yelled out. "Stop! I'm not— I didn't have sex with nobody else."

At this point, I didn't give a shit. She had to pay for all she had done. In my mind, I saw myself tossing her across the room by her hair. Saw me trying to tear her head away from her neck like the accident had done to my son. I wanted her to suffer. Needed her to suffer. I imagined Donovan Junior suffering. Wondered how long he had suffered until the ambulance got there.

The doctors told me he died a painful death. The impact of the wreck had been so bad that a tree limb was the only thing holding my son's head to his body. It was so bad that as soon as he had been pulled from the wreckage, he bled out. Died in the middle of the fucking street like an animal.

I was going to kill this bitch. She deserved no less. I heard other people at the door. Security was trying to get in, but they couldn't. Good thing they couldn't. My anger would have made them my next target.

Then I heard Rebecca's voice. *"Daddy, what you doing to Staci? Stop it, Daddy," she cried.*

I looked down and saw my baby girl's throat in my hand. Shit scared me so badly, I jumped up like a fire had been lit under me. Rebecca wasn't there. Just Staci. Crying. Slobbering from the mouth. Her neck and face reddened from what I had done to her. Her clothes ripped and torn.

If Staci had come home and told me any man had handled her this way, I'd kill them. But there I was, doing to her what I wouldn't allow another man to ever do. When had I become this man? I couldn't believe it. I'd lost my damn mind.

"... she's going to kill you, too," my father's voice echoed in my head.

Staci had taken me there. I was at her job, in her office, attacking her … attacking my wife.

We stared at one another, long and hard. My chest heaved up and down in heavy spurts. Staci was still where I had left her on the couch. In her eyes was fear. I'd never seen my wife look at me that way before. She looked at me like she was in fear for her life.

A loud succession of knocks lit up the silence between us.

"Mrs. Dixon," Amber called out.

"Mrs. Dixon," another voice, this time male, called. "Are you okay?"

Staci couldn't speak. She was shaken to the core and trembling like she realized just how close to death she had come. Sweat beaded at my temples. My eyes burned. My shirt seemed to be constricting against the muscles in my chest and arms. I felt like the room was spinning and caving in.

"The police are here," Amber said.

I heard her telling the officers she had an extra key to the office. Seconds later, Amber pushed the door open with three police officers behind her. Amber looked at me, and then searched the room until her eyes fell on Staci. A few of Staci's coworkers were all in the hallway as well, all looking at me like I'd grown several heads.

"Oh my God! Staci, are you okay?" Amber asked as she rushed to kneel beside my wife.

"Get on the ground," an officer shouted at me. "Now."

I turned to look at the officers. All three white. All three with their hands inching toward their guns. I could just end it all here. With the way the racial tensions were in America, it wouldn't take much for them to kill me on the spot. All I had to do was move an inch. I was tired. So fucking tired. How much more did I have to lose while loving Staci?

I looked from the officers to my wife again. Staci's lips were coated with blood like some kind of fashionable red lipstick. Her hair was wild. Her neck had my fingerprints around it like she was wearing a reddish pink and purplish green choker. She looked like she had been in a fight for her life. Amber held my wife like she was her lover. Had placed herself in front of Staci like she could protect her from me. In Amber's eyes, she no longer saw a man she had a crush on, she saw a monster. I'd become something to be feared, no longer a human.

Chapter 19

As a Black man in the racially insensitive climate of America, my pride wasn't going to allow me to kneel so three white men could arrest me. That just wasn't going to happen. So, there I was, in my wife's office, getting tased within an inch of my life and I still refused to go down. Somewhere between grabbing a cop's arm and shoving him backwards when he tried to use his club on me and Staci screaming for them to let her talk to me, another shock from the other cop's Taser took me down to one knee.

I heard my daughter's voice in my head screaming for me just to lay down. Staci was screaming the same. I saw my life flash before my eyes when the third cop's club hit me in the back of the head. Amber and Jason were holding Staci back, while she screamed for the cops not to hurt me. Tears cascaded down her face. There she was, screaming, fighting, trying to get away to help me and I'd just done to her what the cops were doing to me. She was willing to risk her life and her safety for me even though I'd thought about taking hers just minutes before.

I yelled out for her to stay back. A cop's knee caught the side of my face, angered me further. I probably would have fought my way up, but I swore I saw my son standing next to his mother, one hand on her arm. Staci jumped. Looked around like someone else had touched her. She snatched her arm away from Jason. Glared at the man like he was crazy.

DJ reached his hand out to me. He still had on his school uniform. The blazer with the stitched emblem on the left side, khakis, and brown dress shoes was how I remembered him leaving for school on the morning of his death.

"Stay down, Dad, please," he said.

As clear as day, I heard him. All the other voices drifted away and all I heard was my son. I stopped fighting. For my son, I stayed down.

Crybaby: Sheila
Chapter 20

Awkward silence filled my home. Jerome had come home two nights ago with another woman's perfume in his clothing. He was shower fresh but had told me he was at his office. I knew he was lying. I didn't need Michaela to tell me or prove to me he was.

"He kept asking me had I talked to you," I told my sister. "I knew something was odd about that. He wouldn't tell me the truth about where he had been. Kept saying he was at his office but wanted to know if I had heard from you."

Michaela had a scowl on her face as we watched the news. One of my clients, Donovan Dixon, was all over the news. He'd been arrested earlier for going to his wife's office and assaulting her. I think it was safe to assume that my next suggestion for them would be a legal separation. Their marriage was in peril, and I was afraid no amount of counseling I gave them would help.

I stared at the pictures Michaela had shown me. I looked up at my sister through blurry vision, then back at the photos. No one else was in the photos, but they proved that Jerome hadn't been at his office like he had said. He'd lied to me. The fact that he had lied about being at a hotel told me all I needed to know.

"Did you see the other person?" I asked.

Michaela nodded. She had a mug on her face that told me she was disappointed in Jerome. Probably just as hurt as I was. Every now and again, anger flashed across her features. She had an eyepatch over her right eye. There were scratches on her face that told me she had been in a fight. I asked her about them, but she just kept shrugging me off. I knew how Michaela could get when she was annoyed, so I let her be after a while.

"Why no pictures of them?"

"Because."

"Because what? I want to see the person fucking my husband."

"Sheila—"

"No, I want to see them. I need to see the person who doesn't give a fuck about my vows and fucked my husband." I snapped.

I felt my anger rising like a volcano on the verge of erupting.

Michaela sighed. "Were you this mad at Jerome? He owes you an explanation, not the other woman."

"Yes, yes I was this angry at him. We've been fighting for two days. I need to know, Michaela," I cried.

I stood and walked over to my sister. Sighing, she shook her head. She was acting as if she was hiding something else. She kept glancing back and forth between the TV and me. When she first came in, she'd been the one to turn the local news on.

"I can't give you any pictures of her right now," she said.

"And why not?" I asked.

"Because I assaulted the damn woman in the hotel," she yelled.

"You did what?"

"She was walking back to the hotel room she and Jerome had made a love nest in. I walked up behind her and then attacked her."

I slapped a hand over my mouth. "Oh my God, Michaela."

I listened as Michaela told me about how she had been trailing Jerome and finally figured out how he had been hiding the other woman. The woman would show up to the hotel before he would, and it wasn't until she had seen them working out together in the fitness room that she figured it out. Jerome had gotten careless. So she had Jillian pretend to be staying at the hotel to strike up a conversation with the woman.

My older sister ran a hand down her face and nodded. "That slut bitch was all smiles while she was outside talking to Jillian. Smiling like she was in love, as if she didn't give a damn Jerome was someone else's husband. And I know she knows he's married. It's the same woman I saw at the park that day when he was running. He showed her his damn ring."

My face was burning, but my insides were cold as ice. Jerome was cheating me. I felt like I was about to hyperventilate. Grabbing my chest as if I was clutching a set of pearls, I gasped as I backed away from my sister and took a seat.

"Sheila," she called out to me. "Are you okay, sis?"

I couldn't speak. Couldn't fucking breathe. I felt as if I was fighting for that last gasp of air just before I was about to drown.

"Why?" I asked.

I shook my head and stopped myself. Was no need for me to ask why. Was it?

"This is … this is my fault," I said as I looked up at Michaela. "I did this."

She was already shaking her head before the words left my mouth.

"No. No. No, you did not do this. It's not your fault that Jerome decided to say fuck his vows and stick his dick into another woman. Don't you do this," she said as she rushed to sit next to me. She pulled me into her arms, rocked me. "Do not blame yourself for what Jerome did. Please don't. Mama did this same shit when Daddy left. I won't allow you to beat yourself up over this."

Something inside of me had broken. It was as if I could feel my heart breaking. I was crumbling, falling apart at the seams. My tears were mixed with anger, hurt, regret, fear.

"I can't do this," I cried.

I couldn't think about Jerome loving some other woman. Making love to some other woman. I didn't want to imagine him holding her, talking to her. Jerome's smile was enough to light up any woman's day. I just didn't want to think about him smiling that way at another woman. Making another woman laugh at his, sometimes, corny jokes. I just couldn't stand the thought of his naked body moving sensually against another person, period! All of it was threatening to drive me mad.

So much so that I jumped up from the couch, walked over to the mantel above the fireplace, and with a one-armed sweep, knocked every picture to the floor. I kicked over an end table.

Pulled at my own hair. Screamed like a banshee before I snatched our wedding picture from the wall.

"Sheila," Michaela screamed my name.

I heard her, but I didn't. Somewhere in the back of my mind I'd snapped.

"Who is she?" I asked.

"I'm not telling you anything until you calm down."

"Who is she?" I yelled, spittle flying from my mouth.

Michaela balked. Took a step back, almost as if she was getting into a defensive position.

"You need to calm down, sis."

"I am calm."

I stalked to the kitchen. Grabbed my purse and headed out the door. I didn't hear Michaela asking me where I was going. Didn't see when she hopped in my car with me. I paid no attention to her after I got on the expressway and she begged me to slow down. I was out of my mind with grief.

By the time I made it to my husband's office, my mind was already made up. He would tell me what I wanted to know, or I would show him a side of me he probably forgot existed. All I needed to do was confront him with the pictures so he wouldn't be able to lie to my face anymore. I had the pictures Michaela had taken. Had grabbed them on my way out the door.

"Sheila, sis, please think about what you're about to do," Michaela pleaded.

"I have thought about it," I said.

"You really want to do this in public?" she asked.

"Since he won't talk to me at home, I'll do it where he is."

I parked in front of the office building, not really giving a damn if I would be towed or not. I snatched the glass door open. Since it was late afternoon, only the security guard would be manning the front, but I was surprised to see Clark walking out. Any other time, the fact that Clark was six foot three, one hundred ninety pounds of lean chocolate would have given me and my sister something to talk about.

But today, today he was the enemy. Clark was dressed in tan slacks, wing tipped red shoes, and a red dress shirt that was straining against the muscles in his upper body. Clark was a walking Instagram model. The kind that women and men lost their minds over on social media and thought they would never actually meet in person most times. His took one look at my face and stopped dead in his tracks.

"Where is he?" I asked.

"Where's who?" he asked.

"Jerome. Where is he?"

"I'm … I'm not sure actually. He left around lunch time and didn't come back to the office today."

Clark looked at my sister and nodded a greeting her way before casting his glance back in my direction. The pity in his eyes told me he knew more than he was willing to let on which also told me he had known of Jerome's cheating long before I'd had proof.

I asked him, "Did you know about his cheating?"

Clark shook his head. "Listen, whatever is going on between you and your husband is between you and your husband. I have no desire to be in the middle of it."

"You lied for him on the days I called here looking for him."

"Not one time have I lied to you, Sheila. You called and asked where he was. I told you where he told me he was going. All I can do is tell you what he told me. If he was lying about that, that's on him," Clark said.

"So you're telling us you had no idea Jerome was fucking around on my sister?" Michaela asked.

Clark's brows furrowed and he seemed to get a bit frustrated. "Doesn't matter what I thought or had an idea of. Jerome comes in, he does his share of the work, he cuts out. Sometimes he goes to the new office in Smyrna. Whatever else is going on isn't my business. I'd like to keep it that way and like to not bring personal business to this office. That's not a knock at you, Sheila, but I'd say the same to Jerome. We worked hard to build our brand, I won't have anything take down all my hard work."

Michaela held up her hand. "Hey, we get it, but you see she's hurting. You don't have to be an asshole about it, Clark."

He sighed. "Look, I'm not trying to be an asshole. I know this is a fucked up spot for anybody to be in, especially Sheila and Jerome, but this is still my place of business."

I turned to walk out. I couldn't bear standing there anymore. Clark didn't have to outright say anything, but the fact that he was so defensive told me that no matter how he tried to deny it, he knew something.

I couldn't drive back home. My nerves had me jittery. As Michaela drove me home, I tried calling Jerome again. His phone rang until it went to voicemail. I called him three more times and got the same result. I knew he was sending me to voicemail and that hurt more than anything.

I wondered who she was. Wondered what she had over me that would make him intentionally ignore my phone calls. He hadn't even called home. I slapped my tears away.

"Can I ask you something?" Michaela asked.

I said, "Yeah."

"Why now?"

I turned my head to look at her. "Huh?"

She gripped the steering wheel with her left hand, and ran the right one through her long hair.

"It's been years that you and Jerome have been on the rocks. You saw this coming long before now, but all of a sudden, out the blue, you decide you want to fight for your husband and marriage. For a while, I really didn't think you gave a damn," she said. "And earlier, why did it seem like you were relieved to find out about the other woman?"

"Because now I know. I don't have to wonder anymore," I said.

She frowned while shaking her head. "Yeah, I get that, but there is something I feel like I'm missing here."

Sitting up, I stared straight ahead. She was right. She was missing something. What was going on between Jerome and I had been brewing for years, but sometimes it took a wakeup call to steer people in the right direction. My wakeup call was no different than a person finding out some horrible news and deciding to change.

"On the night he didn't come home, the night of our anniversary, earlier that week, I found out I'm pregnant," I said.

My sister whipped her head around at me so fast, I had to yell at her to keep her eyes on the road.

"What?" she asked.

"Yeah. I'm about sixteen weeks pregnant. I actually thought I was dying of something. I'd gotten so sick and finally had to suck it up to go to the doctor. Only to find out I'm carrying Jerome's child. That news put so many things in perspective for me. And you know my weight has been up and down for years, so it was easy for me to hide it from you and him. Not to mention, my period has always had a mind of its own."

"Sis, why haven't you told him?"

"I was going to that night, but he never came home, and then with all that has been going on between us … I don't know if he's going to leave me or not."

"That's no reason not to tell him he's going to be a father."

"I have no intentions of being a single mother," I said.

"You know Jerome wouldn't let you do this alone, Sheila."

"I don't want to be a damn statistic. I don't want to become Mama. Have my whole life dedicated to working—"

"You're being a fucking hypocrite right now," Michaela snapped. "All you fucking do is work!"

"Yes, but that's different. I'm not a mother. If Jerome leaves me and I have this kid …" I let my words trail off as I shook my head.

"So what does that mean? You telling me you want to have an abortion?" she asked.

"I need to know if he's going to leave me before I decide to have this baby."

"You're sixteen weeks already."

"I have up until twenty-four weeks to decide."

Michaela kept shaking her head. The expression on her face was akin to disgust and disbelief.

Finding out I was pregnant changed so many things for me. Jerome and I hadn't had sex in about four months, so it came as a surprise. To know I was carrying life inside of me made me reevaluate everything. Jerome had always wanted kids and I had all but refused to have a child. I guess God had other plans.

That whole week all I did was think back over my marriage. So many things I needed to make sense of. So much Jerome needed to be honest with me about. Had called my big sister and talked to her about all that had been on my mind minus the baby. I had always been afraid to give my husband children. I didn't think I'd be much of a mother. And in no way did I want to give a man children, and then have him make me a single mother. No way could I imagine being a single mother. That fear made me keep my pregnancy a secret.

"You're selfish, Sheila. So fucking selfish right now," Michaela said as we pulled up to her place.

I hadn't been paying attention to the fact that she wasn't even headed in the direction of my home.

"You can call it what you want, but for as much as I love Jerome, I can't risk it. I refuse to become a single mother," I said. "I refuse to become our mother."

"And what if you do decide to work it out for a while, and then a few years from now, you end up divorced. Then what?"

I shook my head. "Jerome won't leave me if we have a child together."

"So why not just tell him now?"

I couldn't face my sister. Couldn't tell her the truth. She would think I was using my child as a pawn.

"I can't. Not now."

"Because you don't want to be a single mother, you won't give this man a chance to be a father? I'm sure Jerome would gladly take custody—"

"You want me to go through forty weeks of carrying a child just to hand him or her over?"

Michaela parked in her driveway and then looked at me like I'd grown two heads. "I just beat a woman's ass for you because I thought you were fighting for your marriage," she said.

"I am," I yelled.

"I can't fucking tell. You're going to use your unborn child as leverage against your fucking husband?"

"I love Jerome with everything in me," I cried. My tongue was so thick, it felt like I was barely able to talk. "But I don't think you understand how scared I am to do this alone, Michaela. I can't be Mama. I can't." I slapped my tears away. "Believe me, I am fighting for my marriage. My whole life I thought I had it all under control. I thought I had it all together. Then the doctor told me I was pregnant, and I realized I didn't. I took a look over my life, saw that my husband and I were strangers in our own home."

Michaela cut in. "That ain't his fault."

I nodded. "I know."

"You can't get an abortion just because you and Jerome may not work out, sis. He deserves to know you're pregnant. No matter what is going on right now, there was a time when you were all he wanted. Should he have stepped out on you? No, but you have to take responsibility for your part in this. It's not your fault he's cheating on you, but you do have to take responsibility for the fact you helped push your marriage to this point."

I gave a sarcastic chuckle. "So it's not my fault he's cheating, but it is my fault for everything else?"

"Pretty much."

"That doesn't make sense."

"Think about it a while, and it will," she said before hopping out of the truck and slamming the door behind her.

Something In My Heart: Staci

Chapter 21

I closed my eyes and thought back to a time Donovan and I used to be happy. Our wedding night. We ran off and got married. Didn't give two shits that his father had a conniption on the other end of the phone when he found out. Neither of us cared his mother didn't want the daughter of a drug addict as her daughter-in-law.

That was the only time Donovan had stood up to his father. Told him he had to accept me or risk losing his only son. That was before Bishop Darryl Dixon's illegitimate offspring showed up on his doorstep one Sunday afternoon …

I just knew Deborah Dixon was going to flip her shit. But she didn't. She looked at the little boy like he had been born with the name Damien and 666 carved in the back of his head. For a second, I thought she was going to spit on the boy. But no. She moved to the side and told him to come in.

In walked a young man who was the spitting image of his father and his older brother. If I didn't know any better, I'd have thought Deborah was the boy's mother. He was tall and stocky. Carried an apprehensive mug on his face that said he wasn't sure what to expect. Donovan wasn't as welcoming. Looked at the boy like he had contagious diseases and then turned to walk away. I stayed behind. I wanted to hear what the boy had to say. He had been bold enough to show up, so I knew he had a lot to say, and judging by the way Donovan and Deborah had reacted, they'd known about the child for a while.

I remember Deborah's hands shaking as she poured herself some coffee. The woman's hands trembled so badly that she damn near dropped the coffee mug. Both me and Darryl Dixon II rushed to help her. She jumped like scalding hot water had touched her when the boy's hand caught hers. She jumped back. He jumped. The mug fell to the floor and shattered. Big chunks of it flipped and flopped across the room.

"What do you want?" she aggressively asked the boy.

Looking stunned, he stuttered, "J-Just want t-to talk to the m-man who fathered me. I don't want money or to make a scene. Just think I-I deserve a conversation," he answered.

"For what?"

Deborah's face was a myriad of emotions. She was in pain. She was angry. She was saddened. She was shocked.

"If you want money, just name a figure. We'll write a check," Donovan's voice came into the room.

I'd thought he'd gone to his father's office, but there he stood. Dressed in a black suit, looking like someone's bodyguard or a hired assassin. The scowl on his face said he wasn't amused. I stepped back just in case my husband decided to fly across the room and yoke the young man up. I saw it in his face. Donovan was ready to fight. He never thought he was good enough for his father, so this boy posed a threat. There was another son who Donovan thought could take the love his father never gave him.

I looked back at Darryl the Second. He stood up, shoulders back and straight. He never took those copper-colored eyes off Donovan's identical ones.

"I don't want your money. I have my own. The man, your father, has been depositing money into my mother's account for years. We haven't spent a dime. You think I want your money?" he asked, almost as if he was offended.

"Then what do you … want?" Deborah asked again. This time she didn't hide the tears falling down her beautiful face.

Darryl turned back to Deborah. "Just to talk, Mrs. Dixon. I only want to talk."

I swallowed when Donovan stepped farther into the room. He was as cool as a northern winter's night. Hands in his pocket, he walked slowly. I stepped in front of him. He stopped. I laid my hands on his chest. He calmed down a bit. Took his hands from his pocket, then folded them across his broad chest.

"Talk about what?" Donovan asked Darryl.

"I'm off to college soon. I don't know who I am really. I just know my mother tells me that man is my father. Other people in my family whisper about it. I'd like to know who he is," Darryl said, then nodded toward Donovan. "I'd like to know who you are, too. Would like to know if we have things in common. If we think the same. Even if I can't talk to him, I'd at least like to talk to you."

Donovan hadn't been expecting that. I saw when his face softened a bit. It was only for a second though. Darryl nor Deborah caught it.

"Why can't you just leave us alone?" she asked Darryl.

Darryl looked at Deborah. He was genuinely concerned with the way he seemed to have rattled her. I could tell by the way he swallowed and then glanced at the floor before looking back at her.

"I wanted to, and I did. For twenty years, we, my mother and I, we have. She's been fighting me for the last thirteen years, telling me to leave it alone. But I don't want to leave it alone," he answered honestly. "I told her then that because I was still a child and under her roof, I'd respect her wishes for me to leave well enough alone. But I'm twenty now.

Just got my first apartment, all on my own." He said that like he was proud of that fact. "I'd like to look the man in the face who lent his semen to make me and ask why he never took the time to acknowledge me."

His last few words made Deborah gasp.

"You should listen to your mother and just leave this alone," Deborah whispered frantically.

"Why? Don't I have a right to even that simple answer?"

"No," Deborah shouted. "Look, I'll put more money into your mother's account, j-just … just don't come back here," she pleaded.

Donovan looked at his mother. "You've been putting the money into her account?"

"Yes! God … damn it to hell! Ain't that enough? Your father's money is my money and I make my own money. I can do with my own money as I please. That woman whored with my husband, but I have enough good in me to know it takes money to raise a child! I did my part damn it!"

My eyes widened. Donovan's arms dropped. He blinked slowly in his confusion. "You did your part?" he repeated her words as if he hadn't heard them the first time.

"You were paying my mother to go away?" Darryl asked.

"I was paying that whore to keep her mouth closed! The least she could have done was keep her son away from us," Deborah shouted, then clutched the pearls around her neck. "Oh, Jesus, forgive me," she rushed out in a whisper.

That was the day I understood that the Dixons weren't as polished and well put together as they liked everyone to believe.

"Ma, why would you do that?" Donovan asked.

"Because your father wouldn't! He wanted nothing to do with the boy."

"And you?"

"I didn't want him to be raised in the filth Calina called a home! Don't I get some credit for that? All she had to do was keep him away from us."

Deborah slapped her hands across her cheeks, slinging wetness away from her face. It could have been just me, but Deborah was acting like something more was bothering her about this whole thing. She wasn't acting like a woman who didn't want to be bothered with her husband's bastard child. She was acting like a woman with something else to hide. I couldn't call it, but when the bishop pulled into the garage, her eyes went wild, and she fell back into the chair behind her.

"You shouldn't have come here," she said to Darryl.

"Ma, you okay?" Donovan asked, concern now etched on his face where anger had been just moments before.

I remember the moment the bishop walked in. He was whistling a tune that only he knew. I'd never heard the song before. Darryl looked at me. I looked at Donovan who had gone to stand next to his mother. The bishop rounded the corner. One hand in his pocket, twisting the ring of keys around his pointing finger, he stopped in the archway separating the foyer from the sitting room.

He took me in and grunted. Took one look at Darryl and his eyes turned to slits. He then looked at his wife and son.

"What is this?" he asked Deborah.

"I-I don't know. He just showed up," she said.

The woman was still clutching her pearls in a death grip.

"Can we help you?" the bishop asked Darryl.

The boy seemed to be shell shocked. For mere moments, he just stared at his father. Stared at him like he was some rare artifact. The bishop did have a rather larger than life personality. I understood Darryl's hesitation. There he was, face-to-face with the man who was his father, a man he had never met before. I could see how it could be a bit overwhelming. What I didn't understand was how a man of God could look at his flesh and blood like he meant nothing to him.

Darryl got himself together. Walked over to the bishop and held his hand to him to shake. The bishop looked unimpressed and didn't bother to take the young man's extended hand.

"What do you want, boy?" he asked Darryl again.

Dropping his hand, Darryl gave a wry smile. "I wanted to talk to the man who fathered me. Was hoping we could—"

"We can't do nothing. Don't you see my wife and son over there? By the way, Donovan Dixon is the only son I have. Let's not forget that. I told your mother to abort you, but she thought keeping you would make me feel something

for her. It didn't. She was something I did twenty years ago and nothing more."

Darryl flinched but kept his composure though his right fist balled at his side. The bishop saw it and chuckled.

"Think twice before you make that mistake. You walked in here, they'll carry you out on a stretcher," he threatened.

The smirk-like sneer on his face said he meant it, and when he pushed the bottom of his suit jacket back to show he was armed, it was my turn to clutch my imaginary pearls. I knew the bishop had grown up in the Cabrini Green projects, but I thought that he had left the hood behind. Apparently, when God called him to minister, he forgot to tell him to leave the guns back in Chicago.

"Darryl," Deborah called out. Both her husband and his bastard son turned to look at her. She cleared her throat and clarified, "Bishop, don't do this. Just say something to him so he can leave here and not come back."

The left corner of the bishop's upper lip twitched while he looked at his wife. "Why in hell did you let him in here?"

Deborah stood. "What was I supposed to do? Turn him away? That ain't Christian."

"Was your husband a Christian when he got my mama pregnant?" Darryl asked.

Donovan stepped in between the boy and Deborah. "I think it's time you leave now," he told Darryl.

Water had clouded Darryl, Jr.'s eyes. He ignored Donovan for a second. "Was he?" he asked Deborah again.

She didn't answer, so he turned back to the bishop. "Guess your heart belongs to God and your dick belongs wherever it lands."

"The devil is a lie," the bishop spat. "You got ten seconds to leave on your own. After that, you don't have any more choices."

Darryl chuckled. There wasn't shit funny, but he chuckled. "She told me you were an evil man. Told me you used God to hide behind your bullshit. As a fellow Christian, I didn't believe her. I just knew that a man as powerful in the word of God as you were, that she was probably wrong. I watched you every Sunday on TV, imagining standing by your side. For so long I thought my mother to be bitter and angry. And she is, but now I see why."

"Five," was how the bishop responded.

Darryl had five seconds to leave. There was no doubt in my mind that the bishop would indeed physically remove him.

Donovan touched the boy on his shoulder. Darryl knocked his hand away.

"Don't touch me," he told Donovan, then looked around the room. "One day, one day you're all going to regret this."

The bishop stepped forward. "Two."

Darryl made his way to the door, but before he opened it, he spit on the floor. "Vengeance is mine sayeth the Lord," was all he said before he walked out and slammed the door behind him.

Those were the thoughts that gave me the extra fire I needed to face those two hypocritical assholes by the name of Bishop Daryl and Deborah Dixon.

The tears wouldn't stop falling. My face, along with Donovan's, was all over the news. Someone had pulled out their cell phone and recorded the cops trying to take down Donovan. I could only bring myself to look at it once. It was worse than what I'd thought it was in the office. I was screaming in the background for them to get off my husband. Fighting with Jason and Amber, trying to get to the man who had just physically assaulted me.

America would never understand a Black woman's plight. Black men could damn near kill Black women, but seeing white men manhandle them—white men who had a history of racial bias toward them—would always put us in protector mode. There was nothing in me that wanted to see Donovan handled by the police that way.

The way the news had spun it, people would think Donovan had tried to kill me.

Technically, he did try to kill you, my mind screamed.

I ignored my thoughts. I sat next to Donovan's mother while his father spoke to the family's attorney. I would have been numb except for the chill already in the room. Donovan's mother had given me the cold shoulder from the moment we had all shown up to the attorney's office together. I couldn't get the way the police had tased and wrestled Donovan to the ground out of my mind. In all honesty, he could have been killed. I wouldn't have been able to live with myself had that happened. In that moment, the fight we'd had didn't matter to me. Donovan wasn't some monster. He was my husband.

My face burned. Throat was sore. Between being attacked in the hotel and the fight with Donovan, my body was in pain and angst I couldn't describe. I was hurting. Not just physically, but mentally and emotionally.

I'll wait for you at the hotel. Need to see you. Need to make sure you're okay, Rome's text came through.

I don't know if I can make it anytime soon. With his family, I sent back.

I said I'll wait. Please let me see you. I need to know if you're really okay. The news said he choked you. Physically assaulted you. Let me see you.

I ran a hand over my hair. I still had on the clothes from hours before when my husband and I fought. *Oh, dear God, how did we end up here?* I thought.

Rome had been texting me nonstop. So had other friends and associates. Everyone had seen the news. My father had even called me. I was so emotional that I'd answered the phone. Told him I was okay and would speak to him later. He wanted to know if what they had said on the news was true. I lied and told him it was blown out of proportion.

One of the reasons I was so hesitant to see Rome was because now he knew my real name. He knew my husband's face. He knew the real me. I was certain that would change things.

"It could take about another hour before they release him," Bishop Dixon said as he walked back over to us, jarring me from my thoughts.

"Why so long? We paid the bail," I said.

"The charges being thrown at him are pretty serious," the attorney said.

Chad Lowery and his identical twin, Saigon, were the best defense attorneys money could buy in the Metro Atlanta area. They came at a steep price, but they always got the job done.

"A lot of people owe us favors," my father-in-law said. "We can't get anyone at the district attorney's office to pull some strings?" he wanted to know.

Chad frowned a bit behind his wire-framed glasses. "I don't need you to say that in front of me again."

I looked up to see Deborah's cold eyes on me. The woman looked at me as if she wanted to fight me. I prayed she wasn't stupid enough to start any shit with me. I was ready for her tonight. Tonight, I would give her what she wanted.

"Probably don't have any more favors to ask. He used them all keeping her out of prison when she killed our grandson," she spat.

She was right. Donovan had used every resource at his disposal, including the twin attorneys, to keep me out of prison. He had his father and his father's people calling in favors all the way up to the governor to keep me out of prison. I walked out of the courtroom with only probation.

Deborah's face was red, eyes misty. Her only son had been handled like a dog for the world to see. I didn't know what I was expecting, but it wasn't for her to go there, and definitely not now.

I gave the woman a slow blink, then tilted my head to the side. "Excuse me," I said.

"How much further down this damn rabbit hole will you take my son?" she asked. "Haven't you done enough? Since the moment he decided to hook up with you, I knew it was a mistake. Knew you would bring him nothing but pain and misery just like your junky mother did Christopher."

Before I could catch myself, I'd drawn my fist back and knocked Mrs. Deborah Dixon off the bench she was sitting on onto the floor. I hit her so hard, her hands flew up, legs flew open, and she fell backwards hard enough to knock one of her pearl earrings out of her ear. I didn't even notice one of her shoes had come off as well.

"I'm sick of you," I yelled as Chad grabbed me, and Bishop Dixon grabbed his wife. "I'm so tired of your holier than thou bullshit!"

"I know she did not put her hands on me," Deborah growled as she got up and kicked her other shoe off, then tried to get away from her husband.

Deborah fought against the bishop's stronghold like the ghetto hoodrat she once was. All that prim and proper woman of God shit had flown right out the window.

"I did, Deborah. I put my hands on you," I taunted.

She kept trying to get her husband to let her go. I wished he would. I would drag her ass up and down this attorney's office so help me God. This would be the day I made Deborah Dixon remember just who the hell I was and what bloodline I'd come from. I was still angry about so many things, including that woman attacking me in that damn hotel. Deborah would take that ass whupping, too.

"I will beat her ass," she snapped, practically foaming at the mouth.

"Try me if you want to," I threatened. "For you to have once been my mother's best friend, you have been nothing but an evil cunt to me anytime you saw fit. You always thought you were better than my mama."

"Your mother allowed drugs to take her to hell just as you're doing with alcohol. I never had to think I was better than her. I was, and I *am* better than she is. I never once abandoned my son or my responsibilities as a wife and mother."

I smirked. "You didn't have to. Your husband did for you. Keep pretending you don't know about his bastard son on the other side of town, wench!"

"Okay, now that is enough," Bishop Dixon's booming voice sounded around the room.

I was ready for him, too. He could get in on the verbal lashing I was giving his wife. They were so full of shit when it came to all this mess. For Deborah to try and pretend she was better than me, for her to tell me that I should accept Rebecca with open arms, it was all a bunch of bullshit. I had to calm down. Needed to get my bearings about me.

"You're right. It is enough," I said over Chad's shoulder; he was still holding me back. "I've had enough of your wife turning her nose up at me every chance she gets, and enough of you whispering in my husband's ear telling him I ain't good enough for him. Screw you! Screw the both of you."

Bishop Dixon's light eyes narrowed. "You best watch your mouth, girl," he warned.

"Or what?" I yelled. "You always hated the fact Donovan married me."

"And he's living to regret it every day," the bishop said. "You need help only God can give you, girl."

"The same God you needed when you made a bastard child on the other side of town?"

"That's enough."

My head whipped around to see Donovan standing in the doorway of Chad's office. Saigon was behind him, his long hair fanning around his shoulders. My anger simmered as I took in my husband's haggard appearance. He glanced at his parents. Did a double take at the bruise that was swelling under his mother's left eye, then turned his gaze back to me.

"Go home," he said to me. "We'll talk when I get there."

For a while, even though he had asked me to go home, all we did was stare at one another. Fresh tears pooled at the bottom of my eyelids. This was the end of us. I felt it deep inside of my soul. There was nothing else left for us to fight for. He knew it. That was why he couldn't keep looking at me. The man in front of me was broken. I was broken. We were broken. No matter how hard we'd tried, we were doomed from the start.

Donovan said to Chad, "You can let her go."

"You're good?" Chad asked me.

Taking a deep breath, I nodded. Saigon stayed where he was. He had strategically placed himself between me and Donovan as well.

Chad let me go, but kept a hand on my upper arm. He picked up my purse and escorted me from the office.

"You haven't been drinking, have you?" he asked me as he walked me to my car.

I frowned. "What? No."

I was offended. Taken aback actually. The fact that I hadn't left his presence except to go to the bathroom told me how low they all thought of me. Couldn't say I had anyone to blame for that but myself.

"It's a valid question, Staci. Just want to make sure you're fit to drive home," he said.

I shook my head, snatched my arm away from him, and then got in my car. I slammed the door, making Chad jump back a bit. He ran a hand through his long hair before walking back into his office. Thunder ripped across the sky just as my phone rang. Since my phone automatically connected to my Bluetooth, it told me the number calling, which meant it wasn't a contact saved to my phone.

I answered, "Hello?"

"You're not home."

The voice on the other end stilled me. I almost swerved to the other side of the road.

"Mama?"

"Saw the news from where I was. Donovan really do that to you?"

"Mama, where are you?"

Her voice was low, kind of raspy. She kept clearing her throat like it was filled with mucus.

"Outside of your house. Calling from this cell phone I bought," she said. "Came to check on you."

"Stay there, Mama. Don't go anywhere. You hear me?"

My body was trembling; heat coursed all through me, causing my armpits to sweat along with the palms of my hands. I was crying now. It had been months since she had made contact with anyone, almost a whole year to be exact.

"I ain't going nowhere. Not until I see you alright," she assured me.

"Okay, okay," I whispered, then blew my horn at the car in front of me that hadn't moved even though the light had turned green.

I could hear the remnants of who she used to be in her voice. That southern belle quality was still there despite all the drugs had done to her. I wondered what she looked like. Had she gained weight? Lost any? Did she still look as beat up as she did last time? I broke all kinds of traffic laws to get home as quick as I could. I saw her as I came up the long, winding driveway. She was sitting on the front steps. I wondered how she had gotten there. Her hair was unkempt, although it looked as if she tried her best to comb it.

There was a scar on the side of her face that hadn't been there the last time I saw her. She stood on shaky legs as she saw me drive up. She'd lost weight, a hell of a lot of weight. She looked like the wind would blow her over. The dress she had on was too big for her. I could tell the tennis shoes she had on used to be white, but now they were so caked with grime and dirt that they were a different color altogether.

Her eyes held a sadness that I couldn't quite put into words. As I parked, she pulled out some Chapstick to apply to her full lips. I yanked my purse from the seat next to me, then hopped out of the car. Delilah tried to smile when she saw me. A closed mouth smile that told me she was still ashamed of the teeth she'd lost on the side of her mouth after one of her dealers attacked her.

She kept running a hand over her hair and brushing down the front of her clothes like she was trying to make sure she looked presentable. Her eyes held water that she refused to let fall.

I rushed over to her, not caring how dirty her clothes were or what she smelled like. I hugged my mother like I would never see her again. She wrapped her frail arms around me. I could feel the tremor in her body as we held one another close.

For a while, no words were spoken. Just tears, pain, regret, and relief. Before that moment, I'd had no idea if my mother was alive or dead. Anytime she pulled a disappearing act, I feared I was never going to see her again.

She pulled away first. Her eyes looked me over. Delilah cupped my face, turned my head side to side.

"You look worse on the pictures from the TV," she said.

I frowned. "What?"

"Saw ya pictures on the news. They said Donovan did all this to you."

My heart sank. The photos the cops took shouldn't have been on any news site. I was considered a victim of domestic violence, yes, but no way should my life had been playing out like an episode of the Rihanna and Chris Brown show.

"Don't believe everything you see on the news, Ma," I said. "Come on."

I rushed to unlock the front door, thinking she was following me. I turned to find she was still standing in one spot.

"Come inside," I told her.

She shook her head. "I don't belong inside of all that."

I frowned. "Huh? What? I don't understand what you're saying."

She looked down at herself, then back up at me before glancing into the open door to my home.

"I'm dirty," was all she said.

"Mama, stop being silly and come on. This is my home. You can come inside. I don't mind."

"Donovan told me not to come back."

My spine stiffened and I stepped back down the stairs to face her. "You've been here?"

She nodded.

"Where was I?"

She shrugged. "I don't know."

"When?"

"Few months back. I came to see you," she said, then wiped the tears falling down her face. "He told me I was dirty. Said I couldn't come in because—"

I shook my head, grabbed my mother's hand, and then ushered her inside. The burning rage I felt inside of me was hot enough to make me spontaneously combust. How dare Donovan turn my mother away when she had come looking for me?

I kicked my shoes off in the foyer like always. Dropped my keys in the bowl on the table next to the door.

"Have you eaten?" I asked her.

"Had some soup at the shelter," she answered.

"Are you hungry? Let me get you some food."

"Okay, but I should wash up first. Can't sit at your nice dinette table and eat like this. Let me wash my face and stuff first."

My mother kept looking around like she was afraid something or someone would jump out at her any minute. She kept moving her feet and looking at the floor. She was acting as if just being in my home was tainting it.

"That's fine," I said to her.

"I-I-I got some dirt ... Donovan ... he don't like dirt of the floors he said."

"He isn't here, Mama. I'll clean it up before he gets here."

She nodded again. "Just give me a rag and some soap—"

"No. No. Come with me upstairs. I'll help you get clean."

She didn't put up a fight. I took her into the guest bedroom I often slept in. I ran the bath hot just as she used to like it. I put some of my oils inside of it and some organic bubble bath. I helped her to undress. Almost cried at the sight of the scars on her body. Damn that. I did cry. She had lost a lot of weight, but she was still a woman. Her breasts still had some plumpness, although not as much as they once had. The stretch marks from my birth still tattooed her lower abdomen. Burn marks, cuts, scratches, and bruises decorated her inner thighs. Her hips still had some of their roundness, but she had scars on them, too.

I had to close my eyes, swallow, and catch my breath. I reached over to turn the water off. Once she stepped inside and sat down, I grabbed her soiled clothing from the floor. Tried to ignore the blood stains in her underwear as I did so. I walked downstairs and dumped her old clothes in the trash. Walked back into the guest room. Grabbed a pair of my underwear that still had tags on them, some socks, and a nice maxi dress that I knew she would be comfortable in.

When she called my name, I walked back into the bathroom. She was sitting with her knees pulled up to her chest, one arm stretched out to me. In her hand was her washcloth. It took me back to a time where there was only her and I. We had no food. She had no money. She left home for an hour. When she came back, Bishop Dixon was bringing her home. Said he had found her wandering around.

Mama looked like she was high and out of it. She walked past me into the house with her head held down. She headed right for the tub. I spoke to the bishop for a moment, and then headed to find her. As soon as I walked into the bathroom, she held both her hands out. In one hand was a wad of cash. In the other was her wash rag, as she called it. She had fresh bruises around her neck.

"You get you some food," was all she had said to me.

There was no need for me to ask what she had done. But I was happy the bishop had found her before she could do anymore. I took the money. Washed my mama's sins away as she cried.

Just like now. I walked over and knelt by the tub, taking the white towel away from her hand. I lathered it with Dove soap and helped to wash her. Just like the old days when I was a little girl.

She cried. I cried. We cried together …

Chapter 22

The kitchen smelled of baked salmon, wild rice, and steamed kale. After I helped my mother to bathe, she rinsed off in the shower. I went to the bathroom in another room to freshen up. My face, neck, shoulders, and chest told of my physical battles. I could no longer tell which battle scars belonged to the stranger in the hotel or the fight between Donovan and me.

One thing was for certain, my mother had been right. The pictures the police had taken of my face, arms, neck, and chest were all over the news and social media. Megachurch, Bishop Dixon's son had assaulted his wife. The media was having a field day at my expense. I turned all communication with the outside world off. For now, it was just me and my mother.

I smiled as I watched her eat. She was hungry, I could tell. Not famished, but hungry nonetheless.

"Where have you been?" I asked her once she had eaten half of the second helping of food I'd fixed her.

She looked up at me, took a napkin, and wiped her mouth. "Around. Here and there."

That was always her answer. She would never come right and tell me exactly where she had been.

"Why don't you come live here with me, Mama?"

She was shaking her head before I could finish the question. "Don't want to see no man putting his hands on you. Don't want Donovan looking at me like I'm the scum of the earth either."

"Donovan doesn't … this is not something we do. This physical violence stuff. And Donovan doesn't hate you."

She kept shaking her head. "No. I'll be fine where I am."

"Will you at least let me put you in a nice rehab facility?"

"I came here to see you. To check and assure you ain't in no trouble with Donovan. To make sure he ain't like his daddy," she said. "You look like you went twelve rounds with somebody. Sure you okay?"

"Yes, Mama."

"Why he hit you like this?"

"He didn't hit me."

"What's all this then?" she asked, waving her hand around as she pointed at me.

"I hit him and things kind of got out of hand."

"Y'all fight each other?"

"No."

"You just said—"

"This was a one-time thing. Some things are going on and emotions got the better of us."

She grunted. I'd cut most of her hair. Brushed what was left back into a full, bushy ponytail. Her skin wasn't as ashen and gray as once before. Some of the color was coming back. I looked at the track marks in and near the crease of her elbows.

"You're still using, Mama?" I asked.

"Don't ask me questions you already know the answer to, Staci. I ain't strong like your father. My demons yet chase me. Ain't no god done saved me," she snapped.

"Do you want to stop? We can get you some help ..."

My mother looked at me like I'd offended her. I often wondered how my father could just run off and leave her behind. He left, got clean, and never came back. How could a man who claimed to love a woman as much as my father claimed to have loved my mother do such a thing? How could he make a conscious decision to not only leave his wife, but his child behind as well? I didn't understand it and I didn't ever think I would.

"You think I don't wanna stop? I can't. I've tried, and each time I try I fall harder than I did before. God must don't want me to change. If He helped Chris, then how come He won't help me? I figure this is all His will," she stated matter-of-fact.

"I'm not much of a religious person myself, but—"

"You married a preacher's son," she blurted out, cutting me off.

"I know, Mama."

"Don't come preaching to me. I don't wanna hear no preaching."

"I wasn't about to—"

"You living fancy and free. Ya demons can't chase you behind castle walls."

I frowned. If only my mother knew how untrue her words were. Part of me wanted to take this time to yell, scream, cuss, and fuss at her. She did this to me! She and Christopher Reynaldo left me to fend for myself as a child. How many times had my mother forced me to become the parent? How many of my things did she sell and pawn to get a fix? How many times had I borrowed money to help her get a fix just so her night terrors wouldn't keep the both of us up at night?

After high school, I wanted to run so far away from this place, but I couldn't. My heart wouldn't let me leave her behind. I had a full ride to Harvard, but I couldn't leave my mother. So, I opted for Georgia State instead. By doing that, Donovan opted to forgo his ride to Harvard as well. He didn't want to leave me.

Thinking about Donovan brought my anger at my mother down. When it came to my husband, I'd gone from abused to the abuser. It finally hit me. I sat back in my chair and swallowed. I coughed once as I thought back. I thought about how Donovan would sneak me alcohol. I remember the very first time he did so. It had never occurred to me until this very moment, that I had done to Donovan what my mother had done to me.

It was a sobering moment.

"I-I just want you to be okay, Mama," I whispered. "That's all I want."

"Then take me as I am. This is all that's left of me," she said.

I was just about to respond when someone rang my doorbell. I grabbed a napkin and wiped my eyes as I headed toward the door.

"Who is it?" I yelled.

"It's your father, Staci. Come to check on you."

I sighed. The last thing I expected was for Chris to show up. It was the last thing I needed, actually.

I yanked the door open. For a second, Chris acted as if he had seen a ghost. His eyes widened a bit, and then his mouth parted like he was struggling to breathe.

"Donovan did this to you?" he asked, shock and dismay written all over his features. "Where is he? I'm going to kill him," Chris said before brushing past me and stalking into my home.

"Excuse you," I said, almost stumbling over.

"Donovan!" Chris yelled out.

"You can't just shove your way into my home!"

"Donovan!"

Chris paced the foyer as he yelled for my husband. His fists were balled at his side, and he was breathing fire through his nostrils it seemed. His face had reddened and the vein in the center of his forehead throbbed.

"He's not here," I said, rushing up to him.

"Then where the hell is he? Call him. This is unacceptable and I don't give a damn who his father is."

"You're a pastor," I said.

"Yes, I am. So, I'll say a prayer after I finish laying hands on him. Look at you. Look at your face, Staci."

"It's not what you're thinking," I said quickly.

"The hell it ain't," he yelled back, shaking his fist as he did so. "I promise on all that is good and holy, he will pay for this!"

"Christopher," my mother's soft voice called out.

She stood just outside of the foyer, twisting one hand in the other as she looked at my father. He was completely caught off guard. His mouth hung open. All the anger that had just been raging inside of my home dissipated. Chris's shoulders slumped, and he looked like all the fight had been sucked out of him.

"D-Delilah," he said, like he couldn't believe it was her.

Mama ran a hand over her hair, a signal that she was used to her hair being down. She gripped her ponytail, and then ran her hand over the front of her hair. Her eyes were watering. She was trying to smile, but I knew she was self-conscious about her missing teeth.

"Yes. Yes, it's me," she said.

"Where … where you been?" he asked.

She shrugged one shoulder. "Here … a-and there."

For a second, there was complete silence between the three of us. I watched my father as he watched my mother. He took timid steps toward her. He kept blinking rapidly like he was afraid she was going to disappear into thin air.

Once he reached her, he stopped.

"I-I-I …" he stopped and shook his head, "I couldn't find you. I looked. This last time, I looked. I promise." Chris's voice croaked like he was choking back tears.

Mama said nothing. But the smile left her face and what replaced it was something akin to resentment.

"You, you kept moving. You wouldn't let me find you and help you," he said.

"What was you gone do when you found me, Christopher? Take me home to live with you and your new wife? Your new daughters?"

His breath caught like he had been slapped with a two-ton brick.

"Hmm? You kept coming to look for me, kept coming to find me. But what was you gone with me? Put me in a rehab? That's all you 'bout could have done. Probably all ya new wife was gone let you do, right?"

Pain resonated in every word my mother spoke. With each word she leveled at him, it seemed Chris took a blow to the heart.

"You know I wouldn't have——" he started.

"I don't know nothing," she interrupted. "Don't know nothing, but what you done showed me. You left us, and I ain't really care 'bout you leaving me, but to leave our baby behind, our child … that fucked me up. You knew I couldn't raise her alone. Knew you was always stronger than me. But you left us. I can forgive ya for leaving me, but ain't nothing you can say that's gone make me forgive you for leaving her," Mama said, nodding her head once in my direction.

Chris dropped his head. His chin on his chest. He stood there like he was being scolded by his parent. It was only when I saw tears drop from his face to the floor that I realized he was crying.

He looked back over at my mama. "I'm sorry. If I could do things all over again, I would."

"But 'cha can't, now can ya? Luckily, our child had some fight in her. She got on well enough without either of us. Your new daughters, I know they happy to have you around. You was a good daddy even when drugs had ya. I know they ain't wanting for nothing," Mama said, her voice soft as a cloud, sweeter than honey. "I don't wish you no bad luck. Just wish you wouldn't have left her behind, Chris. If you was gone go get clean, you coulda come back for her. I woulda let 'cha. I wasn't no good for her. I wasn't. I don't care about you being sorry. And we can't change nothing now. Don't want no help from you. So once I leave here again, don't come looking for me. Stay on with your family."

Delilah turned to look at me. Those hot tears rolling down her face matched mine. I was hurting for her. I felt like a kid caught between her parents fighting.

"You got a room I can go lay in?" she asked me. "I ain't feeling too good."

I nodded and wiped my face with the napkin.

"Wait, Delilah, please. Don't do me like that. I made a lot of mistakes. Listened to the wrong people. I thought she … I thought Staci would be okay with Donovan," Chris said.

My mama looked at him. "Her face look like she okay?"

I said, "Mama, Donovan—"

"Stop lying for him. He just like his damn daddy," she snapped, her voice raised a bit.

"I'm not talking about now," Chris said. "She had Donovan back then. I thought with him and his family … thought she'd be fine. Thought they'd help out. They told me they would."

"Well, they lied," she said, then staggered a bit.

I rushed to her side. "Let me help you get into bed."

"Just show me where to go. I can get there myself."

"Delilah," Chris said.

"I don't want to talk to you, Chris. Not right now. Just let me lay down."

"I'm sorry. I swear to God I am," he said. "I've been trying to right my wrong, but neither one of you will let me," he yelled. "Staci barely wants to talk to me, and you—"

"Me, what?" Mama spat. "You can't bring back some of the things you took away from me, Chris. So don't come here trying to help me or none of that. I'll be fine. I been making it without you all these years. I made it then. I'll make it now. I even made it when those men came and beat your son out of me."

Gasping, I dropped the hold I had on her arm. Chris made a sound akin to a wounded animal in the wild. All of our faces did something, contorted in ways that looked as if we were all in some kind of physical pain.

"All that … blood," I whispered. "I thought it was just from the beating they gave you. You told me …"

"I know what I told you," she said. "Wasn't no need to worry your little mind no more than it already was. I made it. I survived. Without you," she snapped, staring my father down, putting the final nail in the coffin of their friendship. "I'll find a room on my own," she said to me as she made her way down the hall.

I'd never seen a man as hurt as Christopher Reynaldo was in that moment. If I didn't hate him so much, I probably would have held him or helped him up when he fell to his knees. Probably would have lied and told him it wasn't his fault when he put his face to the floor and whispered some unintelligible words to God.

But I didn't. I left him alone in the foyer to fight his own demons, just as he had done to me and my mother.

Chapter 23

"So you're not coming?" he asked.

"I don't know. I have a lot going on right now," I said.

"Why did you lie to me?"

I knew that question was coming, but I played it off anyway. "About what?"

"Your name. Who you were. Who you're married to."

"Like you told me your real name."

"Rome is closer to my real name than Piña is to yours."

"I didn't expect us to see one another again after the club."

"But we did. And you kept the lie going."

Sighing, I looked out my window. "Okay, Rome."

"My name is Jerome. So, technically, I didn't lie."

He was still in the hotel. Had called me after I stopped responding to his texts. It was an hour after my father had a mental breakdown in my foyer. I assumed he had left since I heard my front door open and close. I was exhausted, so arguing with Rome about my name wasn't in my plans. Both of us were silent. I heard the news playing in his background. I could hear them talking about what had happened between me and Donovan.

"Will you turn that off?" I asked with way more attitude than intended.

"He really do all that to you?" Rome asked.

"No, remember your sister-in-law attacked me in the hotel hallway just days before?"

"I don't remember all those bruises and scratches."

"Because you ran off as soon as she told you she was going home to tell your wife you were fucking me."

"Piña … Staci, don't do that to me."

To hear Rome call me by my real name took some of the fight out of me.

"You left me. Showed me my place in your life."

"You wouldn't have done the same?"

I had a moment of clarity. I couldn't front like I didn't get scared when Donovan told me he was on his way to that hotel that night. But that was only because I knew Donovan would have tried to kill Rome.

"That's what I thought," Rome said after I didn't answer.

"Just please turn the news off. I'm sick of people talking about me and my husband."

"You're a victim of domestic violence. One of the most revered bishops known to Christianity is the father of the man who did it. This is going to be news for a while."

"Yes, but that doesn't mean I have to watch it or listen to it, Rome. Turn it off."

"Come make me."

"Stop being childish."

He was quiet.

I said, "My mom is here."

The TV quieted down in the background or he turned it off.

"Seriously?"

"Yeah."

"How is she?"

"It's been stressful. Trying to get her to let me put her in a rehab center. Then my sperm donor showed up. It was emotional for a while."

I told him about all the words that had been spoken. Told him about my mother not really giving a damn about anything my father had to say.

"I never knew how hurt she was that he moved on," I said. "I mean, I knew she wasn't happy about it, but to hear her actually voice it out loud with such disdain … it broke my heart."

"I know what it is to have one parent be taken away because of a habit. So, I can see both sides here."

"My dad walked away from us. He left us behind so he could get clean and then he just left us there. Married a white woman, had two more daughters, and didn't show up again until I was twenty-six."

"Yeah, but doesn't he get credit for getting clean?"

"No. I mean, I applaud him for wanting change, but what about us? Did he have to abandon us?"

"Maybe he figured you were close to adulthood and could take care of yourself regardless of your mother's shortcomings."

"He was in and out of prison for years leading up to that point. He had left us long before then anyway."

"So what are you mad about? If he was gone before he actually walked out that last time, why the animosity?"

"You don't understand," I said, felling anxiety rising with each word spoken.

My father, Christopher Reynaldo, decided to go and clean himself up. I wasn't upset about that part, but did he have to completely walk away from my mother and I? Did he have to move on the way he did? Moving on wasn't the bad part. The bad part was that he completely abandoned us. My mother got served divorce papers that she didn't know were coming. She was completely blindsided. The whole time my father had been in prison the last time, my mother was under the assumption that he would come back, just like he'd always done.

But he never did. I remember Delilah signing those papers. Tears pooled at the bottom of her eyes, but they never fell. I threw the tantrum. I screamed and asked why. I hit my mother, blaming her for sending my daddy away. I remember she and I fighting, exchanging blows because she wasn't just going to let me hit her. I swung, and she swung back until she was too tired to do so. So, she held me until I got tired as well. We ended up against the wall in the front room, her holding me as I cried. Then I held her until she stopped crying.

I told Rome all of that. I didn't even realize I had been speaking out loud.

"Then because I felt bad about hitting my mother, I asked Donovan for some money," I said.

Rome asked, "Why?"

"So Delilah could go get her fix."

"Damn, Staci ..." was all he said.

"She got so high that night that I thought she'd killed herself. I remember the needle sticking out her arm while she was laid across the bed. I thought she'd killed herself. I was so scared. Crying, begging God just give her … us, one more chance. Told God if he just let her live, I'd never drink again."

"Wait. You were drinking at sixteen?"

I nodded like he could see me. "Yeah."

I hadn't meant to tell him that. Hadn't meant to mention my long fight with alcohol. God kept his end of the deal. He allowed my mother to live. I broke my end of the bargain. Years later, God took my son.

I heard Rome moving around in the background. Water was running or he could have been pissing. I wasn't sure.

"I notice you drink a lot when we're together. Do you have a drinking problem, Staci?"

"What the fuck kind of question is that to ask someone, Rome? I could have been drinking to quell the guilt behind cheating on my husband."

"I seriously doubt that," he said.

"How would you know?"

He was quiet a moment, then asked, "Are you coming to see me?"

"No."

"Why not?"

"Told you my mother was here."

"She can't be alone for about an hour or so?"

"I'm not coming to see you."

"I'm at a hotel down the street from your house."

"No."

"Come see me."

"No, Rome."

"Fuck you then."

"No. Fuck you. Where is your wife?"

"I don't know. I left work when I saw you on the news. Came to our old spot, then left when I remembered my sister-in-law knew where it was."

"How did you know where I stay?"

"Simple Google search, Staci Dixon," he said, reminding me that my face and name were all over the news.

"You should be home with your wife."

"Let me see you. I just need to make sure you're okay."

"You want to fuck me."

"Yes. After I make sure you're okay."

"I'm going through a lot."

"Let me take some of the pain away."

"No. Go home to your wife."

He grunted. "Shut up, Staci."

"Come make me."

"Stop being childish."

We were quiet again. For as much as I had on my mind, I couldn't pretend like I didn't want to see Rome. But I didn't know if I wanted to leave my mother alone in my home. After all, she was a drug addict. I didn't want to come home to find some of my things gone. I knew that was wrong to think, but we had been there and done that.

"What hotel are you in?" I asked.

"Embassy Suites near the airport. Not my normal kind of hype, but it's better than I expected."

I walked down the stairs, then made my way to the guest bedroom. I knocked once and got no answer. I twisted the knob, cracking the door. My eyes widened in surprise. On the queen-sized bed were my mother and father. My mother was asleep with her head on his chest. His eyes were wide open.

I put the phone down by my side. "What are you still doing here?" I whispered. "I thought you were gone."

He shook his head once. I couldn't read what was in his eyes. They just looked blank. He was looking at me, but I could tell his mind was somewhere over the rainbow.

"Let her sleep," Chris said to me. "We'll all talk when she wakes up."

I didn't argue. I shut the door just in case he changed his mind and tried to talk to me. I still was in no mood to have a decent conversation with the man.

"Hello," I said, putting the phone back to my ear.

"You coming?" Rome asked.

"Yeah."

We hung up, and I grabbed my purse and keys. Donovan still hadn't called or came home. I doubted that he would. The expression on his face told me we were done. My heart told me the same. The day had been stressful, and I was hoping that, like always, being around Rome made everything better.

The roads were still slick with rain and it drizzled a bit as I backed up and drove down my driveway. The weather looked how I felt inside. Dreary. Dark. Gloomy.

It didn't take me that long to get to the Embassy Suites. I got a ticket to park and then made my way inside to the elevator. The atrium-style lobby was filled with people milling about. Getting up to the sixth floor took no time at all. Room 624. I passed a white couple in the hall. They were stumbling, tipsy, and happy.

I knocked on the door of room 624. Waited a few seconds, then knocked again. Rome opened the door. He had the phone to his ear. Still dressed in tailored slacks, square-toed, red bottom dress shoes with his red dress shirt hanging open. His wife beater displayed the muscles in his chest.

"What time did she stop by?" he asked whoever was on the other end of the phone after taking my hand to pull me inside of the room.

Rome locked the door, then put the latch on. His locs swung around his shoulders. He walked like tension was locked in his shoulders. Even though he kissed me, when he pulled back, I could see the bags underneath his eyes. The room smelled of him, which meant he had been here for a while. Sandalwood and something spicy was the way I always remembered his scent. It always made my nipples hard and mouth wet. Rome's scent was an aphrodisiac.

I walked farther into the two-room suite which had a sitting area that sat off from the room that had a king-sized bed. There was a TV mounted on the wall across from the bed over the brown dresser. A desk was off the side of the dresser. A gray chair with earth toned circles sat in the corner next to the window and diagonal to the bed.

I kicked my shoes off and sat on the bed. I checked my phone again to see if Donovan had called. He hadn't. I didn't know why I was waiting on him to call. By now I should have known better.

Rome paced the sitting area as he talked on the phone.

"So Michaela was with her?" he asked, then nodded. "What else did she say?"

Rome yawned, then stretched.

"I know, Clark. I know, man. It's not my intention to put you in the middle of anything and you know, with as hard as we worked to build our brand, I wouldn't do anything to fuck us up right now. … Trust me, it won't happen again. But don't forget that before now, you used to be the biggest whore Atlanta had ever seen. Don't forget how many times I had to lie to your wife before she left your ass."

Rome chuckled. I laid back on the bed. My mind was all over the place. I was wondering how Chris talked my mother into allowing him to come in the room with her. My mother and I still had a lot of demons between us. We had brushed so many issues underneath the rug. It was odd that I had no problem signing up for marriage counseling to try to fix me and Donovan but had never thought of the idea to help me and my mother's relationship. That would be something I would work on after all the dust had settled.

Rome laughed at whatever Clark had said on the other end of the phone. Then he sobered. Told Clark he feared his marriage was over. Told his friend I was in his bed now and that he didn't think he would be going home tonight. I had no idea what Clark said back to him. Heard Rome confirm to him that I was the woman on the news. Yes, the one who had gotten attacked in the hotel and the one Bishop Dixon's son had assaulted.

I stared up at the ceiling. Thunder rumbled across the sky again. For some reason, that calmed my soul a bit. I got up, walked to the window, and drew back the shades. Rain had started to fall. I stood there for a few minutes. I watched people run to and from their cars. I could see the lights in other hotel rooms going out. Wondered how many lovers and adulterers were about to make love, fuck to the sound of the rain.

When lightning flashed across the sky, I went to lay back on the bed again. Rome told Clark that he was going to speak to him later. They said a few more words, then Rome ended the phone call. Rome turned the lights out in the sitting area. They were already out in the room. I kept my eyes closed when I felt his presence in the room. He moved a few things around on the dresser. I heard him unzip his duffle bag. I opened my eyes. After grabbing some underwear and a smaller red bag with toiletries, he headed to the bathroom.

My phone vibrated. My heart rate accelerated. I just knew it was Donovan.

It wasn't.

It was the man who had donated sperm for my birth.

Your mother wants to know if she can have water and fruit, his text read.

I sighed. **Of course she can**, I sent back.

A few seconds passed. The toilet flushed in the bathroom. The shower came on.

She wants to know if it's okay to stay the night, he sent.

That's fine, Chris.

Are you ever going to forgive me? I miss you calling me Dad.

Not my fault.

I know and I'm sorry.

Stop apologizing. Nothing will change.

The bible speaks on forgiveness. You should read your word and heal.

I frowned. My fingers moved across my touchscreen keyboard rapidly. **Don't come preaching to me, Christopher. You want forgiveness? Go to God. This is all you get from me. Take it or leave it.**

You don't have to be so angry at me all the time.

Look, you have your family. You had two little girls to replace me. They call you Dad. Be happy with that.

You're my daughter, too, Staci.

I had no choice in the matter.

Don't be this way.

My frown deepened. I sat up and pulled my jacket off. The rain was falling harder now. Sounded like the skies had opened up and flood rains poured out.

I laid back down and asked, **Where's my mother?**

She's eating pineapples, a small salad I found, and drinking water.

That's good. She has an appetite.

Yeah. She looks good.

I didn't think she did, but I wouldn't spoil his happiness.

Where are you? he asked.

Out.

I know that. Are you safe?

Yes, Christopher, I'm safe.

He didn't respond after that. I scrolled through old text messages. Found the last one Donovan sent me. The last message he sent me told me he was on his way to the hotel just before that woman had attacked me.

Where are you? I sent to Donovan.

I laid the phone on the nightstand next to the bed. The shower went off. Rome moved around the bathroom doing his hygiene thing. I thought about Donovan. Picked up the phone to call him. The phone rang four times before he sent me to voicemail. I tried again and got the same thing.

Chapter 24

There was once a time Donovan and I were happy together. Before we lost our son … before he became just a memory. A picture in a frame. I felt myself getting emotional. My throat swelled and I choked back tears. The oddest thing happened while Donovan and I were fighting earlier. I swore my son touched my arm. One minute I was screaming for Donovan to stop fighting and lay there. The next I felt the warm touch of a hand on my arm that didn't belong to Jason. I knew he thought I was crazy with the way I'd jumped away from him.

Just like I knew the bishop was probably filling Donovan's head with all the ways he could leave me and keep his money. God knew I never saw Donovan and me where we were. Never thought we'd go at one another like we did today. It was safe to say that all the respect we had for one another was gone. Donovan made that clear today. A few years ago, you couldn't have paid him to come to my job and carry on the way we had today. Yeah, he'd shown up early on in my career to check one of my male coworkers about the way he spoke to me, but nothing like today.

I thought back on the times he and I used to laugh and smile at one another. We would flirt with each other from across the room. Even those times I got too drunk at societal functions, he'd take my hand and lead me out. If I couldn't stand up, he'd scoop me up in his arms. There had always been love in his eyes … or had it been love?

My thoughts quieted down. My mind went from seeing the love he had in his eyes to the pity. The hurt. The pain. The tiredness. That night he had been tired. He carried me from a charity event in his arms. I was pointing up at the stars, amazed at them like I'd never seen them before. Donovan gazed up, then glanced back down at me. He smiled. At the time, I thought I saw love, unconditional love in his eyes, but no. Now, now I knew there was something else there.

The plastered smile on his face had been fake. He put me in the back of the truck, and I remembered the way he stopped before going around to the driver side. He rubbed his eyes with this thumb and pointing finger like he always did when he was tired. He pinched his nose, then lifted his chin in the air to take a deep breath. I was too out of it to think about the fact my drinking had been weighing on him. Even when he was enabling me, I never stopped to think about how my habit was affecting him.

The light from the bathroom brought me back to the present. Steam followed Rome from the bathroom like a jilted lover. It chased him while he walked away without a care in the world. For the last few years, that was how I felt about Donovan. The more I chased him, the easier it was for him to walk away.

He pulled the white towel from around his waist like he didn't care I was seeing him fully naked. That was how close we had gotten. He moved around me like I was no longer a stranger. I loved the way his locs mopped around his shoulders. Was sad when he pulled them back, using two stray ones to tie the other ones away. He did that effortlessly, like he had been doing it for years.

My eyes were half-mast as I watched him put oil on his body. Anytime he oiled his arms and chest, his abs constricted. I took in the globes of his ass in the mirror when he bent to oil his legs and thighs. The best part was when he ran his hands up and down his abs, then over his dick. My body came alive at the sight of it rising to life. He made it jump, and it bobbed up and down.

He walked over to the bed. I flinched when he ran his hand up my thighs, then snaked them around to the inside of them. My breathing deepened as the rain fell harder.

"I like Staci a hell of a lot better than I do Piña. Every time I called your name, that song by the same name about piña colada came to mind," he said.

His voice was low and even, husky like he was on the precipice of arousal.

I smiled a bit.

"Turn the light off in the bathroom," I said.

He asked, "Why? Don't want to face me head-on now that all the formalities are out of the way?"

I shook my head. "Don't want you to see the bruises," I answered honestly.

"They don't bother me."

He raked his fingers up my inner thigh until he reached the heat between my legs. His fingers brushed against my underwear. He could feel my wetness. I knew that by the way he grunted, then licked his lips. With ease, he hooked his fingers and moved my panties to the side. My breath caught, and I tensed when his fingers slipped between my folds.

"Relax," he said.

"I am," I lied.

"You're not."

He was right. All sorts of tension was riding me. My mind was on everything from what happened between Donovan and I to my mother and father. It was even on the woman who had attacked me in the hotel. Even still, I couldn't take my eyes off Rome and everything that made him a masculine male.

While he used one finger to rub around my clit, the other expertly coaxed it out of its hooded covering. I was so wet that his fingers were easily saturated in my juices. It was odd the way my body responded to him. One minute I was sad about the bruises my husband had given me, and the next, Rome had my pussy wet. It made me question if I needed male companionship so badly that I could push what had happened earlier to the wayside and indulge in carnal pleasure.

I knew the answer to that. Since the day Rome and I first exchanged voicemails and then emails to the moment we met at that club, we'd had undeniable sexual chemistry. This time was no different. I almost jumped out of my skin when I felt his breath on my yoni. The feeling was so intense that I gripped the comforter.

I was gazing down at him as he looked up at me. "Want me to stop?" he asked.

My tongue darted out and licked my dry lips. I shook my head. He kissed my yoni lips. I whimpered. Back arched a bit as he kissed them again. And then again. When his tongue flicked out to lick between the folds, it was as if he was French kissing my pussy. I went to grab his locs, but he caught both of my wrists and held them.

Rome's tongue explored my insides like he was searching for the secret to my Nile, and when my hips lifted off the bed, he sucked my clit into his mouth. Between the moaning and the humming he did while sucking on it, the vibrations had me gritting my teeth and fighting to catch a breath.

Water rimmed my eyelids. "Shit. Rome … ahhhh, fuck."

I tried to back away but couldn't. The grip he had on my wrists was ironclad. My hips kept pumping up and down off the bed, trying to get away from the mind-numbing pleasure. Rome pulled away. Blew cool air onto my clit that made me scream out. He kissed my yoni again. Tilted his head and made love to my pussy like it was a work of art.

He kept groaning and licking his lips as he looked at it.

"You have a beautiful pussy, Staci," he told me.

"I know," I said.

Rome let my wrists go, scooped his arms under my thighs, and pulled my face closer to his. With intense aggression, he let his mouth ravish me. I had a handful of his locs. My hips had a mind of their own. One minute I was trying to back away from him. The next I was grinding my pussy on his face.

"I'm … coming," I cried out.

He moved one arm, slipped two fingers inside of me. My muscles clamped around them. The orgasm was mounting. It traveled from the tips of my toes, cramped the muscles in my thighs, and then settled in the pit of my stomach. As Rome fingered me, his mouth never stopped sucking on my clit. It was like his tongue was a suction and each breath he took intensified the pleasure I received.

I was starting to love Rome. And I knew I shouldn't have been feeling that way, but he was putting a move on me that I wouldn't soon forget. He made me feel emotions I hadn't felt in years. No way I could deny myself that anymore. Was I being selfish? Yes. But I no longer cared. Sometimes I felt like I was the wife from that movie *The Bridges of Madison County*.

I was stuck between duty as a wife and chasing after the love I deserved from a man who wasn't my husband.

Rome came up and kissed me. I could taste me on his lips. He always loved when I sucked and kissed on his lips after he would perform oral sex on me. Told me his wife had a hang up about it. Didn't like for him to try to kiss her after he would eat her out. I loved that shit. Loved the pure, unsoiled taste of me on his lips.

I wrapped my arms around his neck. As our tongues danced, I imagined Rome was my prince. I imagined I'd found the right frog this time, even though he didn't belong to me. I wondered what his wife would think if she knew Rome's dick was several inches away from breaking skin with no condom on. I no longer cared. It was clear he was dancing on that thin, gray line as well.

To one another, we were forbidden fruit, and every chance we got, we took a bite out of the other with no care of the consequences.

He pulled back from the kiss and gazed down at me.

"I need to get condoms," he said.

"I know."

It was like he was toying with the idea of saying fuck it all. Go in raw, the aftermath be damned. We kept staring at one another. He didn't make a move to go get the condom. I didn't move my thighs from around his waist. I gave his locs a light tug. Brought my head up a bit to suck on his bottom lip.

He gave something akin to a guttural groan. His body jerked when I kissed his Adam's apple, then bit down on his neck. That was his undoing. That was when he made the decision to say fuck it all. For as selfish as it was, I wanted him to put a baby in me. I'd gone and lost my damned mind, clearly. But, in that moment, I didn't care.

My back arched and I sang a song of pleasure that I was sure could be heard in the hall despite the storm raging outside.

"Fuck me, Jerome," I begged in his ear.

He made some kind of sound that told me he was struggling with the decision he had just made. He was inside of me. Raw and unrestricted. That shit felt so fucking good that I saw lightning behind my eyelids.

"Please fuck me," I begged.

I needed him to fuck the pain away. As his dick got harder, continued to swell inside of me, I rocked my hips upward. I needed him to move inside of me so badly that I had no shame. My wantonness was put on display. It had been too long since I'd felt a man in the raw. I was about to come undone.

"Staci … Piña … Staci, please," he aggressively whispered, "don't make me do this."

"Do it," I whispered while sucking on his ear, then I bit down into his shoulder.

He jerked again. This time he gave me five hard, deep thrusts. The thunder clapping outside did little to hide the sounds of my satisfaction. Jerome's strokes were so damn good that I was afraid nothing could be make feel ashamed for the nasty, sex-filled requests that spilled from me mouth.

I asked him to fuck me like he hated me. He did. He went long, hard, and deep. So deep, I had to beg him to take it easy.

Told him to fuck me like he loved me. He obliged. Slowed down his frantic thrusts but stayed deep and short, stroked me into a frenzy.

I asked him to stop. I wanted to just feel him pulsing inside of me. He stopped. Caught his breath while he kissed me.

He and I had always been nasty together, nasty like Donovan and I used to be. When it had come to sex, my husband and I never had any hang-ups. We'd started exploring as teenagers and never stopped. Not until … not until …

"Staci, stop," Jerome barked out.

I ignored him. Kept dipping then rocking my hips as I clamped my thighs tighter around him.

My nails dug deep into his back. He threw his head back. Locs went flailing backward like some tendrils on a cat o' nine tail. He yanked me down a bit, put the back of my knees into the creases of his arms, and fucked the fuck out of me.

His balls slapped against my ass. He was so deep, he was breathing for me. The look of unmitigated pleasure on his face told what was about to happen. I reached for him, but he ignored me. I lifted my hips and gave him a better angle. He shook his head angrily. Then cursed. Thunder and lightning danced across the sky. As the thunder rocked the halls of the Embassy Suites, Jerome rocked the walls of Staci Dixon.

He knew what I wanted. So he gave it to me.

"Fuck. I'm coming, Staci. Oh my fucking God, I'm coming," he roared.

His head fell back. The muscles in his chest and arms strained. The vein in the center of his forehead looked as if it was about to pop.

"I feel you. Damn, I feel you," I cried. "Come inside of me," I coaxed.

He was shaking his head like he was fighting with the thought. I leaned up, snatched him down by his locs, and brought his lips to mine. My thighs wrapped back around his waist. Every thrust he threw at me, I threw it back like I had something to prove, and when his body jerked, I knew I had him.

He pumped harder, faster. Made sounds that told me my pussy had taken him to heaven and brought him back down again.

Am I Wrong?: Jerome

Chapter 25

Walking into my home felt foreign to me. I knew why, so there was no need for me to pretend I didn't. I stayed in that hotel room with Staci for another day. She left to check on her parents a couple of times, but for the most part, she was there with me. She told me she wanted to let some of the media hype die down. Her job didn't want her to come back for a while. So, they made her take all the vacation time she had accumulated over the years.

I learned all of that while listening to her phone conversations. I even heard when she stepped into the hall and left her husband messages. Got annoyed when she stepped into the bathroom to do the same. He was ignoring her, and she was still chasing him.

Yes, my sister-in-law had attacked her in the hallway, but I saw the fresh bruises he had given her as well. That bothered me. But I kept my mouth closed. I was too busy thinking about the fact I'd left come stains inside of her. We'd both made a decision I wasn't sure we could live with, since we hadn't really thought it through.

I heard my wife in her office. I didn't know what we would or could say to one another at this point. But I told her long ago that if I got the notion to cheat on her and actually did it, it was time to walk away. I dropped my bag, then picked up the mail to see what had come for me. Bills. Credit card offers. More bills.

The TV in the front room was playing. A terrorist attack had happened in some other part of the world. That would be the talk of all the news channels for a while. I had no desire to see the trauma other people would suffer behind the attack on my TV. Leave it to news channels to not care how a terrorist attack would trigger the victims of old attacks. I switched my TV from CNN to Fox 5. At least with the local news channels, I'd get some local news thrown in with the breaking news.

I could hear the low hum of the central heat going. It had been raining in Atlanta for two days and now the cold air had come in. Atlanta weather was odd like that. We really had no winter, and then on the first two days of spring, winter weather settled in. Nevertheless, it would probably be summer by two in the afternoon.

Sheila's office door opened. I heard when she walked out. Heard her sniffles. I put the mail on the table, then spread my arms over the back of the couch. I braced myself for what was about to come.

"So this is it?" she said.

Her voice was low, shaky. Didn't carry that authoritative tone it usually did. I didn't want to look over at her. Didn't want to see her crying.

"I don't get a chance to fix us?" she asked.

I answered, "I don't think we can be fixed. We've moved past that stage."

"Please don't do this," she cried. "You have to give me a chance to fix it."

I sighed and stared straight ahead. I'd left my future children inside of another woman. I'd subconsciously made my decision.

"Give our family a chance," she said.

Family? What fucking family? I'd been trying to create a family with her for years, and each time she shot me down. And now, now she wanted to discuss family? Wanted me to give our nonexistent family a chance?

"Our family?" I repeated. I snapped my head around at her. "You call this—"

I stopped at the sight of the tear-stained face. Her hair was a bit unkempt. She wasn't the well-put together therapist and businesswoman I once knew. She looked like she had been in a fight with love and lost. She had on shorts with a thin tee-shirt. There was a slight pudge in her stomach that I hadn't noticed before, but her weight had always been up and down so that wasn't unusual.

"Sheila, this isn't a family. We're not even the same husband and wife we used to be," I said.

A bit of the anger and bass had left my voice. I hated to see my wife crying. It always ate away at me. To know I was a part of the reason the tears were falling down her face made me feel even more guilt about the time I'd spent away from home with Staci. I was living two different lives at this point. I didn't know where I wanted to be.

Staci and I had talked about things ... said things ...

If I left her, she would leave him.

We could run away and never look back.

She and I had imagined life without a Donovan or a Sheila. We imagined her carrying my child. The shit was wrong, no doubt, but that was where my head was. Clark had told me not to let new pussy come between me and my wife. However, at this point, Staci had become more than new pussy. She was in my head. Occupied my thoughts where only Sheila used to be.

"Who is she?" Sheila asked. "And don't lie. Michaela told me about the incident at the hotel."

Dropping my head, I ran my tongue over my dry lips. "Sheila, stop."

"No. Tell me. Who is she? Who's the woman my sister assaulted because you were committing adultery?"

I stood and glared at my wife. She swallowed and held her head high. I could tell a new wave of anger was replacing her sadness. Clearly, she hadn't been watching the news. If she had, she would have been able to answer her own question by now.

"No matter what I had going on, I never cheated on you, Jerome. I had plenty of opportunities."

I dipped my head forward to make sure I'd heard her correctly. "Excuse me. Say that again. You had what?"

She nodded and turned her lips upwards. "I could have had my pick of any well-respected doctor or lawyer in Metro Atlanta, but I chose to be a damn football wife," she spat. "I could have chosen jobs overseas or anywhere in the world, but I chose to stay and become a goddamn football wife! I had to sit in rooms with snooty-ass white, Asian, and Latin bitches who thought you deserved better than a Black woman as a wife. There I was with several degrees in my field, and I had to be subjected to that bullshit."

"What the hell does that have to do with you bragging about—"

"I'm not bragging about anything. I'm saying you never once thought about how your career affected me. You like to brag about how you weren't like other ballers, about how you were a 'good man' like that wasn't what you were supposed to be. Like you weren't supposed to be a good damn husband to me. You hung around with Clark's whoring ass and all the other ballers. Think I don't know what they thought of me? Like I didn't overhear Clark telling you, you could have your pick of any other race of woman in the room and you chose a fat, Black girl."

I took a deep breath. I knew the time she was speaking about. The Falcons were in their prime. Winning games left and right, parties every night. We were in a room full of what they called exotic women. Clark had been drinking when he said that to me. I put him in his place, but I hadn't even known she heard him. That would explain why she was so indifferent when he or any of my teammates and their wives had come around.

My wife and I stared one another down.

"Why didn't you say anything, Sheila? You know you could have talked to me about anything, and I would have handled it," I said.

She shrugged one shoulder and shook her head. "Don't you remember? I did, Jerome. I said something. I told you about all the things those women were saying about me and all you told me was to ignore it. But that didn't work for me. So, I went back to my work. That was how I chose to ignore it among other things. And now we're here. Even after you retired, we're still here. Yet, you act as if this is all my doing. It isn't."

"I never cheated on you with any of those women. If someone, anyone said anything untoward toward you, I corrected it."

"I know you, Jerome."

"I never cheated with any of the women who were shoved in my damn face, Sheila. I always, always came home to you."

A new stream of tears rolled down her face. She made an expression as if my words were hurting her.

"I know my husband. I. Know. You."

I didn't know why she kept saying that. Anytime she did, it made me a little more uncomfortable.

"Sheila, I didn't—"

"You hear me, Jerome, but you refuse to listen," she said.

I tilted my head and studied her. For the life of me, I couldn't figure out if she was playing with my head or not. She rubbed her hand over her stomach, then looked at me before turning to walk away. My phone buzzed. I was set to ignore it until the number on the screen made me pause. I didn't pick up until I was sure Sheila was out of sight.

"Are you out of your fucking mind?" was how I answered.

"You weren't supposed to fall in love," the voice on the other end of the phone taunted.

"I told you to never fucking call me again," I snapped.

"Tsk. Tsk. Tsk. Now come on, Jerome, after all the drama we've gotten into together, I can't call an old pal?"

I walked into the hall to make sure Sheila wasn't within earshot before I entered the guest bathroom and shut the door.

"What do you want?" I asked.

"You actually fell in love with Staci Dixon. I can't believe it. Does she know?"

"Does who know what? Have you been stalking me?"

The person on the other end of the phone let out a cackle that would wake the dead. "Nigga, please," they spat.

"Then how do you—"

"How do I know you're fucking Staci Dixon? Well now, that's for me to know and you to find out. Does Staci know it was you who ran her off the road that day?" they asked, then laughed.

"The day she thinks she killed her son? She know that was you?"

"Shut up."

"I watched your ESPN special a few months back. All your old teammates bragging about how you were the good guy. How you never slept around with other women on your wife," they said, then laughed manically.

My body tensed, shoulders felt like the weight of the world had taken a seat on them. I was Atlas. The world was my burden. My eyes watered and my vision blurred.

"Why don't you just leave me alone? I paid you."

"That you did, but do your friends and wife really know why you quit the league so suddenly? How is that guilty conscience working for you? They know you really quit because you ran that poor woman off the road while I was sucking your dick?"

"Go to hell."

"Been there. Done that. How's that beautiful wife of yours?"

"If you come anywhere near my wife, I will kill you."

"Are you threatening me, Jerome? Don't do that. Don't threaten me."

"Don't come near my fucking wife!"

"Does she know you went through her files to find information on her client? That you found out that Staci likes to go on chat lines and get off?"

"Shut up and stay away from my wife if you know what's good for you."

"What would happen if she found out? Talk about six degrees of separation … or was it?"

I hung up when I heard Sheila walking down the hall. After flushing the toilet, I turned the water on to make it seem as if I was using the facilities. I threw cold water on my face, and then stared at myself in the mirror. All my past demons danced behind my eyes. I swallowed down the massive lump in my throat.

I opened the door just as she passed the bathroom. She didn't look back at me. Just kept going by doing whatever it was she was doing.

My phone buzzed twice. Two text messages came through. One from Staci telling me she wouldn't be able to see me this weekend because something had come up. The other one chilled me to the bone. I swallowed down the bile in my throat and gripped my cell so tightly that it threatened to break in my hand.

Vengeance is mine sayeth the Lord, was all it read.

I Keep Forgetting: Donovan

Chapter 26

Five days later …

"On Thursday, March 21st, a video surfaced of my husband being arrested in my office. That same night, photos leaked of what appeared to be the outcome of a fight that my husband and I engaged in. However, on March 17th, I was attacked in the hallway of the W Hotel in Midtown. While I did not file a police report, there is video footage of the incident and Officers Tyrone Beatty and Paul Gyser were the responding officers. The photos leaked to the press are not a result of my husband physically assaulting me. They are the result of an attack that had occurred days prior …"

I watched the TV mounted on my front room wall as they replayed my wife's face over and over. She was dressed in her best attire, a cream-colored business suit with a red blouse underneath. Her hair was pulled back into a bun with a red ascot tied around her neck to hide the bruises there. The pearl earrings in her ear set the whole dutiful wife look off. I stood beside her, her hand in mine as she told half-truths to save my ass.

My eyes were red. The navy-blue tailored suit I had on complemented Staci's attire.

My wife and I stood side-by-side on the TV at a press conference put together by my father's PR representatives. Bishop Dixon wanted to make sure we got ahead of the melee before it spun out of control. It wasn't just my reputation on the line, it was his as well. As the son of one of the most decorated and noted Bishops, according to his PR reps, it was imperative I cleaned this mess up.

"The quicker we get ahead of this thing, the better," Joyce had said.

Joyce had been my father's secretary and anything else he needed for years. She was probably the only woman my mother could trust around my father.

So, we jumped in front of it. Used a room in the mayor's office to hold the press conference.

Joyce was careful in who she invited as far as press. She invited the news stations and blogs who would post whatever she wanted them to. She wanted those who would take what Staci had said and run with it. Not to mention, she had gotten the two police officers who had come to the hotel to corroborate Staci's story.

"So what about the video we saw of the fresh blood on your lips?" a reporter asked.

Staci dropped her head for a second, then looked back at the camera. She bit her bottom lip to keep it from trembling.

"Sadly, I tried to hit my husband, and when he went to block the hit, my hand bounced off his arm and into my lip," she lied.

Her eyes were lined with water. We were the 2016 Ray Rice and Janay Palmer.

"Will you please turn that off?" Staci asked.

I turned my head to look at her. I hadn't even heard her come in. She was dressed in a white mini dress that hugged her curves and breasts. Something I hadn't seen her in before. Her hair was bone straight and parted down the middle. It had a shine to it that said she was fresh from the salon. Yet again, the thought of her fucking another man made fury ride up my spine.

I turned back to the TV and took a sip from the water bottle in my hand. "Why?" I asked.

"We were there. Do we have to keep looking at it?"

I didn't respond to that. I watched her shapely ass when she walked around the couch and made her way over to the window.

"What in hell you got on?"

She glanced at me from over her right shoulder. "A dress," she replied, sarcastically.

I rolled my shoulders. For the past few days, she had been walking around in her own world. Hadn't said much to me. She stayed locked in her room or in the guest room with her mother whom I didn't want here.

"Your mother still in my house?" I asked icily.

"Our house," she corrected me.

"Whatever."

"Yes, she is. She's my mother. I'm not putting her out."

Delilah had been just as standoffish as her daughter. She'd speak and then disappear behind a closed door. I had no problem with the woman other than the fact she kept disappointing my wife. In the past, anytime Staci reached out to her in hopes of helping her to get clean, her mother had broken her heart. Because of that, the last time the woman showed up at my door, I told her to leave and never come back.

"I don't want her here," I said.

"She's my mother, and I don't appreciate you not telling me about her showing up before."

"You'll get over it."

"You're so worried about my mother and yet we haven't talked about our own elephant in the room."

I clicked the TV off and looked at her.

"Did you cheat on me, Staci? That's all I need to know. If you did, we're done."

She shrugged. "I don't care one way or the other. Doesn't matter. It's time we stopped delaying the inevitable. You already have another child outside of this marriage. So, whether I have or haven't cheated on you isn't the issue. You lost respect for me. A long time ago you did or you wouldn't have fucked my best friend nor procreated with her." She gave a half shrug. "So I don't care. We can be done. Get your attorney to draw up papers."

I frowned while studying her back. I hadn't really looked at my wife in years. I couldn't deny that the feminine curve of her back and the outline of her hips and thighs in the dress she was wearing stirred something in me I hadn't felt in years. I stood, set the bottle of water down on the coaster on the table. She tensed a bit when she saw my reflection walking up behind her in the window. I stopped a few inches behind her. It broke my heart a bit to know I'd instilled fear in her, fear of me. Fear that I would hurt her. Again.

"I often wonder where we would be if D-Three was still here. I wonder if we'd be this miserable or if we'd be as happy as we used to be," I said while watching her reflection in the window.

"Were you ever really happy, Donovan? I remember all those times when you would have to clean up my vomit after I would drink too heavily or the times you would have to carry me out of charity events. Were you ever really happy with me? You chose to let Harvard go to stay behind with me."

"I loved you. Would have taken on the world for you. Would have forgone a trip to heaven if it meant staying with you."

She nodded. She knew I wasn't lying. I had my flaws, but I loved the fuck out of Staci once upon a time. I wasn't sure if I still loved her with the same passion, but I knew I still felt something.

"I stole our son away from you ..."

I glanced out the window when she said that. The trees were vibrant with green colors. The sun was shining, but judging by the way the trees were swaying, the wind was blowing hard. Our lawn people were going about their day, doing their jobs. One man was on a riding mower. Another had a leaf blower, while one small, Mexican woman was busy planting whatever flowers Staci had ordered.

"There was a time, even before we lost our son … I couldn't wait to hate you, Staci," I confessed.

She stiffened a bit. Shock decorated her features.

I kept going. "I loved you so damn much, so damn hard. Went against family. Fought my parents tooth and nail for you. I loved you so damn much I couldn't wait to hate you. Your love had me so warped, I'd go against God for you. I needed a reason to hate you. Needed a reason to get the spell you had worked on me off. There was a time … you were so drunk, so damn out of your fucking mind with alcohol, that I asked myself why I couldn't let you go. I was jealous of that fucking bottle. All you did was give me a reason …"

She turned to look at me. She was about to speak, but I held my hand up.

"You always chose that damn bottle over me. I asked, begged, pleaded, cussed, threatened you, fussed with you to leave it alone and you wouldn't. Your love for the alcohol took precedence over your love for me."

She shook her head. "No, it didn't, Donovan."

I knew she would deny it. "Remember how you would cry and beg your mother to stop? Always asked her why she didn't love you enough to stay clean?"

Staci fidgeted around like my comparison of the two addictions made her uncomfortable.

"That's different. I can stop anytime I want to," she said in a low voice.

"Then why didn't you? If that's the case, you're proving my point. If you can or could have stopped anytime you wanted, that either means you didn't care enough about me or RJ to stop or you intentionally chose to keep hurting me, because, again, you didn't love me enough to stop."

"In her defense," I heard behind us, "it's not about loving or caring enough."

I turned to find Delilah standing there.

"Mama," Staci said. "You need something?"

"Nope. Was on my way to the kitchen when I heard y'all talking," Delilah said to Staci, but she kept her eyes on me. "The first time Christopher and I went to cop, we had on suits. He had just come from the NFL draft. He had no takers. I went dressed up because I just knew at the time they was gonna sign him. They didn't. Back in college, we used to smoke weed, we did a little PCP, stuff those white kids would give us. We were the 'good' Black kids. Not like those 'other' Blacks. We went to this building. There was a hole in the door. We slide the money in, they slid the product out. They couldn't believe people who looked like me and Chris was buying drugs. They made us take tests to prove we wasn't no cops or nothing. First time, I had to smoke right there. They gave me the good stuff, too. I took it to the head. We needed that hit. Needed to take off the sting of Chris not getting drafted and the fact that job I had been promised for being one of the good Blacks was given to a white girl who had just gotten out of a halfway house."

Staci said, "I didn't know that."

Delilah nodded. "Lots you don't know. Thangs ain't never go quite right for me and Chris growing up, but once we got out our neighborhood, got to college, we just knew things would be different. And it was for a while. For a while, we had it all together. We had left the pain of our pasts behind. Left the abuse we suffered as kids, all that. We were riding high."

I asked, "What happened?"

Delilah looked out the window like she was seeing her life flash before her eyes in the windowpanes.

"Life," she said in a huff. "Them drugs get a hold of you and it ain't about if you love somebody enough to let go. Not while they got you in their grip. This shit, the drug addiction, the alcoholism, it's a disease. It has to be cured. When I first started, it was about getting a good feeling you know. It was about being taken away from all my stress, all the ills life had given me. Me and Chris would get high and everythang would be okay. Then we needed to keep getting that high so we could function. It was all good at first ya know. We could get high and nobody knew it but our closest friends. Then life happened. I got pregnant. Had a baby kicked out of me."

"Another one?" Staci quipped.

Delilah nodded. "Yup."

"Before me?" Staci asked like she was either in awe that there was a baby before her or in shock.

Delilah nodded. "Yeah."

"Who did it?" I asked.

Delilah looked at me. I watched as the light in her eyes slowly drained. A storm brewed behind her eyes.

"The man who was the first to introduce me to drugs and alcohol," she said.

Staci started, "Chris wasn't—"

Delilah was already shaking her head. "No, your father and I were introduced to drugs by someone else. We had our little clique we ran with. Thought we was better than the other Black kids even though we came from the same hood they did. I ain't used to talk this messed up. Had better speech in me. We faked it after we made it, but life caught up with us. Guess it wasn't meant to be."

"What wasn't?" Staci asked.

"For Chris to go to the NFL. For me to get that job in that financial firm. No matter how far we ran, our demons caught up with us. People who were 'sposed to be our friends turned their backs on us." She looked at me. "I see your mama and daddy doing well. Funny."

The way she said that shit made me uncomfortable. Like she knew some things about my parents I didn't know. The sarcasm in the word 'funny' was palpable.

"What does that mean?" I asked as I folded my arms across my chest.

"What's what mean?" she asked.

I noticed her top lip had turned upward a bit as she stared at me. It was as if she was looking at me but seeing someone else. I made a move toward her. She jumped back. Did that like she was afraid I was going to hurt her or something.

"I'm not going to hurt you, Delilah," I said. "I never have. You know that."

"I don't know nothing," she snapped. "You did that to my baby's face and neck. Don't know what you capable of."

My brows furrowed. I looked at Staci who moved closer to her mother.

"Mama, Donovan isn't going to touch you," she told her.

"He better not. Bet not touch you again either. I ain't got too much to live for. Don't mind doing time," the woman said with a glare in her eyes that made her threat clear. "You just like him, you know?"

My jaw twitched. "Just like who, Delilah?"

"Yo damn daddy."

"What has my father done but try to help you?"

"Help me?" she repeated like she couldn't believe I'd said it the first time. "When was this so-called help 'sposed to had come? Where was I when it came? When it get there?"

"You can't help people who don't want to be helped," I said.

"Yo mama and daddy don't help nobody but themselves. Funny how they like to sit in that big, fancy church and act like they gots it all together," she mumbled. "They left me and Chris to rot when we needed 'em most."

"It's not my folks' fault you're strung out, Delilah," I snapped.

"Donovan, stop," Staci demanded.

"Tell her to stop. Sick of her looking at me like I've done something to her, then speaking about my parents like they're evil. They didn't put the drugs in her hand. Be mad at the person who introduced you to drugs. Go find them."

Delilah stood straight up. Her lips screwed up into a scowl. You would have thought the room we were standing in was filled with cow shit or something.

"I don't have to or need to go find nobody," she said.

I said, "And just for the record, I don't think drug abuse or alcoholism is a disease. I think it's a chronic choice. Every day you wake up and choose to shoot that crap up your arm and every day Staci takes a drink, she chooses to. It's not a disease. A disease is cancer. Choosing to do drugs and alcohol are not. You have a choice and every day you make the one that's most important to you."

"That's enough, Donovan," Staci snarled.

"It's alright," Delilah said. "He gone get his wake-up call soon enough."

I frowned. "What the hell is that supposed to mean?"

"Just what I said. One day you gone see yo daddy and mama for who they really are. And as for the person who introduced me to drugs and alcohol … It was your father, of course."

Breakdown: Staci

Chapter 27

My mama's words shut Donovan down so hard that all he could do was stand there and stare at her. Donovan's face hardened. I couldn't quite explain what I felt. I was so damn stunned that the fact my mama had basically just said Donovan's father had stomped a baby out of her didn't register just yet.

"You're a liar," Donovan barked at her.

My mama turned and headed back to her designated room, but not before saying, "The truth don't need no defending, Donovan."

"I want her out of here," he said with a little too much bass in his voice for me.

"She's my mother. She isn't going anywhere," I said.

"The hell you say. You get rid of her, or I will."

"You'll have hell on your hands if you try."

The threat in my voice was real. If he tried to put my mother out of the house I helped to build, he would be in for one hell of a fight.

I knew my husband and he hated to be threatened by anybody. The scowl that adorned his features told me he was going to call my bluff. That was until his cell rang. The house phone started next, and then my phone.

Something was wrong. Donovan snatched his phone from the table.

"What's up, Pete?" he answered.

I picked up my cell. It was a number I didn't know.

"Hello," I answered.

There was no answer.

"Wait, what?" I heard Donovan say. "When? Did Monet get out? I'm on my way."

I watched in horror as Donovan snatched up his keys and wallet.

While I held my cell phone to my ear, Donovan told me, "My shop is on fire. Pete got out, but he says Monet is still inside. I'll be back."

I nodded so fast my head resembled a bobble head doll. For the first time in a long while, Donovan kissed me. It was only a peck on the lips, but it shocked him just as much as it did me.

We stared at one another for a few moments.

He was the first one to break the silence. "I'll be back."

I realized the person on the other end of the phone was just breathing.

"Hello?" I said again.

The person on the other end said nothing.

I didn't have time for crazy-ass people. Ever since the news conference, we had been getting strange calls from reporters and random people alike. I hung up. I prayed that Monet was okay. She was a single mother who Donovan had hired from the church. She was very respectful and not once tried to come on to my husband like so many of the others. I said another silent prayer, then headed for my bedroom.

I was halfway up the stairs when someone rang the doorbell. I blew out steam, then turned around. I hoped it wasn't one of the stupid reporters who had camped out near the end of our driveway again. One had even ordered pizza just so I would open the door and he could get a picture of me. I looked through the peephole to see little Rebecca standing there. She was alone.

"What the hell, Tara?" I mumbled as I snatched the door open.

She would wait until Donovan left to pull some shit like this. Tara knew Donovan would rip her a new asshole if she had dropped Rebecca off like this without calling first.

"Ms. Staci," Rebecca cried.

She was smiling, but there was sadness in her eyes. Looked as if she had been crying or it could have been the pollen that decided to show up. Rebecca had always been allergic to the stuff. I was happy to see no reporters were out there.

"Hey, Becka. Where's your mother?" I asked.

Rebecca's long, red, wavy hair was unkempt. It was as if she had dressed in a hurry as she had on two different shoes and Doc McStuffins pajamas.

"She's in the car."

I strained my neck and saw Tara's BMW hiding behind Donovan's G-Wagon.

"Why is she sitting in the car?" I asked Rebecca.

She shrugged hard and whimpered, "I don't know. Can I come in? Did you cook, Staci? I'm so hungry."

The way she said that tugged at my heartstrings. She sounded tired and restless. What in hell had Tara been doing that she hadn't at least fed the child?

I ushered Rebecca in. "Come on in."

Rebecca rushed by me. "I saw Daddy leaving. I'm happy you-ya-you were here. I don't want to go back with Mommy tonight. I'll be good. I won't say a word. I won't cry. I won't do anything bad. Just let me stay with you, Staci. Please," she whined and begged.

Frowning, I knelt in front of Rebecca. A strong odor of stale urine assaulted my senses. I blinked, then backed up a little. Tara hadn't even bathed the girl?

"It's fine. You can stay. But do me a favor, okay?"

Rebecca nodded.

"Go to your room. Remember how I showed you to run your own bath water?"

She nodded again.

"Go start it for me and I'll be right up, okay?"

"You pr-pr-pr-promise?"

I nodded. "I promise."

"I don't want to be alone in the dark again."

"No worries. No dark rooms here. I promise."

When Rebeca rushed in to hug me, I fell back on my ass. Something had happened to her. Something had changed in the child and it worried me. She wasn't so happy-go-lucky anymore.

"I love you, Staci, and I knew you loved me, too. Mommy said you hated me, but I knew you didn't."

I held her in a hug. I closed my eyes and felt like shit for all the times I'd been indifferent toward the child.

"Go on now. I'm coming. Let me talk to your mother for a second," I said.

Rebecca rushed up the stairs. I got up and stormed out the door. Tara stepped out of the car before I got to her. She was dressed like she was on her way to a runway in Paris. That angered me further.

"What the hell, Tara? What's going on?" I asked.

"Nothing. Brought my child to see her father," she said.

Tara lit a cigarette, something I hadn't seen her do since high school. The funky bitch blew smoke in my face.

"He got you good, huh?" she asked, while staring at the bruises on my face, neck, chest, and arms.

While her child looked homeless, the cunt stood in front of me in name brand shoes and clothes. Her hair was done while her child's hair looked like it hadn't been combed in days.

"You brought this child over here filthy and hungry and you're standing up here like nothing is wrong. Donovan would snap your fucking neck if he was here," I snapped.

"No. He saves that kind of shit for you," she said snidely.

I cut my eyes at her. "Tara, don't play with me."

"What? I ain't got no money to feed the little crumb snatcher," she said casually.

"That's a lie and you know it. The redneck in you is starting to show."

She grunted. She knew I was right. She was starting to act like her folks over in that damn trailer park near Stone Mountain. They were the epitome of hillbilly rednecks. From the tobacco chewing grandfather, to the incestuous uncles and brothers.

Tara's mother never took care of her. Tara didn't know how to love a child no more than a cat knew how to fly. She stared me down as I knew my words shook her to the core. Took a puff of her cancer stick and then blew smoke in my face again. I slapped the cigarette from her hand.

"You should be ashamed of your damn self," I yelled at her.

"For what?" she asked as if she was clueless. "I can't take care of her no more, Staci."

"The hell do you mean?"

She glanced around, then shook her head. "I only had her because I thought he was going to leave you."

I cocked my head to the side. "Say what?"

"I didn't sign up to be no single mother like most you Black bitches around here. Y'all like that shit. Y'all applaud it like it's some kind of badge of honor. Not me."

If I'd had words to describe the look on my face, I still wouldn't have been able to describe the look on my face. I knew she was attacking Black women as a collective because I'd attacked her redneck upbringing, but it still stung.

"Since he's still here with you, y'all can take care of her. I'm not cut to be anyone's mother."

"Tara—"

"Oh shut the hell up, Staci! You won, okay? You won."

"Won what exactly?"

Tara looked around for a moment. Her eyes were wild, pupils dilated. It looked as if she was fighting with her words, like she was trying to make up her mind about what to say next.

"Don't matter. Take care of my baby for me. I have to get out of here."

No matter what Tara was saying, there was something in her eyes that told me she wasn't telling me everything. She was skittish, looking around like she was afraid of her own shadow. Tara had done the most fucked up thing a friend could do to another, but something in me felt like she was in trouble. I touched her arm.

"Tell me what's really going on, Tara. Let me know. Even though we're no longer friends, let me help if I can," I told her.

She snatched her arm away. "You want to help me? Take care of my baby. Tell her I'm sorry, but I gotta go."

Before I could say anything else, Tara hopped in her car, backed up, and sped away like the devil was on her ass. I was left standing there trying to figure out what the hell was going on.

Chapter 28

About an hour later, after I fed Rebecca—she bathed herself; said she didn't want me to do it, which I respected and allowed her to wash herself—she was helping me to bake cookies in the kitchen. My mama had come out of the room. She told me she wasn't sure how to treat the little girl. Wanted to make sure I wouldn't be hurt if she showed her too much love. I told her it was fine. Treat Rebecca with the same kindness and respect she would any other child. That was during dinner. Rebecca ate three pieces of chicken, two helpings of rice, and a spinach salad. She told me she hadn't eaten in two days. I asked her why, and she only shrugged.

I texted Donovan and told him we had an emergency at the house. He hadn't texted or called back yet. I wasn't surprised being that his business was on fire with one of his employees stuck inside.

Once the cookies were baked, I sat down and braided Rebecca's hair while she ate a few. Yes, there had been times when I gave her a cold shoulder, but there was no way I couldn't care for her wellbeing. She was still a child, my husband's child. As much as that hurt me to say, it was what it was.

Rebecca was quiet and content. Wasn't as bubbly as she normally was. I wanted to ask her what Tara had done to her, but figured the girl needed to just rest for a while. When I was done, she laid on the couch and watched TV, quiet as a mouse. Normally, she would be talkative. She would be all over me, asking questions, trying to comb my hair, asking me about this and that.

I went to Donovan's office and grabbed his good rum. After everything that had been happening, I needed a strong drink. I'd had a few drinks over the past couple of days, but nothing that got me the buzz I needed. I texted Rome. Told him I could probably get out to see him later. He and I hadn't been able to really talk since our last encounter in the hotel. He'd been acting a bit strange, but I figured he was upset I couldn't get out to see him earlier.

That same number that I didn't recognize from before called my phone twice more. Each time, they said nothing. Maybe Donovan had another mistress. At this point, I didn't give a damn.

I sat in my husband's office and drank damn near the whole cantor of rum.

The first drink took the edge off.

The second drink got me going.

The third one took me to where I needed to be.

By the time I realized my head was swimming, the bottle was down to its last two fingers of rum.

"Fuck," I whispered.

I hadn't planned to do that. I panicked. What if Donovan had come home and found me in his office damn near drunk again? Rising, I got my bearings about me. I was about to walk out, but looked down to see Rebecca was standing there.

"What's …" I took a deep breath to steady myself, "what's wrong, Becca?"

"He said you have to stop drinking now. It's impo … impa … um, important," she said.

"Huh?"

"My friend? Remember? I told you about him. He said you gotta stop now. He says you and Daddy are going to need one another."

I frowned at the child. Her and her damned imaginary friends. I pet the child on the head, and then stumbled out of Donovan's office.

"That's nice," I said to her.

I staggered to the kitchen, bumping into a few walls along the way. I needed water to take the sting of some of the rum away.

"Please don't drink no more, Staci. RJ really hates it when you drink," Rebecca said.

I froze where I stood. The water bottle fell from my hands, and I swore, in that instant, I sobered up a bit. "What did you say?" I asked her.

"RJ, he hates it when you drink. He said to stop now. You have to. It's imp– you just have to stop now."

I moved closer to Rebecca. "Did Tara tell you to say that?" I questioned.

Rebecca looked scared. I was scared. My heart was beating so hard, I felt as if I was about to pass out.

Rebecca backed away a bit. "No, no. RJ told me to say it. He's my friend. He protected me from Mommy's bad friend. He told me to hide, and I did. But he says you have to stop drinking your tea, Staci. It's important.," she whined.

She said so much in so little time that nothing was making sense to me. *Bad friend? What bad friend? And how in hell did she know about RJ if Tara didn't tell her?* I didn't believe in any imaginary friends. Tara had put her up to that shit. I knew it.

Rebecca's eyes were wide with terror, and she was shaking her head while crying. "No, no. I promise. She didn't tell me. Please let me go, Staci.

Let me go. I won't say anything else. I promise. You're hurting my arm," she squealed.

I hadn't even realized I had grabbed her arm. I'd damn near yanked her from the floor. Apparently, I hadn't been thinking those questions, I'd asked them out loud, all the while grabbing and yanking on Rebecca. I heard the front door open and close, then saw my mother rushing into the kitchen. She was yelling for me to, "Let the child go!" Donovan came jogging around the corner. He took one look at me and then his child who was crying for dear life.

My mother grabbed Rebecca out of harm's way.

Donovan charged at me. "You aren't going to take another child from me," he snarled through clenched teeth.

Donovan was angry. So much was going on. Too many things happening at once. I was drunk. He could smell the alcohol. I had to go. This was the last time. I would never lay hands on another one of his children and put them in harm's way again. I was done. No more chances. "You have to get the fuck out," he yelled.

Bruises were on Rebecca's arms where I had snatched her up. Had I put those there? I couldn't remember. As Donovan dragged me—yelling, kicking, and screaming through the foyer of our home—Rebecca was yelling for him to stop. She didn't want him to hurt me. But he had seen the bruises. He smelled the alcohol. I had to get the fuck out.

"No, no, no," I heard Rebecca screaming.

She fought out of my mother's hold and rushed for her father. Grabbing his big arm, she held on for dear life. Sweet, little redheaded Rebecca, the little girl who I'd given my ass to kiss at every turn, was fighting for me.

"Noooooooo," she screamed. "Dadddddyyyy, noooo. She has to stay. She has to stay. RJ sayyyyss she has to stay," she kept screaming.

Rebecca's squeals and yells were so loud, they were deafening. Donovan stopped. He had dragged me down the first two stone steps of our home, but he stopped for Rebecca.

He was breathing like a raging bull as he looked at his child.

Rebecca stopped screaming. Her face was red and wet with tears. "Staci didn't put these bruises on me. Mommy did, Daddy. Mommy hit me. She always hit me. She hit me with a belt, Daddy. Staci didn't do it!"

Before You Walk Out My Life: Jerome

Chapter 29

"Why are you here?"

Those were the words I asked the man in front of me. For the past week, he had made my life a living hell. Between the phone calls, the text messages, and the threats to expose me, I was ready to kill him.

He smiled at me. Perfect, white teeth set against plush lips made my eye twitch. He had a lady killer smile. It could lure even God into the bowels of hell. His smile had lured me out of my comfort zone.

"Wanted to pay an old friend a visit," he answered coolly.

To those on the outside looking in, we looked like two normal Black men having a friendly chat. However, if they looked closer, they'd be able to see the tension, feel the storm brewing.

"I told you to leave me alone, to never call or contact me again," I spat.

He shrugged. "I changed my mind."

"You used me."

"No more than you used me. And, hey, that accident? Well, that was a strange twist of fate." He laughed. "The gods were smiling down on a nigga with that one."

I looked around, wondered if someone would recognize me. I took as many precautions as possible. I had on a fitted cap with sunglasses. Tried to be as incognito as possible. Told him to meet me in public, at Southlake Mall. The mall was nowhere near as busy or popular. It gave me great cover. We sat in the back off in a corner near the kids' carousel. The pale green and beige color of the tables and floors made the mall look like something out of a 70's sitcom. There were very few people in the place. It almost looked like a ghost town. Most of the shops in the mall had been closed. It was skeletal compared to more popular malls around Metro Atlanta.

I turned my attention back to the man sitting across from me. His nails were longer than the average male as they tapped on the beige-colored table. Women loved what he could do with his fingers. Men loved what he could do with hands. Wheat-colored Timbs were on his feet. He had on black, baggy jeans and a black, button-down shirt with a cleric's collar. The muscles in his arms caressed the fabric of his shirt. Hair lined like he had stepped out of the barber shop before meeting me. Waves in his fade glistened atop his head while copper-colored eyes held a mischievous twinkle.

His skin was smooth and clear. A golden brown that made his eyes stand out even more.

There was an arrogant, smug smirk across his lips when he asked, "How does it feel?"

"How does what feel?"

"To have fucked me and my sister-in-law?"

His words felt like a fist that caved my chest in. Sweat beaded my temples. I took my glasses off to rub my eyes, and then put them back on. He knew something about me that no one else did. Bile rose in my throat.

"It happened once," I said.

His upper lip twitched in the corner before he asked, "Did it?"

My fist banged on the table. Women walking past us jumped and then rushed forward. He sat unmoving.

"What do you want?" I asked him again.

"I need some help is all. Need to get close to Staci Dixon."

I shook my head. "No."

"You don't actually love another man's wife do you, Jerome? That's pretty sad. Violating another man's wife like that is so beneath you." He took a deep breath like he was bored. "Especially since you have a beautiful wife at home."

"I told you to leave my wife out of this."

"Or?"

He was challenging me. He knew he had the upper hand. Knew I didn't trust him.

A slick smile spread across his face. His perfect white teeth shone at me. That smile told me he didn't have good intentions. Daryl Dixon, Jr. was a dangerous man.

"Leave her alone, Darryl," I said. "Staci has done nothing to you."

"She was in the room when they all disrespected me. She said nothing. Just stood there. She's as much of a Dixon as the rest of them. I need to get to her to get to Donovan. You're going to help me."

"You planned it," I said to him. "That whole thing, taking that route home, all of it. You planned it …"

I didn't even have to say what the 'it' was. He knew exactly what I was talking about. It was something that had haunted me for the last six years. I thought back to the day of the accident.

We met at a bar. I needed to tell him I couldn't see him anymore. What had happened between us was a done deal. I couldn't risk losing my wife. Couldn't risk her finding out the real me. Didn't want her to hate me the way her sisters hated her father. My sexuality had always had a big asterisk beside it. In college, I played around with roommates. Had sex with a few men here and there. Had sex with women, too. Knew what I liked. Knew what I didn't like. Lived life on the downlow, hiding my bisexuality, until I met my wife. She was different. Something—wasn't quite sure what it was—but something drew me to her.

I felt safe with her. Felt at ease. She was easy to love. I no longer had to hide. I could just be with her and be at peace and I was. Those demons that chased me around, they stopped when I met her. I called them demons because that was what my parents had called them. I met Sheila and those so-called demons went away. I didn't have to struggle anymore. With Sheila, I had peace. I was good.

For a long while I was, but then I met Darryl. He was at a party the Falcons had been throwing. Women surrounded him like flies on shit, but when he caught my eye, we both knew the deal. It was easy to slip away. Say a few words to one another no one thought anything of.

I went to the bathroom. He followed. He handled his business while I handled mine. When everyone had left and we stood at the sink washing our hands, a look passed between us. It was easy for one down low brother to spot another. Neither of us was living our truths, but we knew the play. Numbers were exchanged. We hooked up a few days later.

I hadn't fucked a man in years. That shit felt new and exciting. Darryl was just as tall as me, just as masculine. Darryl knew how to touch me in ways Sheila hadn't—couldn't. Darryl brought me the comfort of a man. Fucking him was an adrenaline spike. A feeling that I knew I couldn't enjoy too much of. I had to stop. So, I did.

The day we met at the bar, Darryl was cool. Told me he understood. Asked me to drive him home. I did. His head ended up in my lap as we took the long way to his home.

In hindsight, I remembered Staci and a white woman at the bar. They were drinking. The white woman kept buying her liquor. Staci kept drinking. At the time, I thought nothing of it. We left right after they did. Again, thought nothing of it. They went their way, we went ours. I still didn't know how Darryl had timed that shit. But as his head bobbed up and down in my lap, I came around a curve too fast. I yelled for Darryl to stop. He grabbed the wheel. I thought he was trying to help me control the truck. I knew better now. My truck swerved into the other lane. Everything happened in slow motion. I swerved into her lane, she swerved trying to avoid impact and lost control of her car.

The crash was loud. I heard when the trees bent the metal. I finally got control of my truck. Fumbled to tuck my dick back into my pants and hopped out of the truck. The smell of oil and gas permeated the air.

The rain made it hard to see as I rushed across the street. The woman in the car was bleeding from her head. A tree branch had pierced through her upper thigh. The little boy's neck looked like it had been mounted to a tree limb. He was alive. His eyes were on me. He was crying and reaching for his mother.

The woman moaned. "Help … him," she barely got out.

"We need to get out of here," Darryl said.

"We can't leave her here," I yelled.

"We can. Someone will help. We've been drinking. We gotta get out of here," he said. "Look. There are no tire marks. No one is out here. No one can prove we were here. We need to go before someone comes around that bend," he argued.

I couldn't get caught there. Couldn't lose all I'd worked for. Couldn't lose my wife. How would I explain the other man in the truck with me and what we had been doing at the time of the crash? I had to go. Darryl and I jumped back in my truck and left the scene of the crime.

"I thought you were trying to help me steer the truck the right way, but you used me to hurt her," I told Darryl.

Darryl smiled coolly, then said, "Cry me a fucking river, nigga. You're no better than me. You got a guilty conscience—"

I cut in. "Her son died!"

"Retired from the NFL and then started stalking the woman yourself."

"I didn't stalk her."

"Bullshit."

"This obsession you have with your brother and his family is sickening."

"No more sickening than you realizing your wife was Staci's therapist, going through her files—"

"You blackmailed me into finding out where they had moved."

After the accident, I left Darryl alone. Cut him off, cold turkey. Three years later, he popped back up with pictures of he and I having sex. He needed something from me. How he had found out my wife was his brother's therapist was beyond me, but he did. I found myself in my wife's home office going through her patients' files. In the process, I stumbled across notes on Staci's files that she had been a member of some chat line. She'd told my wife everything. From the fake name she used to the name of the chat line. So, that whole story about the flyer of Khemetic Konnections being on my car was a lie. It wasn't a coincidence that Staci and I met.

I told him, "I'm not helping you to do this shit. I've done all I'm going to do."

"Please don't tell me you think you're any better than I am. If I'm sick, you're demented. Who fucks the woman they almost killed? The woman whose son they killed?"

"Shut up," I growled low.

"We different sides of the same coin. Who was better, Jerome? Me or my sister-in-law? Huh?" he taunted, then laughed.

It was almost maniacal.

My lips twisted and fists closed as I pushed my chair back. I was seconds away from beating him into the ground until he laid a gun on the table. That sinister smile that only belonged to him etched across his features again.

"Feeling froggy? Leap," he dared me.

We stared one another down like rams did just before they clashed head-on. I was ready to risk it all.

He looked up. Smiled. "Talk about six degrees of fucking separation and now it's all going to come full circle," he said.

He waved at someone behind me. Turned that lady killer smile on. He nodded. I turned around and my heart fell out of my chest.

There stood my wife, with tears in her eyes. She had stopped halfway to us, and it made me wonder how much she had seen and how long she had been standing there.

"Oh, yeah. Figured you'd tell me you wouldn't help. So, I invited your wife to lunch with us," Darryl said.

I stood so fast, the chair toppled over behind me. Sheila stood, not blinking. Her arms were folded. She had come out of the house in

Uggs, yoga pants, and an oversized tee shirt. Her eyes were red and puffy. Before I could say anything, she turned and walked away.

Darryl stood. "Vengeance is mine sayeth the Lord."

His sneaky chuckle made the hairs stand up on the back of my neck. He still had a gun. I turned, ready to knock the shit out of him regardless, but he was already headed for the exit. He strolled through the automatic sliding exit doors like he was the king of kings and never looked back.

Chapter 30

I found my wife sitting in her car near the Macy's upstairs entrance. She sat staring straight ahead. Tears fell down her face. I knocked on her window. She didn't move. Just sat there like she was staring at things I couldn't see. I was relieved to see the door was unlocked. I slid in next to her.

The silence enveloped us like a cocoon.

"It's not what you think," I said.

"Don't," she said. "Don't do that to me, Jerome."

I looked at her, and then stared out ahead of me like she was doing. I didn't have any words for her. Didn't know what she was thinking. She had closed herself off to me.

"I remember the first night I saw him," she finally said.

I slowly turned to look at her.

"Seen who?"

"Him. That man you were sitting with. I've seen him before. The night at the party. I remember it. Remember the look you gave him. It solidified things for me."

I frowned. "I don't understand."

Licking her chapped lips, she turned to me. "I know you, Jerome. I've always known you. Took me a while to admit it to myself though. In college, I knew you then. I couldn't place why your aura was so familiar to me until the night of that party. But once I saw that look that passed between you and him, all the other times I'd seen you give men that look made sense to me. My father … he used to have that same look. There were times, when I was a child, I'd see my father with this intense gaze in his eyes. There was a difference in the way he looked at men. It's a look somewhere between disgust and desire—" She stopped talking like it pained her to continue on. "Yes, I know my husband. I've always known you. To find out it was another woman you were cheating with was a relief."

She used the back of her hand to wipe her nose.

"Thought it was a man. Thought you were going to leave me for a man like my father had done my mother. I'm not going to become my mother. You could have told me. You could have. I don't know what I would have done. Don't know if we would have been married or what, but, one thing is for certain, you would have had my support. You deceived me, and I hate you for that. I hate you for making me love a lie."

"But it wasn't a lie. I do love you," I said.

"Do you? How dare you try to put all this shit on me, knowing damn well you had skeletons in your closet? Oh how easy it was for you to boast of not fucking other women when it was a ..." she lashed out at me, slapped me in the face so hard I swore spit flew from the corners of my mouth; I had to grab her wrists to keep her from doing it again, "man you fucked around on me with."

"Stop," I barked out, holding her wrists in the air.

She spit in my face. That simple move told me how low she thought of me in that moment. I'd never seen my wife so out of character. I closed my eyes as the mucus slid down my cheek.

"All I needed was proof. I couldn't be sure until I had proof. I thought Michaela would provide that, but what do you know? Jerome was really fucking another woman this time."

I let one of her wrists go, and then wiped her saliva from my face. She reached into the backseat and pulled an envelope up front. She shook the contents out and there was her proof. Pictures of Darryl and I having sex.

"Guess I should be grateful you used a condom," she said sarcastically. "I hate you. I hate you for making me out to be the villain. Was I wrong in some areas? Yes. Could I have been a better wife? Yes. But I had to protect myself, Jerome. I had to. And I was right. I was fucking right. I hate you so fucking much."

"I'm sorry."

Those were the only words I could muster. There were demons chasing me that only she had silenced. I told her as much.

"Fuck you and your demons. Whatever they are, I hope they fucking chase you down and drown you in your own shit," she said.

I said nothing. I couldn't. I knew no matter what I said, she would use it against me.

"When did you fuck him?"

"What?"

"When?" she yelled.

"Don't do this, Sheila."

"Tell me when."

"It was years ago."

"Tell me when or I swear to God, we're done. We're done, and I'll send a copy of these fucking pictures to every one of your old teammates and clients."

"It was years ago."

"When? What times? What days? Where was I? What lie did you use when you got home? Did you fuck me after you fucked him?"

"All I ever wanted was you. You changed on me."

"When, Jerome? I don't care about anything else."

"That's the problem. You only care when it's relevant for you. Any other time, you don't care about anyone but yourself."

She was silent for a while. She kept staring at her wedding band. Staring like she was trying to remember when and why she had put it on.

"You fucked him, and then came home to fuck me. I bet I can remember the days and nights if I put my mind to it. Those nights when you would come home from the gym. You'd be extra horny. Extra amped. Would fuck me like your mind was somewhere else or like—"

"No. No, I didn't. I never did that to you," I said.

She whipped her head around to look at me. "Did what to me? Did you fuck him, and then come back home to fuck me?"

"You barely let me touch you."

"Yes or no?"

"We lived like strangers in our home. We barely said two words to one another. You're always working."

"You work. You work just as many hours as I do. I never cheated on you."

"You rejected me."

She was silent again. Her eyes never left mine, but she didn't utter a word. Her lips trembled. Her tears kept falling. I reached for her hand. She snatched it away.

"Don't touch me," she said.

"I'm sorry."

"So am I. How long have you been fucking my client, Jerome?"

Another wave of fear, panic took residence within me. There was no way I'd admit to knowing Staci was my wife's client.

"Who?" I asked, feigning ignorance. Sheila swung at me again. I caught her hands and yelled a lie, "I don't know who the fuck you're talking about!"

"Staci Dixon. You're fucking Staci Dixon! How long?" she yelled back.

I frowned. Made a face that said I was stunned. "I-I had no idea she was your client ..."

"But you're screwing her?"

There was silence on my end.

"Are you fucking both of them at the same time?"

The utter look of disgust on her face hurt. That shit hurt worse than any words she could have thrown at me.

"No, Sheila. I haven't been with … That stuff between me and him, it was done more than five years ago. I met Staci about three or four months ago."

"Where did you meet her? How did you just happen to meet my client?"

"Club Egypt."

"Oh, so you go to clubs now?"

"I went that night. You had a night off and decided to hang out with your friends. I was lonely. So, I went out."

"How many times have you fucked her?"

I dropped my hold on her hands. "Can we go home? People are starting to look. Can we do this at home?"

Sheila looked around. More people were pulling into the mall. Some were looking at us, the couple arguing in the car. Some were pretending not to look. I was sure they could see the tears rolling down her face. My wife had come undone. She was using language that was unbecoming of her. She wasn't the polished professional. Her colleagues wouldn't know who this Sheila was.

"He came to our home with those damn pictures. He knew where we lived. You fucked him in our home?"

"Hell no. I'd never do any shit like that."

"How does he know where we live?"

"I don't know, Sheila. I don't fucking know."

"He knew where things were in our home, Jerome. He knew where our bedroom was. Knew about the pictures on the mantel."

I shook my head, anger steadily rising by the moment. "I have never brought that man into our home, Sheila. D is crazy—"

"Oh, so you know him well enough to call him D as opposed to Darryl?"

I chose my words carefully. "That's … Look, listen to me. He isn't right in the head. If he was in our home, he got in some other way. He's dangerous."

"Was he dangerous before or after you fucked him?"

She looked down at the pictures that had flown all over my lap and the floor of the car. Looking at Darryl and I sickened me. Not because of the sex, but because of the way my wife had to find out.

"I need you to just stop for a second and listen to what I'm saying, okay? We need to get home so we can talk," I said.

I had to fight with myself. Needed to come up with a way to tell her about Darryl without revealing all my secrets, too. That made me think about Staci. I had to find a way to tell her about

Darryl as well. She had no idea that he was even after her.

Sheila didn't say anything. She cranked the car and put it in reverse. I was just happy she was listening. I'd find a way to come back and get my truck later, but for now, at least she stopped asking me questions about Darryl.

We didn't head to our home as expected. We ended up at her sister's place. Michaela and I had gotten along fairly well over the years, but judging by the last time we spoke, it was safe to say we weren't cordial anymore. She was standing outside talking to her girlfriend, Jillian, when we pulled up. Michaela's spine stiffened when she saw me. She came charging toward the car, but Jillian stopped her.

I was sure the last thing Jillian wanted was for Michaela to show her ass in front of all the rich folk of the Hidden Lakes community of Metro Atlanta. The posh, suburban neighborhood wouldn't be able to handle the show I was sure she was ready to put on.

Sheila parked the car. Her head hung, shoulders drooped like it was too heavy to hold up.

"You told them?" I asked.

She nodded once. "Daddy's here, too," she said.

I groaned low a bit. I'd only met the man a few times, but he unnerved the fuck out of me. He was abnormally pretty for a man, but the bass in his voice and the absolute masculinity about him made him a walking conundrum. Shoulders wide, hair long, skin pretty, long, black eyelashes shadowed eyes as gray as the sky on a cloudy day, bowed, plush lips, and cheekbones most women wished they had, that man made me uncomfortable.

"You couldn't leave this between us?" I asked.

"You didn't," she snapped, then exited the car before I could say anything else.

I watched as Sheila walked into the house. Wasn't no need for me to prolong the inevitable. I got out and then slammed the door behind me. I slid both hands in the pockets of my jeans. Michaela's eyes burned a hole in the side of my face. She'd never looked at me that way before. For her to allow her father in her home meant that he was no longer the enemy. I was. The tables had turned on me. That woman hated her father with a passion, and now that same hateful passion shot daggers at me from red eyes.

Her breathing was slow, lips tight, and fists were balled. "Why?" she asked.

I stopped, took a deep breath. "Why what?"

"Why did you do this?"

"Michaela," Jillian said. Probably trying to keep her woman calm.

"No. I need to know. I need to know why he would do this to her. I fought for him. Told Sheila over and over to not push you away. Scolded her for not loving you right, for not loving you enough and y-you … you would do that to her?"

I guessed the fact that she had caught the woman I'd been cheating on Sheila with in the hotel had taken a back seat. This was personal for the whole family. They were mad I'd been cheating with a woman, yes. But Michaela had a look in her eyes that said she was ready to kill me now.

Before I could conjure up an answer, I saw a movement out the corner of my eye. Their father had stepped outside. He was dressed in all black from head to toe. Black sweats, black tee shirt that snuggled against the muscles in his chest and arms, and black combat boots. He was dressed like he'd come for a fight. His long hair was pulled back into a messy ponytail. His nostrils flared as he glared at me. His lips were turned down like something stunk.

"I guess this is my payback," he said.

The coldness of his voice made my spine straighten.

"Not sure I understand what you mean," I replied.

"To hear my baby girl broken down like she was this morning on the other end of the phone, I imagined that was how her mother felt when I ran off and did what I did," he said.

I had no response for that.

"You got any explanations for that? Not only did you fuck around on her with one of her clients, but there was a man, too?"

Frowning, I took my hands from my pockets. My pride and ego had already taken a hit, I wasn't about to let him beat me down further. I prayed that motherfucker wasn't about to try to lecture me about a subject he was well-versed in. He must have already known where my mind had gone.

He shook his head, then pointed at me. "Don't even think it. Times were different then. For the life of me, I don't understand why men still hide in closets now. Ain't no reason other than selfishness."

"So it was okay when you did because times were different?" I asked, just to be sure I was hearing him right.

"I didn't say that."

"Oh good." I shrugged sarcastically. "Because that would be fucking hypocritical."

"What I did wasn't right, but at least I have the excuse of the times. What's your excuse? In this day, in this time, hell, especially in this goddamned state, you can be as open sexually as you want to be."

"It doesn't work that way," I said.

"Then tell me how it works."

"With all due respect, I don't have to explain shit to you. The only person I owe an explanation is my wife. Furthermore, no matter what you or anyone else think, at least I didn't walk out on her. That's the only part of your reflection that I'm not."

Michael tilted his head like he had to think about what he was about to do before he did it. Michaela step in front of her father.

"Stop, Daddy. Don't," she said to him.

She said that like she knew what he was about to do even though he hadn't made a move to do it yet. Father and daughter had the same hair, same facial features, same lips, same eyes. That shit was almost unnatural. I'd seen pictures of the man and his wife, their mother, before. If I didn't know it was a man in the pictures with her, I'd have thought it was a woman.

Michael's face was red; eyes had glossed over like he had taken a leave of his senses.

Breakdown: Sheila

Chapter 31

I heard Michaela's first scream while I was in the bathroom. It was so terrifying that I hopped off the toilet. Did a piss-poor job of wiping the urine from my vagina. Jillian's yell for my father to not do that made me forget about washing my hands. Michaela's second shrill scream came as I raced down the stairs. Then I heard what sounded like someone being thrown into the side of the house.

"Michael, stop!" Jillian screeched.

By the time I'd made it back outside, my husband was on his knees on the ground. The side of his head was bloody, and my father's size thirteen boot was connecting to his ribs. Daddy kicked Jerome so hard, I felt it when it sounded like a rib cracked. Blood dripped from Jerome's lips to the concrete garage floor. His face was a mishmash of pain and anger.

"Daddy, no," I cried.

"Stupid nigga," my father growled. "You see, I tried to be respectful, and you would fix your fucking mouth to hurl some malicious shit like that at me."

I had no idea what Daddy was talking about, but whatever Jerome had said to him had obviously set him off.

"Michael," Jillian called out to him again.

Daddy paced as he pointed at Jerome. "He's disrespectful." He spit on the ground like having to even address Jerome left a bad taste in his mouth.

I raced over to my husband, the coolness of the concrete reminding me that I'd taken my shoes off. I remembered this side of Michael Williams. The temper. The rage. I was sure Michaela remembered it, too. It was the same aggression that had attacked her as a child when Daddy had caught her kissing Jillian. The same rage that would knock the shit out of any man who stared at him for too long back then or any man who looked at us for too long. His lethal "What the fuck are you looking at?" would make grown men tremble in their boots. "They're little girls, you stupid motherfucker," would make any male scramble and run.

Daddy was wary of adults around children. Wasn't no spending the night at other's houses, going to parties, none of that. In his mind, adults couldn't be trusted around children.

I saw where he had slammed Jerome's head into the wall. Blood was caked into the cracked brick like it had been strategically painted there. I knelt to help my husband up.

"You need to calm down, Michael," Jillian said. "You know you can't get into a physical altercation with anyone like this."

Jerome got to his feet and stared my father down.

"Please don't," I said to Jerome, warning him to just let it be. "Just come inside. Please come inside."

I knew my husband and I knew my father. Jerome hated to be bested, and to challenge my father would be his undoing. My husband wasn't a punk, but my daddy's demons were way more aggressive than Jerome's could ever be. Whatever monsters Jerome had inside of him would lose the battle and the war if he tried to go up against my father.

Michaela stood behind Daddy as he paced. Tears were rolling down her face. It was safe to say that Daddy had probably triggered her. He had probably taken her back to the day when he beat her with that belt until she couldn't sit properly.

Jillian was in therapist mode as she stood in front of my father who still paced back and forth like a caged animal. Each stride as powerful as the last.

"Michael, you should come with me," she said to my daddy. She looked at me. "Take Jerome inside, Sheila. Let me talk to your father, please."

I knew Jerome wanted to fight, wanted to say something, but I pulled him inside. If he provoked my father again, wouldn't be any stopping him. I led Jerome to the guest bathroom near the kitchen.

He yanked away from me as I closed the door. He walked over to the sink as he snatched his shirt off. The white walls and big mirror above the sink made the small bathroom appear bigger than it was. Zebra print towels and décor made up the design on the bathroom. Everything else was plain from the white porcelain toilet to the white tub and sink.

"Fucking faggot," Jerome muttered.

"Stop. Don't call him that when you're—"

Jerome's head snapped around at me so fast, I almost felt like I needed to physically defend myself. His locs had come undone.

"Say it," he growled. There was a threat somewhere in his tone.

"Don't call him that when you're the one who provoked him," I said, finally finishing my sentence.

"How do you know when you weren't even out there?"

"Daddy doesn't attack unless provoked."

Jerome rolled his eyes at me, then looked back in the mirror. He turned his head to see the gash on the side of it. He was gripping the sink so hard I could hear it straining under his weight. He was looking at himself through the mirror, seeing something I couldn't see. For the first time, I realized I didn't know my husband as well as I thought I did.

Those demons he spoke about earlier were swimming around in his head. I saw them behind his eyes. That same faraway expression my father used to wear was staring at Jerome head-on. His face looked sullen. Sweat pooled his temples. His lips were parted as he took in short bursts of air.

"Jerome," I called out to him.

"No. No," he said.

I was about to ask him to let me see the wound, until he growled out like a wounded animal. He sent one fist after the other into the mirror.

Shards went crashing down around him. I jumped back, remembering I was barefoot. Our world had come crashing down just like that glass. Everything and nothing was what I'd thought it was. I didn't know my husband, but I knew him. Blood dripped from his knuckles. I wanted to help him, but the glass on the floor kept reminding me my feet were bare.

Life was imitating art if you would … I thought about Staci Dixon. God, life had thrown that woman all the monkey wrenches it could, only for them to lead her to my husband. I wondered if she knew. I didn't have any pictures of Jerome in my office. But didn't she know who he was? It was silly of me to assume she was into football. She didn't seem like the type, but my pride wanted her to know who my husband was so I could blame her for his misdeeds as well. Had he never mentioned my name around her? People who carried on affairs always talked about the people they had at home.

Could Mr. Dixon have known about the affair? Was that why he had attacked her in her office? Looking at that press conference … to find out that my husband had been fucking my client, that shit took six degrees of separation to a whole new level. One I wasn't prepared for. I still wanted to talk to Staci. I needed to see her face-to-face. How could she have not known he was my husband?

"Sheila, are you okay?" Jillian asked after knocking on the bathroom door.

I didn't say anything. Just stood with my arms folded as I stared at Jerome.

"Please just say you're okay. Michaela can't keep Michael from coming in here if you don't, and

I won't try. I'm too damn small, white, and fragile to try to keep an angry, Black man at bay."

Jerome's head jerked up and he stepped toward the door. I moved over in front of the doorknob.

"I'm fine, Jillian. I'm fine." I put a hand on Jerome's chest and shoved him back. "Stop," I said to Jerome. "He'll kill you."

I remembered what Mama said happened to my father's parents after a while. Remembered her thinking back to the night my father came home covered in blood. Michael Williams wasn't afraid to kill. There was a point of anger you just didn't push my father to. Jerome had damn near tipped those scales.

I thought back to the day I visited my father. Thought back to the one question he wanted me to answer.

"Do you really know your husband like you say you do?" he asked.

I diverted my eyes. Looked at the floor, the pictures on the wall, and then back at my father.

I nodded. "I know him," I said barely above a whisper.

"How? Are you sure?"

"He's your reflection."

Daddy's face hardened and his lips turned downward. "Meaning?"

"I watch him. Watch the way he looks at women he's attracted to. Watch the way he looks at men ..."

Daddy grunted.

"I remember the times I would catch Mama watching you. She was never too bothered with the women who were enamored with you, but when a certain kind of man stared at you for too long, she'd get real uncomfortable. But not more than when you would stare back. There was a look in your eyes I didn't understand then, but Jerome has that same look."

"Has he been with men?"

I shook my head. "Not that I know of."

"You sure?"

I shrugged.

"I know his kind," Daddy said. "Know the look of yearning and wanting. I know the look of that closet door he's hiding behind. Why do you think he barely comes around me?"

"Says he doesn't know how to react to you ... with what happened to you and all. Said you make him uncomfortable."

"I wonder why. I make a lot of so-called straight men uncomfortable. Ask yourself why."

As I watched my husband now, there was no need to ask why. I got my answer. I had my answer all along. I just refused to acknowledge it.

Jerome had been bested by two men who lived their truths. Darryl had exposed him, and my father had brought him to his knees. To a man who had lived most of his life in a closet, that had to be soul crushing to his pride and hell on his ego.

Jerome tried to get past me again.

"I'm pregnant," I said.

He stopped. Looked down at me as his locs curtained his face. He frowned. "What?"

"I'm pregnant."

Jerome twisted his neck as if it was sore. "When? How? Are you sure?"

"I'm four months pregnant. Do the math. Think about the last time we had sex."

His lips pressed together in a slight grimace. His mouth opened and closed like he couldn't find the right words to say.

"I don't know what you and Staci had going on other than sex, but I hope that was all it was. I don't plan to become my mother. Before I allow you to walk out on me for another woman or a man and leave me a single mother, I'll have an abortion."

Jerome's eyes protruded from his head and his nostrils flared. "What the fuck?"

"You heard me."

I didn't know what would become of me, Jerome, or our marriage, but I knew one thing for certain, I would control my own fate and be the narrator of my own story.

I told him as much. However, he didn't get to respond. There was a loud knock at the door.

"Sheila, you'd better come and look at this. You and Jerome."

The panic in Jillian's voice alarmed me. I turned to open the door. Jillian's face was red as she turned and powerwalked back down the hall. I followed her with Jerome close behind me. I walked into the front room. There Jerome was, his face plastered all over the screen with pictures of his infidelity for the world to see.

Whatever Happens: Donovan

Chapter 32

"She didn't do it, Daddy."

Those words had stopped my rampage. I wasn't thinking straight. Had just come from my office, which had burned to the ground with my secretary inside. I walked into my home to hear my daughter screaming and crying. All I could think about was how I wasn't there for RJ. I heard the fear and absolute terror in the shrill cries of my daughter.

To rush into the kitchen and find that Staci was the reason, yet again, that a child of mine was in pain lit a fire in me that couldn't be extinguished.

Not until I made Staci pay. Not until she got the fuck out my house.

Staci was as drunk as a wino. So drunk that she could hardly sit let alone stand.

"Mommy did it, Daddy. Mommy hit me. She always hit me. She hit me with a belt, Daddy. Staci didn't do it!"

Those words stopped me. The way Rebecca held on to me, trying to defend a woman who hadn't been the best to her, broke my heart. But not more than hearing that Tara had been abusing my daughter. How had I not seen it? How had it gone unnoticed for so long?

"Why didn't you tell me?" I asked Rebecca after taking her back inside.

Delilah helped Staci up. She wasn't my concern at the moment. My daughter was.

"She said if I told, she would take me away and I would never see you again," Rebecca cried.

I thought back to all those red marks I'd seen on Rebecca. She lied to me. Told me she'd fallen at school or that a bug had bitten her. I was so angry at myself for not paying more attention. I had to ask God if he was playing some kind of cruel joke on me. Why would he send me two women to birth my children who had so little regard for them? What the fuck had I done to deserve such a cruel fucking fate?

I was tired. Soul was weary. It had been a long time since I'd had some peace. As I knelt in front of my daughter, I looked her over. Turned her head side to side to see if I could see any more bruises. When I was sure there weren't more, I picked Rebecca up and carried her out to the car with me. I dropped her off to my parents, and then headed to Tara's place. She and I needed to have a coming to Jesus talk. I didn't call her. Didn't want her to know I was coming for fear she may run off.

But when I got to the house, she was gone and so was everything in it. The shit seemed so odd to me. It was so unlike her to do anything like that. I tried calling her and got no answer. No matter how many times I called, she still didn't answer. There was nothing I could do about it at the moment. So, I went back to my parents' place.

My pops wasn't home. I walked in to find my mother holding a sleeping Rebecca in her lap. There was a fire going in the fireplace. Georgia weather was just that fickle. The house smelled like apple pie and friend chicken with a faint scent of fresh Pine-Sol in the air. Mama was in the living room, sitting in Pops' La-Z-Boy by the big, bay window.

"The baby was bone tired," Mama said. "Was talking about RJ being her friend. Was Tara really beating on this child?"

I blew out steam, ran a hand down my face, and sat down. "That's what she told me."

"Fix it, Jesus," Mama gasped.

"I don't know what I've done for God to be this cruel to me."

"Don't you put this mess on the Lord."

"Everything happens according to God's plan, right? So, if this ain't God's doing, whose is it?"

"God isn't the author of confusion, son."

"Then who the fuck is? Because if you're telling me that God allowed the devil to come in and do this, then it all comes back around to it being His doing. Am I wrong?"

"The Word doesn't work like that, baby. You can't take it and turn it into what you want it to mean."

I had a good mind to tell her that was what most Christians did.

"I don't understand any of this," I said instead.

"I know, baby. I know," Mama said. "But God ain't ever put more on us than we can bear."

I didn't have time for that pacifist Christian bullshit. "Listen, I need Rebecca to stay here until tomorrow. I need to get home and handle Staci."

Mama frowned. "She's drunk again."

"Is it okay if Rebecca stays here?"

Mama nodded. "Becka told me Staci's mama is there."

I nodded. Mama's nose wrinkled, and she pushed her tongue against her top lip. Her face blanched, and then she cleared her throat.

"You got an alcoholic and a drug addict in your house, son. Be careful," she said. "We told Christopher to leave Delilah alone a long time ago. He didn't listen. She almost killed him. Now I'm telling you the same thing. Leave Staci where she is before it's too late, son."

I didn't respond, not verbally. I'd heard that speech before. There was a time when I thought my mother wouldn't be pushing the same divorce agenda my father had been, but I was wrong. So, I just nodded before making my way out.

I made it home just as the rain started to come down. Dusk had settled in, and the skies were darkening. I heard Staci and her mother talking in the kitchen.

"You doing good, baby. You have to stop this or it's gone ruin your life," I heard Delilah saying.

I looked around the counter to see Staci's head in the kitchen sink. It was safe to say with the way her body was lurching forward, she was throwing up. I sighed. Delilah was rubbing her back. Staci made a godawful sound. Sounded like something between sobbing and throwing up her entire digestive tract.

"I can't do this anymore," Staci cried.

Delilah got some paper towels and helped her to wipe her mouth. Staci turned around. Her brown face was flushed, eyes red and watery. She slid to the floor.

"I need help, Mama. I need some help," she cried.

Delilah sat on the floor next to her daughter. She wrapped her arms around her shoulders while Staci sobbed.

"I know, baby."

"Please help me," Staci whispered between cries. "Please help me …"

Two hours later, the house was quiet. I'd left Staci and her mother to their own recognizances. I needed time to think. Monet had left behind four children. No one knew how the fire had started. Pete said she had called him just minutes before saying she thought someone was in the office with her. He rushed over to the office, but by the time he got there, it was up in flames. All the other drivers had been out on routes. None of it made sense to me, and I knew the media would be all over it. We just dodged one hell of a storm, and now another one was on the horizon.

I heard Staci moving around in her room. Our bedroom door was locked like always. She was going up and down the stairs. The last time she went down, I got up and went down to see what she was doing. She had on a track suit, her hair was pulled back into a neater ponytail, and she had on Nike tennis shoes. In her hand was a black bag. I watched as she pulled it to the sink then opened it.

She pulled out bottle after bottle after bottle of alcohol. Any kind you could think of from wine to gin to tequila to bourbon to rum, she had it. She lined each bottle up on the counter, and to my surprise, she started pouring the contents of each bottle down the sink. She was silent, a stoic expression on her face.

I stepped around the corner and startled her. She almost dropped the bottle she had been pouring from. She stared at me for a long time, but no words passed between us. She went back to pouring out the contents of bottles. I moved to the pantry, opened the door, and looked behind the boxes of cereal. I pulled out the small basket of travel-sized liquor she'd collected over the years. Went in the cabinets above the oven and removed the bottles she had there, too.

When I turned back around, she was watching me. I walked over to the sink, helped her to empty the bottles.

"You find Tara?" she asked.

I shook my head. "No."

"Is she really gone?"

"Looks like it."

Staci told me what Tara had said when she dropped Rebecca off.

"She was acting really weird," Staci said once she was done.

"She can stay gone as far as I care. She'll never see Rebecca again."

We were quiet again. So much happened. So little had been done to rectify it.

"Are we over?" she asked once the last bottle had been drained.

"You're going to get some help?" I asked.

"I am."

"You fucking somebody else?"

She moved to the side, out of snatching distance, before she answered. I imagined this was how she felt the first time I came home late. The first time she found out about Tara and me. That scared feeling dancing in the bottom of her stomach same as it was doing mine now. To think of another man touching her in the way only I had made me shiver. I was first. I'd been her only. And now someone had added his essence to my wife's DNA.

"Was it easy for you to fuck Tara and come home to me like nothing had happened? I've always wanted to ask that but was afraid of getting the answer."

I shook my head. "No. Not at first."

She nodded. "You know what I can't get over? I always looked at Rebecca and got an odd feeling around her. The red hair and all. Tara started to act differently. Didn't want me around the little girl. That was around the time you made me feel as if I was as barren as a desert, too."

I could have given so many reasons for what I'd done. None would matter. I had to call a spade a spade.

"I was wrong, Staci."

"You went on for years, fucking her and other women … you tormented me. You know that?"

I could feel the vein in my neck rise. My heartbeat sped up. "Tell me, Staci."

She jumped. Moved back a little more, and I realized that demand had come out harsher than I intended.

"I'm sorry," I said. I softened my voice a bit. "I just need to know."

"Why? Would it change anything?"

I rubbed my hands together to keep from balling my fists. Staci got candid for a second. Told me all the things Tara had told her. She told me how Tara had told her all the things I'd said about her. Things that I regretted saying. Things that I'd hoped Tara would never repeat. Things like how sometimes I regretted not going to Harvard. How I wished I'd met Tara first and then things may have been different. How RJ should have been Tara's son and then he'd still be alive.

Staci's voice shook as she spoke. The pain was so tangible it covered me like a cloak and wouldn't let go. Her word shut me up.

"So many nights I laid in the guest room because my husband shut me out. I was so … fucking lonely, Donovan. In so much pain. Every time I closed my eyes, I saw our son. I had nobody to talk to. I was a pariah. You had a support system. All I had were those bottles."

She was vulnerable. For a second, she and I were those teenagers again. I was her boyfriend back in high school. The one who'd finally seen firsthand what she had to endure so I stole liquor from my father's stash and took it to her.

"What was I supposed to do?" she asked barely above a whisper.

She spoke like her tongue was thick and her throat was dry. She'd indirectly answered my question. My lips turned downward, and I looked everywhere but at her. Every time I looked at her, I saw another man touching, kissing … holding her. That shit forced me to take in deep breaths to try to contain my anger. Somewhere in the deep recesses of my mind I didn't think Staci had it in her. I didn't think she had the gall to fuck another man. That shit mortally wounded my pride. Tore my fucking ego to shreds.

But I had opened that door.

"You let him fuck you raw?"

I didn't know why I had asked that question. I was lying. Yes, I did. I needed to know if she had done to me what I'd done to her. The one thing that I wouldn't have been able to handle was her carrying another man's seed. That shit was hypocritical, but I'd be damned if the woman I called my wife walked around carrying another man's child.

"No, Donovan. I never let him fuck me raw," she said.

There was something about the way she glanced at the wall then back at me that made me feel like she was lying. Or that could have been my guilty conscience. I didn't know. All I knew was, my wife and I had come to a standstill in our marriage. Either we were going to divorce, or we were going to get it together. I had no idea if I was going to be able to get over another man being inside of her, touching her, holding her, kissing her, fucking her. I wanted to kill that nigga. So help me God, I wanted to kill that motherfucker.

Could I look past her infidelity like she had done mine? The next few days would give me my answer. Every social media network, blog, and news station would air our dirty laundry for the world to see.

Anonymous: Darryl Dixon, Jr.

Outro

"This just in, Bishop Darryl Curtis Dixon has been arrested on charges of rape and aggravated assault. A young woman, whose name we can't release, has accused the bishop of rape. The nineteen year old is a member of his church and she alleges that the bishop raped her on more than one occasion in his office on the church grounds. This is startling information only because it seems as if Bishop Dixon and his family have been hit with scandal after scandal. Just mere days ago, his son was in the news for assaulting his wife, a few days after that the bishop's son's shop went up in flames just hours before photos of his wife carrying on an affair with retired Atlanta Falcons player, Jerome Thibodeaux, hit the net …"

Nothing is ever what it seems. Nothing is true, everything is permitted, but vengeance is mine sayeth the Lord.

The End … is only the beginning.

Dear Readers,

If you have come this far then you're probably pissed at me, huh? I left so many cliffhangers in this book, but I had to. This story of Staci, Donovan, Sheila, Jerome, and the supporting cast is only the beginning, an introduction if you would. Just so you know, Darryl isn't finished by a long shot. He is going to turn Metro Atlanta on its head until he feels every one of those Dixons and the people who love them have gotten their just due.

There are many more secrets to be revealed and drama to unfold. So, you already know there will be a part two. No worries, all your questions will be answered then. I want to thank all of you who have taken a chance on me and have enjoyed my work. It is now 4:45 a.m. in Metro Atlanta on a Tuesday morning and I'm signing off for now.

NikkiMichelle resides in Metro Atlanta, Georgia by way of Lexington, Mississippi. Carried by her love of reading, she began writing at the early age of twelve and has been on a journey of "trying" to pen the perfect novel ever since (she's still working on that). Her love of writing and wanting to create stories with true to life situations are what inspire her to continue to write stories readers will enjoy with characters they can relate to. You can catch her works in the previously released anthologies *If Only For One Night 1&2*, *Full Figured 3*, and *Girls From Da Hood 7*. Her full-length works include *Tell Me No Secrets* and *Tell Me No Lies*, and the critically acclaimed novels, *BiSatisfied* and *BiSensual*.

www.ingramcontent.com/pod-product-compliance
Lightning Source LLC
Chambersburg PA
CBHW070818190726
48292CB00006B/2043